Dedication

For Cheryl, my friend, and her damn cute dog.

In memory of Gerald Enman, February 5, 1934 - June 13, 2025

What Reviewers Said About Melt

Melt is a witty, fast-paced, brilliant gem of a novel, with a plot that is character-based and a setting that will appeal to urban and rural readers alike: Christmastide in Halifax. Moulton's protagonists are members of a yoga studio who have little in common except that membership, as witnessed by the fact that a reader always knows who's talking as the points-of-view change faster than the weather in Nova Scotia. Throw in a tall, dark and handsome detective named Terrell, a dog with his own opinions named Madoff, a large Greek family, cocaine, and an innocent teenager; make sure there's fabulous food and high drama in every chapter; and you end up with a truly superior piece of work.

Paul A. Barra, Author of *Sgt. Ford's Widow*

"What's going to happen?" That question grabs you from page one—and doesn't let go. *Melt* pulls you in with sharp writing, unforgettable characters, and twists that keep coming. It's a wildly entertaining ride that melts away the world around you until there's nothing left but the story. Buckle up!   Clare O'Connor, Author of *Skateboard Sibby*

MELT

Lotus Detective Series #2

donalee Moulton

Print ISBNs
Amazon Print 9780228637233
Ingram Spark 9780228637240
Barnes & Noble 9780228637257
BWL Print 9780228637264

Table of Contents

Chapter 1.

Luke's balls are itchy.

His left hand, casually resting on his left thigh, is mere inches from his testicles. He could surreptitiously edge his hand forward and find relief.

"Surreptitiously" is not a word in Luke's usual vocabulary. It has nothing to do with IQ. Indeed, Luke is smart enough to read the room before he moves his hand a nanometer. He scans the beige walls, the brown tables, the black gowns, the onyx gavel. A courtroom, he concludes, is not the best place to scratch your scrotum. Luke clenches his legs together to stop the itching. Now he has to piss. Why the

Luke looks up to see the judge looking down at him. "I want to confirm your plea. You understand by pleading guilty to trafficking a schedule one drug you could spend 25 years in a federal prison."

This is not news to Luke. It is not good news, certainly, but it is not a surprise. It is what he has signed on for. Luke's lawyer nudges him. Luke stands up. He returns the judge's gaze without malice or defiance. "Yes, your honor, I understand."

The associate chief justice of the Supreme Court of Nova Scotia quickly and efficiently takes in Luke's demeanor, his clarity of voice. She takes in his blue suit, at least one size too large; his tartan tie, with Value Village written all over it; his left hand, which seems to have a small twitch. She looks into Luke Castle's eyes. She sees what she often sees: fear. What she does not see is hope.

Justice Louise Redmond shifts her gaze to the Crown prosecutor. Then to defense counsel. She reaches for the gavel. "I am not sentencing a seventeen-year-old boy to federal prison before I have a fitness assessment conducted." The judicial mallet hits its thick round oak base. "Under section 672.11 of the *Criminal Code of Canada*, I hereby order a comprehensive competency assessment be conducted on Lucas Raymond Castle. Sentencing will follow pending the results of the assessment."

There is a shuffle of chairs as the lawyers rise. They reach for their files and their briefcases. The court reporter removes the flash drive from the stenograph. The bailiff moves toward the rear door that leads into the judges' private offices. Justice Louise Redmond is not finished, however. She stands. "I would like to see counsel in my chambers immediately." Looking into the public gallery, she locks eyes with an attractive man in a grey suit and black turtleneck that contrasts perfectly with his onyx skin. "Detective Terrell, please join us."

Justice Redmond walks through the rear door without looking back. The two lawyers look at each other and shrug. They turn to look at Detective First Class Michael Terrell. He shrugs.

Luke Castle scratches his balls.

***

Justice Redmond's chambers are not what any of the assembled expected. There is no large mahogany desk, no dark paneling, no velvet curtains. Instead, there is a glass table with a column of black drawers. Cream colored zebra blinds cover the two sets of windows in the room. But it is the large oil on canvas that has drawn all eyes. A contemporary mix of colors—ochre, teal, indigo—that if you look closely reveal a face.

Justice Redmond follows the gazes of the three people in her judicial suite. "Deborah Maurer. *Easter Bonnet.*" Her pronouncement clearly means nothing. "Artist and title."

Everyone nods and grins. The conviviality is short lived. Justice Redmond waves the trio to chairs positioned in front of her desk. At the back of the room, the court reporter sits ready to transcribe the conversation.

"Let's dive in with a simple question," says Justice Redmond. She pauses, perhaps for effect, perhaps internal reflection. "Were you all born yesterday?"

Not a question anyone in the room was expecting. The court reporter's hands hover over the stenotype machine, uncertain whether she is to record this. But there is no uncertainty as to the nature of the question. Opposing counsel look at one another, suddenly aligned. Crown prosecutor Lauren Edwards decides to brave the waters. "We have a confession. A confession we have not been able to shake."

This pronouncement is met with dead silence. The court reporter's hands continue to hover. Clayton Manning decides to go where angels fear to tread. "I have advised my client of his options. Repeatedly. He insists on pleading guilty."

Michael Terrell looks at the floor. Perhaps to encourage invisibility in this space. Perhaps to hide a grin. Justice Redmond takes in both the reluctance and the smirk. She hears the excuses put forward from the experienced lawyers sitting a few feet in front of her.

"Let me be clear. We have a seventeen-year-old kid, and I do mean kid, accused of a sophisticated, masterly crime. And you are all comfortable with that." Three sets of eyes look anywhere but at the associate chief justice of the Nova Scotia Supreme Court. Terrell continues his intimate relationship with the floor; Manning suddenly finds his navel fascinating; Edwards turns her head slightly to the left and bathes in the abstractions of an Easter bonnet.

Justice Redmond, Honey, as her friends call her, sighs. It is a mixture of frustration and disappointment. She raises the index finger on her right hand. The court reporter quietly removes her hands from the vicinity of the stenograph. "Let me be frank. I know this kid did not commit this crime. You know it. I know you know it. What I don't know is why the hell Luke Castle is sitting in my courtroom waiting to be sentenced."

The index finger lowers. The court reporter resumes hovering. "Perhaps you can help me here Detective Terrell."

Michael Terrell is fond of Honey the woman he knows from yoga. Justice Redmond, however, scares the bejesus out of him. "Your honor, we have tried to break Castle's confession. We have not succeeded. He is either very afraid of whoever trafficked those drugs or very protective of someone involved. And we have a confession."

"By law, we must act on that confession," says Edwards. She plows ahead. "And that is not all we have. Let's face it Luke Castle is no innocent. We have his financial records. He's making a lot of money, and he's still in high school. We know he's dealing and has been for some time." The prosecutor regrets the words as soon as they leave her lips.

Justice Redmond shoots her a withering look. It hits home. Edwards withers. "We are not here so you can tell me the law, which, by the way, clearly states supposition is not evidence. We are here so you can tell me how the hell you are going to save a minor from spending the rest of his life in jail. A jail that is filled with the worst of the worst."

"I can offer a reduced sentence—again— if Castle identifies his accomplices." Justice Redmond shoots Edwards another withering look. The public prosecutor pivots. "Identifies the person or people behind this crime."

"I'll speak with my client, again, to drive home the seriousness of this offence and the relief a reduced sentence will offer," says Manning. He looks at Edwards. "Can we offer protection?"

The Crown prosecutor groans. Federal witness protection is difficult to obtain and very expensive, one of the reasons it is difficult to obtain. Another reason: witness protection is offered only in cases where organized crime is involved. In this room, there is no doubt in anyone's mind that this is indeed the situation with Luke Castle. But that has never been admitted. That is why the defense has asked the question in the presence of the judge. Dammit.

Edwards keeps her eyes as far away from the judge's face as possible. "I will check into WP. See if it is an option in this case."

"Let's push for protection," says Justice Redmond. "That kid will not survive jail. He spent most of the morning looking like he was afraid to scratch his own balls."

The assembled take this last statement as a signal they are dismissed. There is a soft clatter of chairs, gathering of coats, files, and phones. As one, they rise and head for the door. "Detective Terrell, would you give me one more moment."

The Halifax police officer turns. The two lawyers look at the judge with a question mark. "Nothing to do with this case," Justice Redmond says. She is lying.

***

"Haven't seen you in yoga this week."

Ahh, so this is Honey behind the desk, Terrell thinks. He's wrong, and he's right. "Surveillance."

"Must be boring."

"Most of the time," Terrell admits. "But I have an advantage."

"So I've heard. You can pee standing up."

The detective grins. It's short-lived. "Can you tell me what is really going on here?" Honey asks. Or it may be Justice Redmond. Terrell isn't sure, and he is not sure how to read the implications embedded in the ten-word request.

There is no point in saying, "Off the record," or "Between you and me." There are

13

no legally kept secrets in a court case. Terrell is not sure how to proceed. He opts for honesty. "There is little doubt the kid is dealing drugs. There is also little doubt he does not have the brains, the bank account, or the balls to import and traffic upward of $6 million dollars in cocaine. And that's all the nose candy we could find. There has to be more."

"Yet this kid is in my courtroom."

"Kid confessed. It's that simple. He was driving the truck. The truck had 150 gunny sacks of flour. Each sack had one kilogram of cocaine."

"That makes him a driver. Not a criminal mastermind."

"Agreed."

Honey looks at the man who outside these walls is becoming her friend when they are mid-cobra poise at the Asana Yoga Studio or halfway through a post-practice cappuccino at Java the Hutt. She knows Terrell will be forthright. She also knows the power dynamic in this room gives her a distinct advantage. It is an advantage she doesn't want, but she does not see any other option than to use it.

"I have a legal obligation to keep innocent people out of prison. I have an ethical obligation to try and obtain that outcome despite obstacles in my way."

There it is. Terrell tenses. He's about to be asked to do something he doesn't want to do.

"Would you like a coffee?" the judge asks. It's not out of the blue. It's a signal the favor is going to be big. Very big.

"Double, double, please." Honey is becoming a friend, certainly a friend of a friend and another two friends. He will hear her out, and he will try to do whatever it is she asks. But, already, he doesn't like it.

Honey talks about yoga; Asana, the yoga studio they both attend; and their yogi friends, three in particular, Woo Woo, Charlene, and Lexie. They tell each other a humorous story or two as they sip steaming cups of coffee and dip vanilla biscotti into the hot liquid. Terrell is relaxed. There is nothing more he can do at this point. Police work has taught him patience. Yoga is teaching him about stillness.

"You know our friends are very clever, collectively and individually."

Terrell nods and dunks his biscotti. Justice Redmond waits. Her biscotti lingers over her mug. The seasoned detective missed his cue, the signal that they were moving from casual conversation to the real reason for this chat. Terrell stops mid-dip. Their friends have many wonderful attributes, and several annoying ones, but collectively they helped him wrap up a grand larceny case several weeks ago. The case was more of a shitshow than textbook police work, but it is now marked "closed" thanks in large part to the three women.

Terrell looks up. He drops his biscotti in his mug. "You can't be serious."

Justice Redmond doesn't say a word.

***

Terrell has raised his objections, openly, clearly, and forcefully. They have been dealt with one by one. The women will do what they did in the last case—bring insight and skill to those areas where they have expertise and experience. They will not work directly with the police, and at the first hint of anything dangerous, they will remove themselves from the investigation, however tangentially they are involved.

"You know they might say 'no'." It is Terrell's last hope.

"Have you met these women?"

'We're asking too much of people who are not in law enforcement."

"We're not asking them to be law enforcement. We're asking them to lend a helping hand where they can and where it makes sense."

"If anything happens to them ..."

"That is your role. Keep them safe."

"Have you met these women?"

Justice Redmond laughs. She gives Terrell a penetrating look. "How is Woo

16

Woo?" Terrell squirms. "Dear god, have you not asked her out yet?"

Chapter 2.

Terrell is not sure what to do with his new marching orders. He is sure though that he has been given marching orders. Despite the informal nature of the conversation, the absence of case lawyers, and the removal of the court reporter, Terrell has no doubt what is expected of him. However, the judicial request, such as it is, poses problems.

The Halifax detective exits the judge's chambers and sends two texts. The first is to his boss, Jennifer Boone. It's one word. "Lunch."

The second text is slightly wordier and more problematic. Usually, he would call Woo Woo and set up a time to meet. Then Woo Woo would call Charlene and Lexie. That's the way things were done when a $60,000 Patek Philippe watch went missing from Vitality+, the gym that houses the yoga studio where the three women, Honey, and now Terrell, regularly practice. But as the judge astutely determined, Terrell has a crush, and he has done nothing about it. Truth is, he likes Woo Woo a lot. That scares the crap out of him.

Terrell's fingers move across the digital keyboard on his phone. *Let's get together after yoga tomorrow.* He knows the women will read between the lines. Something is up. He also knows the women will wonder why the hell the text went to all three of them. Terrell wishes he knew.

***

Inspector Jennifer Boone is already in a booth and halfway through her first cup of coffee when Terrell arrives. The waitress waves as he crosses the pub floor. Cops are a familiar face in the Dry Dock, and Terrell and Boone are regulars. By the time Terrell has tossed his coat on the seat and settled in, a tomato juice is sitting in front of him. (Woo Woo suggested he get more vegetables in his diet.)

"I see that's going well." Boone nods in the direction of the tomato juice.

Terrell ignores the jibe. "Justice Redmond wants Woo Woo, Charlene, and Lexie to help investigate the Castle case."

Boone is halfway to reaching for her coffee mug. She doesn't make it all the way. She sits back, knocks the cup over, and jumps back as coffee spills over the oak tabletop onto the blue leatherette seat and drips onto her right pant leg. Terrell grins. That went better than he expected.

Once dry, Boone gives Terrell a nod, and a sigh. The two cops have worked together for more than 20 years; he knows her sign language and his boss's bodily sounds.

"She's worried about sending a kid to prison."

"Aren't we all."

"Apparently not to the same extent as her honor."

"Okay, so Honey is a superior human being. What the hell does that have to do with the Powerpuff Girls?"

"I'm really not sure. She thinks they can help, and she wants us to have all the help we can get."

"Do you think they can help?"

Terrell gives his boss a look that is somewhere between a kidney stone and the last scene in *The Notebook*. Boone knows exactly what he's telling her—and what he's not. "You're worried about Woo Woo."

"I'm worried about all of them." Terrell leans in. "You and I know this amount of drugs shipped this carefully and this smartly is not amateur hour. This is well organized, well funded, and well enforced. All three of those scare me."

Boone taps the table. Her index finger hits a spot of spilled coffee the waitress missed. Without thinking, the inspector wipes her hand on her already damp pants. "I'm assuming from the urgency of your terse text, saying 'no' to her honor is not an option."

"Let me know how that goes."

"So, we have to involve the women and protect them at the same time."

"I'm Robbery Homicide," Terrell reminds her. "I was only in court today because I'm being called as a witness in another case."

Boone absently plays with the small puddle of coffee under her saucer. "I'm also assuming the women will not see the need for our protection or necessarily pay attention to us."

"They aren't foolhardy, but they're not going to be harnessed," says Terrell in agreement.

"And they know you, trust you." Boone continues piddling with the puddle.

"And I'm Robbery Homicide."

Boone lifts her finger from the tabletop. "Not any longer. As of now, you're on loan to the Drug Unit."

Terrell doesn't know whether to be relieved or frustrated. It's not where he wants to be. It's exactly where he wants to be.

"Why didn't you just ask Woo Woo what she'd recommend?" Boone asks. The thought has just occurred to her. Terrell gives her his kidney/*Notebook* look. "Dear god, have you not asked her out yet?"

***

Charlene reads Terrell's text with a hint of annoyance and a dash of curiosity. As a new co-owner of Vitality+, she's in the middle of moving boxes, overseeing renovations, and making sure Maddox has a comfortable, quiet spot to sleep. She doesn't need anything else on her plate. On the other hand, Terrell is a friend and helping to solve the case of jerkwad's missing watch was fun. Charlene has discovered she likes fun. Perhaps there is another case.

Lexie has the same reaction as Charlene. She's mid-podcast, looking for ways to promote their new gym/yoga studio, and a favor from a straight man doesn't rank high on her list of priorities. Still, she likes Terrell, and he has helped to make her life more interesting. She should be kinder and more open, as yoga teaches. Still, this could be a pain in the butt.

Woo Woo reads the text and cries. Some of the soft sobs are happiness. She has heard from Terrell after roughly a month. Some of the sobs are sadness. It's taken Terrell a month to reach out – and not just to her. Woo Woo doesn't care how busy she is with the new gym, and she does believe in the yoga values of compassion, peace, and kindness. She also knows Terrell makes her heart pound in a way no vinyasa flow ever has. Dear god, why has he not asked her out yet?

***

Associate Chief Justice Louise Redmond sits back in her quilted La-Z-Boy chair. It's been a good day. It's been a miserable day. She has a seventeen-year-old sitting in a youth correctional facility waiting to spend most of his life in a federal prison. Honey has no problem with incarceration. She quite likes putting people who commit crimes in jail for lengthy periods of time. She knows they're not going to be rehabilitated. Not in prison. She also knows Luke Castle doesn't belong in prison, at least for this charge. Dammit, why are people so stupid?

What's bothering Honey is her request of Detective Terrell. Let's be honest, and at her core Honey is honest, what she asked of the detective wasn't a request. He'll do it perhaps because he likes her but mostly because when she speaks people within the justice system jump.

What's bothering Honey is not the response to her request, but the request itself. Why would she ever want to involve three women with no law enforcement experience in a case that is clearly linked to organized crime. At best, they could do a downward dog. That does not fare well against a bullet.

Still, something tickles the back of Honey's mind. Something she can't identify. Something that is perhaps not identifiable, but something that tells her these women will be central to giving Luke Castle back his life.

Daily Thoughts—
Charlene Kurtz

Monday, December 5ᵗʰ

It's busy. The gym is doing well. Members continue to renew, and new members are joining. I've created a database. I'll do a PowerPoint for our bi-weekly partner meeting later this month. I think I'll suggest we do a holiday dinner for the four of us. We should also do that for the staff. I'd add it to the agenda but, by then, it will be too late to organize. I'll send a text to everyone now....

I'm back. Lexie and Kristi have already said it's a great idea. We'll poll staff tomorrow. This will cost us some money, but money well spent. Maybe we could host something at Woo Woo's place. That would be a treat. Madoff is very fond of Aunt Woo's house. He can pretend he's Toto and has been transported to the Land of Oz.

As much as I wanted to wait before renovating the gym, Woo Woo's idea to have a small number of suites for reflexology, massage, reiki, and aromatherapy is a good idea. Lexie went to a salt room. She thinks we should include one as part of the gym and studio offerings. I agree, but I cautioned us about moving too quickly. Kristi seems okay with the different ideas. We're trying to be respectful. This was her business before it was ours. We're the newcomers.

It's nice to have a reason to get up early in the morning that stretches the mind as well as the body. Madoff isn't a fan but wait till he sees his very own doggy area at the gym. It will be in the office, of course, but he'll have a good view of the gym. People will come to pet him.

The cop wants to see us. Wonder what that's all about. Probably an excuse to see Woo Woo. Well, we'd be going for coffee anyway. Perhaps he has a case for us. We'll be like Charlie's Angels only with brains and real bodies. And no reporting through to some man who hides behind a machine. Reminds me of that poem "Yellow Brick Road." (Woo Woo read it to us.)

If Terrell asks us for a favor, maybe I can ask him to do a background check on my recently found half-brother, Sam. That's what a DNA kit from your daughter gets you—a new member of the family. I am not going there tonight. (Would it be legal to do a background check? I'll ask Terrell tomorrow.)

It's going to be another busy day. :)
Sincerely,

Charlene Kurtz

PS He's a psychologist. Which means I'm going to be psychoanalyzed.

Chapter 3.

Kristi has the yoga room ready. The diffuser is emitting a fresh lemon citrus blend; the props are within easy reach of yogis entering the studio; the plastic frog sits in his lotus position at the front of the class, smiling.

It's a full house today, regulars and semi-regulars. This often happens around the holidays. People's schedules are busier than ever, but they are also more aware of the need to make time for themselves: mind, body, spirit.

Reducing stress and relaxing is the theme for the month. Kristi starts the group off in reclining bound angle pose. "Supta baddha konasana." The words roll off Kristi's tongue like this is her first language. In a way, it is. The opening pose, she reminds everyone, is also a breathing exercise. Kristi takes them through several different breathing techniques before they return to their normal pattern of breathing.

From butterfly legs, the group moves to child's pose. This is supposed to be a resting position. Most members of the class would challenge that contention. Sleeping pigeon elicits a few groans and a smirk from Bhodi who has expertly positioned his right shin at the front of his mat and his left leg straight out behind him. But after two minutes even Bhodi is relieved when they move into a supported forward fold. *Paschimottanasana.* Kristi hears the sighs of approval.

It's nearly time to wrap up. Kristi gently leads the group into the pose of the month: melting heart pose. It's a meditative pose intended to mirror the activity of the month. For most people, except Bhodi and Woo Woo, resting chin and elbows on the floor while your rear end reaches skyward is theoretical. Everyone tries though. Terrell doesn't believe it can be done. He refuses to look at Woo Woo in case she proves him wrong.

After savasana, a lovely guided meditation to a snow-capped mountain lodge with a roaring fire inside, the group begins to wiggle hands and feet. They bow and reach for blocks, straps, and bolsters. The after-class call goes out, "Who's going to coffee?" Seven hands go up in the air. It's a large and lively group for coffee.

***

Charlene, as usual, has snagged the corner area with its sofas, fabric-covered chairs, and plumped cushions. Archina treats the group to a plate of chocolate chip cookies, fresh from the café's oven. There is a clutch of hands as everyone reaches for a well-deserved treat. Most of the get-together is spent trying to figure out what Bonnie should get her seventeen-year-old daughter and her 86-year-old mother-in-law for Christmas. *Gift card from Amazon. Pajamas. Mani/pedi.* Lexie isn't sure they were much help.

Terrell is waiting for the sofa crowd to thin out. He's sitting in a chair with a direct view of the front door and Woo Woo's left shoulder. He didn't want to sit next to her, too presumptuous. Now he thinks sitting this far away is too cold. He has no idea why he is thinking these thoughts. He's a fully grown man who carries a gun.

Lexie waves goodbye to Archina and turns to the fully grown man who (usually) carries a gun. She jerks her head at Woo Woo as her friend heads for the washroom. "WTF?" Terrell smiles, pretends the comedian has made a joke. No one is laughing.

When Woo Woo returns, Charlene leans in. She's got a busy day ahead. "What's up?"

"I have a favor to ask. It's not my favor by the way." Terrell, the cop and the friend, is trying not to show his concern and simultaneously trying to show that this is something the women should be concerned about.

"We're not going to like this are we?" says Lexie.

"My fear is you are going to like it."

Woo Woo searches Terrell's face, the first time this morning she's really looked at him. She's good at reading people. "You're worried."

"I am. This is no easy favor, and I cannot give you details here. If you're interested, we'll have to have a much longer conversation."

"Would be nice to know what the favor is though," Lexie says. She has snark comedian down pat.

Terrell tells them about Luke Castle, without giving them Castle's name. "You really think this boy is innocent?" Woo Woo asks.

"I'm not sure he's innocent at all," Terrell says, "but everyone agrees he did not commit the crime he is accused of."

"A crime that will keep him in jail for 25 years," Charlene says. She reaches for reassurance, but Madoff is at home in his bed.

"At a minimum," says Terrell. "You don't come back from a long stint in federal prison. This kid will be eaten alive, or he will survive. The latter may be worse."

"What do you want us to do?" Woo Woo asks.

"It's complicated, and I'm not sure," says Terrell. "I really need to fill you in on the details."

The three women look at one another. It's as if they're speaking telepathically. "Why don't we meet at my place tonight for dinner. I can always do a follow-up PowerPoint," says Charlene.

Everyone nods and starts to gather up dishes, purses, yoga mats. Charlene gives her friends a smile and a wave as she heads for the door and her busy day. Woo Woo leans over and hands Terrell a small bag. "Cranberry muffins. I made them last night."

The detective takes the bag. It's hard to look Woo Woo in the eyes. It's hard not to.

"Oh, for god's sake," says Lexie, "get a room."

***

Charlene is running late. She'd usually stop by the Italian Market to pick up something to serve her guests. Costco is closer. She grabs a lasagna from the prepared foods and some Balderson's cheese to give it extra oomph and that homemade feel. She puts garlic bread in her basket and an almost-ready-to-serve Caesar salad. Lexie is bringing dessert and Woo Woo wine, so Charlene is set to go. At the last minute, she adds some beef liver Nutri Bites (for Madoff) and almond butter cups (for the second round of tea in case the dinner meeting goes long).

It's after five o'clock by the time Charlene walks through her front door. Madoff knows something is up. It's not just the bags with a hint of something special—is that liver?—it's Mama C's energy. Madoff prances to show her how good a dog he will be and to encourage early presentation of a treat. But mostly to remind his owner he has to go out to pee.

This is Terrell's task for the evening. As if on cue, the buzzer rings. Madoff is down the hall and springing into open arms before the detective is fully through the door. Madoff loves Terrell. He plays chase with him, and tug. He gives him extra treats. Mostly though, Madoff loves it when Terrell scoops him up in his arms. He feels safe— and he sees the world from a vantage point not usually available to him: six feet up.

"Am I the first?" Terrell asks after the licking and scratching is concluded.

Charlene gives him a look of exasperation. "No, Woo Woo is not here yet. For god's sake, just ask her out."

***

Madoff and Terrell have the best walk. They took one of the trails near the condo— all the way to the end. Madoff had two poops, fourteen squirts, and too many sniffs to count. He's in seventh heaven even if his walker is a little out of sorts. It might be the Woo Woo thing (he heard Mama C), but it feels like something else. Still, fourteen squirts!

Dinner is almost ready by the time the boys return. There's a beer waiting for Terrell and a Nutri Bite for Madoff. He tries

32

to savor the treat. He fails. The tidbit is gone in one bite. Terrell's beer takes longer. As is the tradition of the foursome, they eat first. Chat about stuff that bothers them, and stuff that doesn't. Sometimes it's a diversion, sometimes avoidance. Tonight, it's pleasant. Everyone knows they will get where they need to go at their own pace.

The pace picks up with tea (chai, green and herbal) and coffee (Starbuck's French roast). Everyone moves to the living room. Resting on the black Gatewood coffee table is a Post-it Tabletop Easel Pad. Charlene hears the unasked question and ignores the silent snickers. "In case we need to take notes." The laughter is no longer silent.

Terrell summarizes what he knows about the case. Luke Castle works for Kimolos Pizza, a local chain with outlets in Halifax, Dartmouth, Bedford, and Truro. Because of its size, and perhaps its link to the drug business, Kimolos has a central warehouse/bakery where ingredients are received, stored, and used to make crust, sauce, and toppings that are then distributed to the ten outlets in the province. One of Castle's jobs is to drive a truck to the Halifax Stanfield International Airport when shipments arrive, load the truck, and take the goods to the warehouse where they are unloaded.

"It's not just flour, tomato sauce, and onions that are being unloaded, though, is it?" Charlene asks.

"Not if what happened early this year is any indication," says Terrell. "Castle was stopped for a routine inspection when he entered a Trans-Canada weigh station. He was carrying 150 gunny sacks of flour. One of them had ripped open. Inside was a vacuum-sealed canister. Inside the canister was a kilo of coke."

"I'm assuming there was more coke inside the other 149 sacks," Lexie says.

Terrell nods. "This is a major drug bust, and frankly a surprise to us. We've known for some time cocaine is flowing into our city and our province in increasing quantities. We weren't looking in the right place. When you're looking at something that large, you're usually looking at the port."

"How did they get the drugs into the airport?" Woo Woo asks.

"My guess is by plane," says Lexie. Sometimes she cannot help herself.

Terrell shoots her a look. Could be a groan for the bad joke, more likely a rebuke for embarrassing Woo Woo. "Roughly 35,000 metric tonnes of cargo arrives at the airport every year. Way too much to check every shipment carefully and no need to check a regular shipment of food manufacturing products for an established Nova Scotia business."

"What about dogs?" Charlene asks. Madoff lifts his head. He does like to be the center of attention.

"It's unlikely dogs would have been called out. No need given what the shipment was and where it was going. Doesn't matter though. Even dogs can't sniff out cocaine in a vacuum-sealed container." Terrell shoots Madoff a sympathetic glance. "Sorry."

"Are you telling us this pizza place has been shipping cocaine into Halifax—in quantity—without the police knowing?" Charlene sounds a little incredulous, and a little more than disappointed.

"Yes," says Terrell. "And no." He explains that Nikolaos Pappas owns Kimolos. He also owns Enigma, perhaps the hottest hotspot in Halifax. A nightclub that boasts 14,000 square feet over three floors. "We assumed Pappas was using the club as a front. We know—although we can't prove it—that he is laundering money through there. Made sense the drug business was tied to that location."

"I still don't get it," Lexie says. "Some kid is driving a truck from the airport. Driver doesn't mean drug lord."

"Agreed," says Terrell.

"What are we missing?" Woo Woo asks. She looks at the detective softly. She knows this is hard for him. Hard to welcome people into the fold who aren't law enforcement. Hard to admit the police didn't get everything right.

"The kid confessed."

Charlene sits up straight in her chair. Lexie curses. Madoff barks.

"He confessed to what exactly?" Lexie asks after several seconds of shocked silence.

"The full-meal deal. Transportation. Distribution."

"You don't believe he had anything to do with this?" Woo Woo asks.

"No one believes this kid could pull this off. Pappas could pull this off."

"So why does a seventeen-year-old confess to something that is going to end his life as he knows it?" Charlene wonders aloud.

***

Madoff has to pee. He's been patient, and he understands that something serious is being discussed: the flipchart is on the coffee table. Still, it's nearly ten o'clock and Madoff has a full belly. There have been lots of treats, and he is fond of lasagna. He nudges Mama C. She's preoccupied. Talking, but mostly to herself.

"I think Madoff needs a quick walk," Terrell says rising and heading for the leash hanging in the front hallway. Madoff follows. He heard his name, and he knows where the leash is kept. Unnecessary as it is.

Woo Woo decides it's time for tea (herbal), and Lexie goes to get the almond butter cups. It may be a late night. Madoff thinks it already is. Charlene is at the flipchart, colored markers in hand. When everyone returns to the living room about ten minutes later, she has written four words on the paper: protection, loyalty, money, fear.

Terrell looks at the board, then at Charlene. "That about covers it."

Lexie is mid chocolate cup. "Let's add confused to the list."

"Reasons why Luke would confess to something he didn't commit," says Woo Woo. Of course, she'd know what this means Terrell thinks. He beams with pride.

Charlene turns to the detective. "Can you rule any of them out, or in?"

"Yes, and no."

"You really need to stop speaking in multiple-choice questions," Lexie says. Chocolate makes her a touch snide.

Terrell lays it out for them. Pappas could be threatening Luke's family, overtly or by implication. Pappas has a reputation for hurting those who hurt him, and Luke has family. His mother, Stephanie, and his younger brother, Brandon. This threat, implied or otherwise, is very real, and Luke Castle is no fool.

Brandon could also be more directly involved with Pappas and his drug business. "Kid's fifteen and cocky. Already had several run-ins with the police. Nothing serious but he likes to push boundaries."

Loyalty is also linked to Brandon. If the younger brother is involved with Pappas, Luke could be showing his loyalty to family. Likewise, he could be loyal to Pappas, or more likely the life Pappas represents. "I'd be surprised if Luke has ever met Pappas," Terrell says. "The man keeps himself insulated from the working bees. Less chance you end up in jail, or dead."

Money is always a motive everyone agrees. Pappas has plenty; the Castles do not. Luke could be willing to sit in jail so his family gets to move out of public housing and into a life with some stability and maybe even a luxury or two. The three women lower their heads. It's not sympathy, it's guilt. They understand privilege and are very aware of which end of the spectrum their lives unfold.

"That leaves fear," says Woo Woo. "I'm assuming anybody in their right mind would be afraid."

"Pappas is a man to fear," Terrell says, "but Castle's lawyer has asked for protection. If the prosecutor agrees, he and his family would be put in witness protection and relocated. That could mitigate the fear. Personally, I don't think the offer will change Castle's plea."

Everyone wants to know why. Even Madoff is curious, although that may be more about the plate of almond cups. Madoff is not allowed chocolate.

"I've interviewed a lot of young men, and old men, and women. I see fear every day. I'm not seeing fear in Luke. My guess is the kid is so far down the chain, if he's even on the chain, there's nothing he would have to offer that could compromise Pappas let alone lead to a conviction. We already have his cocaine. That's the blow."

Woo Woo plays with the tassel on her necklace. "What are you seeing?" Lexie and Charlene shoot her a look. Madoff joins in. (He likes to be included.) Terrell hesitates. "Resignation. When I look at the kid, I see someone who feels he has no choice but to confess."

***

It's late, everyone is getting tired, and the reality of the situation is weighing on them. The women understand what has happened, and they are emotionally entangled, removed as they are. What's missing from Terrell's very thorough briefing is why they are being briefed at all. It's now past 11 o'clock. Everyone agrees more discussion is required. They'll meet in the Vitality+ office after yoga tomorrow.

Madoff has given up hope that he will ever sleep in his bed again. He's stretched on the sofa, snoring softly, his head on Lexie's lap and his back legs on Woo Woo's. Terrell scoops him up gently and carries him to the bedroom. He places him quietly on the bed and lightly rubs his ears. Madoff opens one eye and rolls over. An inch from his nose are two Nutri Bites. Madoff loves Uncle Terrell.

Chapter 4.

Beast has claimed the top bunk. Luke isn't sure why someone would want the top bunk over the bottom bunk, but Luke knows—after only a few days in the Nova Scotia Youth Center—that you don't argue with Beast. He gets whatever bunk he wants.

Luke is fine with the bottom bunk. He can reach the door more quickly to yell for help; although to be fair, Beast has not proven to be a difficult roommate. Aloof and indifferent usually. Definitive about the bunk he's claimed certainly. But at 6'4" and 275 pounds (Luke is being kind here), Beast could be much more difficult and downright dangerous. Luke reminds himself, despite Beast's size, he is only 15 years old, the same age as Brandon. This guy is a kid.

Not for long. Juvie will beat that out of you pretty quickly. Literally for most people in here. Beast is the exception. He's big, and he's a pro. The grapes (Luke is trying to learn the lingo to fit in) say he's been here for eight months without one trip to the infirmary. Luke wonders if maybe Beast will become his friend and protect him. Luke knows he's watched way too many movies. He also knows he will likely be tried as an adult.

His lawyer was by today. Pushing him to recant. That's what they call it. They make it sound easy. No one gets hurt, everyone lives happily ever after. Luke has watched that movie too many times. He knows fiction when he hears it.

"If you don't, you'll go to jail likely for the rest of your life." His lawyer's mantra. Luke likes his lawyer. Even feels bad for him. He's trying to help, and Luke refuses to be helped. Of course, there's stuff the lawyer doesn't know. Stuff that Luke isn't going to say out loud. But he has an insurance policy if he ever needs it.

Luke rubs the spot on his wrist where the handcuffs had been. He's kept quiet. Played by the rules. The ones no one ever writes down. He's protected them all. His family. Her family. But mostly her. Luke's heart aches. His brain has never stopped working though. Tucked inside a toilet inside a warehouse is a piece of paper that will shine a whole new light on what happened the night Luke Castle got behind the wheel of a flatbed truck and $6 million worth of cocaine landed in the evidence room at the Halifax Police Department.

It's not that Luke doesn't want out of this mess and out from behind these walls. He does. He also wants to live. He wants those he loves to be safe. There have never been threats. There never would be. That's not how this is done. Still, Luke could have opted for protection and spilled his guts. That would uproot his family. That would destroy her family. Well, it would destroy her. Trials do that. Nothing is hidden anymore. Everything is hung on the line for the world to see.

Mostly though, Luke wants to do what he feels is right in his heart, not his mind or his pocketbook. This feels right.

Beast lets out something that is midway between a snort and a squeal. Luke doesn't want to know what the hell is going on in the top rack. He holds his breath. After several seconds, Beast returns to his raucous snoring. Luke thinks he might have that sleep disorder rich people get.

A plan. That's what Luke will need to survive prison. He figures he has a month. That's how long his lawyer said the competency assessment would take. Luke will have to go to the Abbie Lane for that. It will be easier for his Mom and Brandon to visit him there. Luke wants to be home with them. He wonders if that ache will ever go away.

Beast moves. Luke can hear the shuffle of sheets as Beast sits up. There is some scratching and a long fart. Luke doesn't breathe. For various reasons. Suddenly Beast is standing in front of the lower bunk, in front of Luke.

"Supper."

This is a pronouncement. Luke is uncertain what is being pronounced. He understands what "supper" means, but the dinner bell has not blasted. Does Beast want Luke to call a CO about dinner? Give him his dinner when it's time?

Beast lumbers toward the door. Luke retreats to a remote corner of his bunk. Beast turns.

"Supper."

The dinner bell rings.

Chapter 5.

Slugs. Kristi Yee has been teaching yoga long enough to have a routine—and an innate sense of what she is about to face. She reads the faces in the room, and the energy. Today the nine yogis stretching halfheartedly on mats and trying to hide yawns means only one thing. *Slugs.*

When a class is sluggish, you have two choices, wind down on energetic poses, open with a longer breathwork, and offer a more meditative savasana. Or you can work the hell outta 'em. Kristi picks door number two.

Now, the theme for the month is restorative, which by its very nature is slower, gentler, more meditative. That doesn't mean there isn't room to nudge. Kristi moves them into thread the needle, left arm under raised right arm for three minutes. This is a comfortable pose. Everyone moves languidly into the position. Kristi suggests, sweetly, they move their left temple to the mat. This intensifies the pose, stretches the neck, and opens the heart.

Archina groans. Terrell grunts. Honey farts.

Kristi tries to hide a smile. Next up, she tells them gently, is vajrasana, a simple sitting pose. "Not that freakin' simple," Bonnie thinks as she struggles to rest her buttocks on her heels without yelping.

To increase their level, Kristi suggests everyone put their hands behind their back and clasp them together in an anjali mudra, or prayer position. Lexie folds forward and collapses. Charlene joins her. Bhodi tries to look serene as he scans the room to see who is paying attention to him. Terrell thinks he might arrest him.

By the time savasana arrives, the group, even Bhodi, is bedraggled, sore, and weary. They are not sluggish.

***

It's been decided the women and Terrell will go to the café for the post-yoga conflab. No need to draw attention to themselves or the meeting. Today, there is a lot of griping, even though Kristi is at the table. It's well meaning. Kristi reminds them it is good for them. Archina suggests they redefine "good."

By the time coffee is over, the day is well under way. Kristi heads for the studio. She knows the four are meeting in the office and knows it has nothing to do with Vitality+. She does not feel left out. These women have formed their own bond. She's part of the group, but not at its core. The same is true of

45

Terrell. Sometimes you are included, sometimes you're not. You are always embraced.

With Kristi's blessing and input, the triad has reorganized and renovated the original office space. This has been expanded to comfortably include three desks one each for Charlene, Woo Woo, and Kristi. A smaller room to the left serves as Lexie's office and a quiet place to record her podcasts as planned for the near future. To the right, past the lunchroom, are two smaller rooms where the storage area used to be. These will be used to offer a range of new services such as reflexology, massage, aromatherapy, and reiki. Vitality+ will, one day, as its name indicates, be more about vitality and less about sweat.

Today, in this room, it is about neither. Lexie dives in. "Not sure how we can help."

Charlene nods agreement and adds. "Or why anyone would want us to help."

"'Cause we can," says Woo Woo. Terrell turns to her and beams. Woo Woo turns magenta. Lexie and Charlene roll their eyes.

Terrell takes a step back. "I'm not sure you can do anything for Luke. I'm not really sure I want you to. This case involves some dangerous people."

He senses the confusion. "You're here because I was asked by someone to bring you together. They believe you can help." The detective holds up a hand fending off the obvious question. "I can't tell you who." He waits a beat. "Does it really matter?"

"Okay," says Lexie, "fill us in." Charlene is prepared for this moment. She has set up a portable projector. On the wall, appears a template: Who, What, When. Under "who" are four names: Luke Castle, Stephanie Kellor (Luke's mom), Brandon Castle, Nik Pappas.

"It's a place to start," Terrell says, "but there are more names."

No one has any direct connection to any of the four names gleaming on the wall. Connections, however, can be made. Charlene offers to set up an appointment with Pappas under the pretext of offering his employees a gym discount. Lexie can reach out to Enigma's entertainment coordinator about a comedy set or a series of comedy nights. "At least we'll be inside. Nightclub staff love to talk."

Woo Woo is going the family route. She'll take a gift basket to Stephanie on behalf of Vitality+. The mother will surely suggest a cup of tea. Perhaps Brandon will be home.

"What do you think we're going to learn that you can't?" Charlene asks.

"Nothing. Everything," Terrell says. "If we can figure out why Castle is lying, we might be able to figure out a work-around. We might even be able to implicate the real leader of this enterprise."

"Who's missing?" Woo Woo asks. It takes Terrell a beat; her eyes are very blue today, almost sapphire.

"Pappas's two sons we think are involved and a daughter-in-law we don't. There's also a second wife and her daughter."

Charlene moves to her laptop, fingers posed. She hits the keys as Terrell calls out the names: Kostas Pappas, Sofia Makri, Dimitri Pappas, Angela Pappas, Mirabelle Fortin.

Quietly, Woo Woo says, "I know Sofia Makri." She feels the surprise in the room. "Professionally. Makri owns Suite and Savory, the gift store in downtown Halifax. She once offered free 10-minute reflexology for customers. I was one of the reflexologists."

It's decided Woo Woo will visit Sofia about another reflexology day, or a gym discount for customers, or both, or something else. It's Woo Woo; she'll figure it out.

"Those are all great places to start," says Terrell, "but first you must seriously decide if you want to start down this road at all. It's not the same as some asswipe who lost his watch."

The responses are immediate—and united.

"The kid needs help. We'll help," Lexie says.

"We'll be careful," Charlene adds.

"Honey has asked us for a favor. It's the least we can do." Charlene and Lexie look at Woo Woo in amazement. Terrell beams.

***

Lexie et al agree they'll tackle their respective tasks simultaneously. That will get answers faster, if there are any answers to get. To be honest, all three women are skeptical they'll be of any help whatsoever. Charlene thinks it's still a good idea—might get them some new business. Lexie is keen to dip a toe back in the stand-up world. Woo Woo wonders if she should make some cherry muffins. Terrell has been working long hours.

Chapter 6.

Mirabelle is growing up. Nik Pappas can barely admit this to himself. He has yet to say it out loud. Still, it is the reality. She has breasts. Now she shows cleavage. At seventeen. He must speak to Angela about this. Then, again, his wife shows cleavage. (She has great cleavage.) We must be careful about the messages we send to our children, Pappas thinks.

It does not occur to him to correct the pronoun "our." It would have at one time. Pappas has been married to Angela for nine years, not blissful years but good years. (The cleavage helps with this.) In all that time, Mirabelle has been living with them full time. She sees her biological father sporadically, and it does not usually go well. He cannot be counted on to parent, and everyone agrees that Mirabelle considers Pappas her father. That makes Pappas happy. Pappas knows what would make him even happier. It is time.

He does not want to jeopardize his joy. Pappas is a smart man. He may not know tweets and grams and posts, but he knows kids talk, and at some point, the talk will turn to parents and what they do for a living. "Businessman" only works for so long, especially if media is splaying your name all over the front page and leading off the six o'clock news with it.

That's what has him concerned about this kid in juvie. Pappas will be blamed for that. Already he feels the increased police presence. More cars follow him home, to the office, out to dinner. Like he's stupid. Pappas knows he's not going to jail, knows there is no link to him and this kid. He's not worried about himself. He's worried about Mirabelle. What if she hears the rumors? Reads some tabloid trash?

Kostas says everything is taken care of and Pappas doesn't need to worry, but you don't build a business without assessing opportunities and threats. Pappas thinks this kid is a threat. Also, Kostas can't take care of everything. He is a devoted son; he works hard and smart. Still there is always something outside your control. Like a daughter who suddenly gets cleavage.

Pappas reaches for his phone. His first call is to Kostas. They plan to meet tomorrow. The second call is to Sofia. He invites his daughter-in-law to lunch. She will have good advice. She had cleavage when she was fifteen.

***

Nik Pappas's secretary pops her head in the office. "There is a woman here who wants to talk to you about gym membership." Pappas gives Zoe a look like she has two heads. "She seems to think she had an appointment. Said she knows Sofia."

Pappas's first tendency is to have Zoe tell the woman he is tied up in a meeting. Then he thinks better of it. Having a good reputation in the community can offset rumors and innuendo. He must be more visible. "Tell her to come in. Perhaps you could make us some of your special coffee."

***

Charlene has dressed like an accountant even though this is not an auditing consult. Two reasons for the attire. One, most of her clothes are accounting adjacent—dark pant suits, white blouses, flats. Two, she feels this ensemble will make her appear more respectable and believable, more businessperson, less weightlifter.

She needs the confidence. Charlene is not about bluster; she's about expertise. (Lexie is bluster; Woo Woo is, well, Woo Woo.) Showing up without an appointment is a first for Charlene. She tries to sound assured, as if there really is an appointment with the drug lord. (Charlene wonders if that's what they should call him.)

So far, so good. The pantsuit has got her past the secretary.

52

While Charlene waits to see if she is making it past go, she checks out the office space. This tells you a lot about a person and how they run their business. Expensive art and you've got a spendthrift and someone who is very pleased with themselves. Art from HomeSense indicates a penny pincher with attention to detail. Guess which one is more likely to cut corners?

The third-floor outer office of the CEO spans the two artistic worlds. It's very clever. Folk art claims the space without dominating. A sea blue painting of a fishing village with cod drying on the line holds center stage above a sofa. A small round table painted by Sandy Charbonneau that features the face of a black cat sits next to the sofa. Magazines are scattered seemingly nonchalantly on the top of the cat's pink nose and white whiskers. Charlene knows differently. This is atmosphere by design. The folk art speaks to the approachable, open nature of the leader and his interest in the local community. It also speaks to eclectic and expensive taste.

Worst kind of client, Charlene thinks. Arrogance isn't going to nudge them to give anything away; a penchant for every detail means little unintended information will be revealed. Clever.

Zoe is back. This time she's wearing a smile. "Would you like a coffee?" she asks as she leads Charlene into Nik Pappas's inner sanctum.

Charlene would very much like a coffee. It sets the tone for the meeting and lengthens it nicely. The folk art ambiance has been scaled back here to one piece, a magnificent sculpture by Brent Dykeman of three happy, grinning, green-blue fish that sits on an incongruously modern plant stand. The other images in the room are family related: graduation photos, children's hand-drawn pictures; vacation shots. It simultaneously conveys an aura of comfort and elitism. Clever.

I'm not going to put anything over on this man, Charlene thinks. (Somewhere in a recess of her hippocampus she admits she has never really "put anything over" on anyone.) The auditor, fittingly, opts for honesty. "Thank you for seeing me. I must admit I don't personally know your daughter-in-law. We have a mutual friend."

Pappas waves a hand in front of his face as if the issue is inconsequential. "I always have time to speak with local businesses."

This gives Charlene the opening she needs. She explains her professional background as an auditor and her new business venture, Vitality+. Then she begins her pitch. She doesn't get too far before Zoe arrives with coffee. A nutty, smoky aroma wafts across the office. Charlene swears the three fish inhale. She takes a sip. "This is heavenly." Both Zoe and Pappas smile.

Pappas takes a moment to thank Zoe and his guest. He explains the coffee is a traditional Greek blend made with finely ground Arabica beans and brewed in a briki. A generous dollop of sugar, he adds, is an essential finishing touch.

And there it is. The man's weak spot. Charlene makes a mental note: pride.

She spends a few minutes speaking about her trip, many years ago, to the Greek isles. She talks with obvious delight about the ocean, the sun, the olives. The people. Charlene focuses for a few extra seconds on Athens where Pappas grew up; the Temple of the Zeus, the central market, the Museum of Cycladic Art. (Charlene has never been to Greece, but she read up on the country this morning in preparation for this meeting. Charlene does her homework.)

Charlene continues her pitch. To be honest, Pappas doesn't seem all that interested. It's like this is pro forma, and he is going along for the ride as politeness dictates. Charlene is about to delve a little deeper into the benefits of a gym membership for employees when Pappas leisurely gives his second wave of the afternoon.

"You have me convinced. I'm in."

The auditor in Charlene knows better than to show surprise, but her yogi third eye is blinking rapidly. This was way too easy. Still, gift horse and all that. "Thank you. I expected, to be honest, a harder sell. You are being very generous."

The enigmatic smile is back. "Employee loyalty is the backbone of our business."

Charlene nods and breathes deeply. Yep, that is definitely bullshit.

Chapter 7.

Terrell is mid-splash. Malt vinegar on deep-fried haddock and fries. Or as his father used to say, "Heaven." He reaches for the ketchup.

"Dear lord, spare me." The voice looking for deliverance is Inspector Jennifer Boone.

"To each their own," says Terrell as he squirts another large dollop of ketchup on his fish and chips.

"I see worry hasn't dulled your appetite."

That stops the 6'2" detective mid-squirt. "What have we done?"

Boone picks up the Chardonnay that is waiting for her on the table. She sips. She looks at her friend. "I haven't done anything."

"Your support is overwhelming," says Terrell. He squirts more ketchup.

Boone raises her hands in defeat. "So, they're doing this."

"Somehow we always knew they would." A forkful of haddock hovers precariously over Terrell's lap. "It's not the doing that has me concerned. It's the dying."

"Surely to god, Pappas is too smart for that."

"Doesn't mean the Pappas wannabes are."

"Point taken." Boone pushes her plate away. "There's nothing for it now. All we can do is watch them very carefully. The women have passed go."

"Charlene has already met with Pappas and has plans to return. Lexie has an appointment with Enigma's entertainment manager tomorrow, and Woo Woo is going to drop in on the daughter-in-law." Terrell shoves a forkful of malt vinegar and ketchup in his mouth. Somewhere a sliver of haddock is hiding.

"I suspect there's more."

"They're going to reach out to the mother and check out the younger brother in the process. They'd visit Castle in juvie if they could."

"They can't, can they?" Boone glances up at Terrell for confirmation. There is a second of panic.

"For most people, I'd say no. For these women, only God knows, and she is remarkably silent on the issue."

Boone lets out a long sigh, part admiration, part dread. She absently reaches for a French fry on Terrell's plate and dips it in ketchup. Takes a big bite. "Lord spare me."

***

Lexie, Charlene, and Woo Woo are plotting. Madoff is napping. The women have decided, well mostly Charlene has decided, that this assignment (that's what they're calling it) requires a formal outline. Charlene has the software. They've listed everyone they'd like to connect with and divided them into two groups: primary and secondary.

In the first group are Nik Pappas, Stephanie Kellor, Brandon Castle, and Kostas Pappas. In the second group, the lesser players, are Pappas's other son Dimitri, his daughter-in-law, the second wife, and the stepdaughter. Charlene also adds legal aid lawyer Clayton Manning. "It's unlikely he will tell us anything, but he might get us access to Luke." Charlene goes back to the keyboard. She adds "Luke Castle" to the list of primary contacts.

The second column, Access, is proving a little more difficult to complete. The women know how they will try to connect with only three people on the list. They decide to take it one person at a time.

Kostas Pappas. On paper, maybe even in real life, Kostas co-owns Kimolos Pizza with his younger brother Dimitri. He has the higher title though: president. Baby brother is VP. Charlene suggests they approach Kostas with the same Vitality+ offer they made to Pappas. Then she nixes that idea.

"Too suspicious." Then she puts it back in play. "On the other hand, we would not just go out to one business offering a discount. We'd go to many. That's how marketing works." She turns to the outline and types in "gym discount" beside Kostas Pappas's name.

"Glad we could help," says Lexie.

Madoff is getting restless. You can only sleep for so long. And surely it is time to eat. Madoff is rarely wrong about mealtimes. The three women get the message and realize they're hungry as well. It's decided they will order in. Madoff gets to decide. They put four take-out menus on the floor. Madoff sits on the Santorini Grill menu. Greek food it is.

***

Terrell is invited for coffee and dessert. That's part of the agreement. The detective has to be kept in the loop, and now the women have a loop. Lexie and Charlene also have their own agenda. Dating apps are so passe.

As Woo Woo puts the dirty dishes in the machine and cleans up, Lexie harnesses Madoff for his nightly constitutional. Charlene prepares for a surprise. By the time dog and walker return to the condo, Terrell is walking up the front steps. Lexie lets go of the leash and the little Westie makes a beeline for his favorite male human being.

He jumps and squeals and licks. Magically a rawhide chew stick emerges from Terrell's left pocket. Madoff rushes into the house and hides the chew stick under the left leg of the living room sofa. Then he rushes back to Terrell for more licks, jumps, and squeals. It is important to say thank you.

As Lexie and Terrell (slightly damp) open the front door, they're hit with a wonderful aroma, something smokey, something nutty. Madoff thinks it might be his chew stick. It's the Greek coffee Charlene has prepared. "I bought a briki after my meeting with Pappas. Best coffee ever."

Her guests agree. They take a few moments to savor their drink and enjoy dessert: honey-fried mini doughnuts. There are three for each of them, and one for Madoff. Charlene puts that aside for later. At the same time, she gets the projector from her office. Subtlety is not her strong suit.

***

The women, Terrell is struggling with a nickname (Charlie's Angels? Three Ninjas? Three Amigas?), are determined to touch all the touchpoints in Luke Castle's life. Three down, eight to go. Terrell agrees, reaching out to Kostas with a discount membership is a safe and fairly sound approach. Kostas and his brother Dimitri have been on the HPD's watchlist for some time, primarily because they are the offspring of Nik Pappas. Dimitri doesn't have the brains of his father or his brother, which makes him more reckless and more likely to trip up. It also means he is more likely to be reined in. For now, Charlene will ask to meet with Kostas. Dimitri will remain on the back burner.

There is much back and forth over the remaining touchpoints. Woo Woo wants to reach out directly to Luke's family with an offer to help. Lexie still thinks they should go through the lawyer. It's finally agreed Woo Woo will contact Stephanie Kellor and ask if they can meet. For now, they'll hope Brandon will be at home when they arrive. She'll make it clear this is about helping Luke. Terrell will give Clayton Manning a call and let him know the HPD is still investigating, using off-book assistance. "Manning will know enough not to ask more," says Terrell.

"He'll need to know a little more," Lexie points out. "We want to meet with Luke."

"There may be another way to do that," says Terrell. "Let's see how the family meet and greet goes first."

It's also decided that for now the wife and stepdaughter can be put on the back burner. Too many steps removed from Kevin Bacon. As it turns out, that was the worst decision the team could make.

Daily Thoughts—Lexie Hill

Wednesday, December 7th

Apparently, the Hardy Girls are on the case. I'm not sure how this happened. Then again, I'm not sure how I came to co-own a gym. Or have a 38-year-old son. Well, I know how that happened; I just can't wrap my head around Nathan being back in my life.

Such as it is. We wave to each other at the gym; sometimes he joins us for coffee after yoga. I want more. I don't know if he wants more. I don't know if he knows I want more. I really don't know how I got here.

But here I am. Strangely enough, I'm happy. I have friends and a new purpose, and it would seem, a penchant for solving crime. In this case, that could get us killed. None of us believe that, of course. Except for Terrell, and he knows more than any of us.

I really, really don't know how I got here.

Doesn't matter. I'm up tomorrow. Meeting with the entertainment manager at Enigma. I'll suggest a comedy night for charity. I could put that on my podcast. If that idea doesn't fly, I'll suggest a Night With Lexie Hill. One of them is likely to be accepted, and I wouldn't mind being in front of a live audience again. Either option will give me lots of reasons to hang around Enigma.

Woo Woo is going to contact the mother. I am not looking forward to that conversation. Maybe I don't have to go. Three of us descending on the poor woman might be too much. I'll try that out. See if they'll buy it. I already know the answer. Tea with mother it is.

The activity for this month is mindful meditation. You sit on a cushion and stare at one spot. Supposed to bring you to stillness, change your brain for the better. It put me to sleep. Maybe that's why I'm still doing these damn daily thoughts. That was last month's activity, and now this month's as well. Maybe that yoga-zen stuff works. Who knew.

I'm avoiding the big issue, maybe the real reason I'm writing at 11:30 at night. Christmas is around the corner. That was easy last year. There was no Charlene. No Woo Woo. No Terrell. Dear god, do I have to get Terrell a gift. If I get Terrell a gift, I'll have to get Kristi a gift. I hate shopping. The easy purchase will be Madoff. I'll enjoy that.

I started a list. There is nothing on it. I put spa stuff for Woo Woo then crossed it off. She already does that. A new projector for Charlene. It would be appreciated I know.

Not creative though. Xed that. These need to be special gifts.

I could get Terrell a dating app. Might help him figure out how to ask someone out.

I'm going to set one intention before I go to bed. Just one.

LH

Intention: Invite Nathan to lunch. Or dinner. Or coffee, just the two of us. It doesn't matter. Just invite your son to something.

Chapter 8.

Sofia Makri is pissed. She's thanking customers as she rings up purchases, greeting familiar faces in the restaurant with a wave, and smiling as she strolls the three floors that are Suite and Savory, but Sofia Makri is pissed. *Covid is killing me.*

Makri is ringing and waving and smiling because she is working, and she is working because yet another employee is off sick with Covid. Or the flu, or RSV. Or a cold. There is a solution: hire more people. Makri is prepared to do that. Indeed, she is paying $3 more than Nova Scotia's $15 minimum wage. Still no luck. People stopped working when the pandemic hit; apparently, they like it. Makri simply cannot find enough staff, which means she is working retail. *Covid is killing me.*

The odd day on the floor is fine; Makri likes to keep a personal eye on the business, and she enjoys seeing customers enjoying the Suite and Savory experience. But this is a business. She is the helm. What she is not is the owner. That would be her father-in-law. That would be a sore spot. Right now, as

Makri waves to a regular sipping soup in Savory, that is a scab she isn't going to pick. There is no point. The University of Toronto MBA grad knows regardless of pandemics she will have to report back on inventory, sales, revenue, profit, labor costs, and anything else her father-in-law demands. Nicely, of course.

Truth be told, Makri would like to buy Suite and Savory from her father-in-law. She has the money. What she does not have is her husband's blessing. Not that Makri needs any man's blessing, but Nik Pappas isn't going to seriously consider any purchase request unless it comes from his son. His favorite son, although no one says that out loud.

In the quiet of their bedroom, usually after a rousing round of grope and tickle, Makri says it to her husband. He dismisses the contention, but he is pleased, and he agrees albeit silently. What he has yet to agree to is bringing the purchase proposal up with his father. Makri is going to give it one more go. She has a bottle of Champagne Henriot Cuvée Hemera 2005 chilling in the wine fridge and a bag of goodies, including the Earthly Body Love Button, from Venus Envy. Kostas will be limp when she is done with him.

If that doesn't get Makri what she wants, she will go to Plan B. Kostas will not like Plan B. His father will like it even less.

It's been several years since Woo Woo has been to Suite and Savory. Little has changed. Three floors invite shoppers to browse through collections of fashion, art, jewelry, crafts, and furniture, often from local or Canadian artists and artisans. Everything is spread elegantly and tastefully over each floor. The message is clear: take your time, find something you love, find something you can't live without.

On the bottom floor, nestled among ottomans with iron bases, poplar sideboards, and fusion side tables is Savory, a café for those who want ambience dished up with their avocado toast. Woo Woo is tempted to have a tea hot chocolate and a few silent affirmations before she seeks out Sofia. Instead, she channels Charlene and gets to the task at hand.

The young woman behind the counter is as elegant and tasteful as the products that surround her. "Camila" is the name on her bronze name badge. Woo Woo introduces herself and asks if Sofia is in. (Woo Woo knows she is in. Lexie followed her from her house to the store.) Camila hesitates, stylishly, for only a few seconds. Woo Woo's geometric mandalas have likely confused her. Could this really be a friend of Sofia's?

It couldn't. But Woo Woo has been rich longer than Sofia. She knows how to look haughty. Tastefully. Camila turns and Woo Woo knows she is in. Step one: completed. Before Woo Woo can truly feel guilty for acting haughty, Sofia is beside her, hugging her, and saying "It's been way too long." Woo Woo wants to believe she is sincere, but Sofia does know her last name. (Aeron, as in Aeron Aerospace.)

"Have you tried our tea hot chocolate?" Sofia asks. Woo Woo wonders who is playing whom.

Once settled in Savory with the steaming liquid bling and a plate of macarons, Sofia takes the reins. "I'd love to believe this is a social call. I suspect it's something more."

Woo Woo blushes. The color is somewhere between crimson and fuchsia. Deceit does not come naturally to her. "I was hoping to interest you in a collaboration, a small collaboration I hope will benefit both our businesses." Woo Woo explains about Vitality+ and her co-ownership. She mentions the renovations they have done, specifically the reiki/reflexology/massage/aromatherapy room. "I was hoping to repeat your customer offer of a couple years ago. I would do a complimentary 10-minute reflexology or reiki session for customers and a discount card for services at Vitality+."

Sofia is interested, especially when Woo Woo says she and her friend, Lexie Hill, will organize the day. Promotion will be basic: signage in the store, in the gym, and postings on social media. Perhaps staff could mention the event to customers. Sofia agrees, although she explains to Woo Woo that Covid is killing her.

That's the aside Woo Woo needs. It opens the door to discussing the personal side of business. Sofia, always professional, does not dwell on the negatives. She makes it clear the business is doing well, but the pandemic has made more than the usual demands. "That must be tough on family life," says Woo Woo as she reaches for another macaron. Cherry. It matches her cheeks.

Suite and Savory's owner is many things. Slow is not one of them. Astute is. Suspicious is. But as Sofia looks at the harem pants and the waxed cotton bracelets, she sees what everyone sees. A nice woman with a good heart who is just a little … well, you know. Fact is, Sofia would like to gripe about her family, and who better to gripe to than this woman who has no connection to her family and unlikely ever to have one. Unless, of course, Woo Woo snorts cocaine. Sofia laughs to herself.

Then Sofia leans in. She gripes.

Woo Woo smiles. To herself.

Chapter 9.

If Woo Woo were here, she'd say this was an omen. Lexie's appointment was for 1:30 with Evan Vickers, entertainment manager for Enigma. The man standing in front of Lexie—with his over-gelled hair, his stressed jeans, and his Metallica tee—is not Vickers. It's Dimitri Pappas. He might well be an omen.

Dimitri stretches out a hand. Nonchalantly. His effort to be cool is not effortless. That's why it fails. Lexie can handle failure. She thanks him for meeting with her at short notice. Dimitri shrugs it off, casually he thinks. Stiff as a board is what Lexie thinks. He could benefit from yoga. She makes a mental note to try and sell him a Vitality+ membership but wonders if drug lords are really the clientele the gym wants.

"Drink?" asks Dimitri. He reaches behind the bar for a bottle of Knob Creek and pours himself a tumbler full. Very cool.

Lexie hesitates. Dimitri on bourbon might be good for the assignment. She asks for vermouth on ice. She has no idea why. It takes Dimitri several minutes to find the vermouth. (Lexie doubts he has ever been behind the bar. She wonders, again, why the hell he's here.) While he's jostling bottles, Dimitri fills in the silence. It's what most people do. Comedians know better.

"So, you want to do a set?"

Lexie upends a stool from one of the faux marble tables and sits down. She takes her time. "I have another idea I think you'll like."

Dimitri stops rattling bottles. "All ears."

"How about a comedy night, not just a comedian." Lexie pitches her idea: an evening of laughs and local talent. There could be two sets, and after each set people would flow from comedy central to another bar in Enigma: the lounge, the club, the pub. "Win, win" says Lexie succinctly. She can play cool, too.

"What's your win?" Dimitri wants to know.

So, not as inane as he would first appear. Lexie has the, feigned, decency to blush. She tells him about Vitality+ and her new role. "I will make some work-out jokes. They'll be prefaced by the fact that I own a gym. Although I'd like you to keep that between the two of us for now."

Dimitri grins. He obviously likes coloring outside the lines. "Sign me up for a membership."

Apparently, drug lords will be part of the clientele. "How does the idea sound?"

The youngest drug lord likes it. They discuss specifics—how many acts, how long each act should be, headliners, theme. Dimitri asks good questions and has good ideas. Lexie thinks there may be more to Mr. Gel than appeared at first.

"Next steps?" she asks.

"I have to run this up the chain, chat with staff, check the schedule. I'll get back to you."

It's unclear whether Dimitri chafes at the chain or this is just business as usual. Lexie yanks the chain. Gently. "I appreciate that—and I know about running things up the chain. I have three business partners, one agent, and my mother. Who apparently has final approval on everything."

"She should meet my father," says Dimitri. He takes a long swallow of Knob Creek. The casual tone is still there. What's new is the rancor.

"I'm the youngest," Lexie says. "I think that makes it worse. Last egg in the nest."

"I can't stand being the baby. Never taken seriously. Fuck 'em." Dimitri makes no attempt at nonchalance. This is old-fashioned bitters. Lexie wants him to continue. She nods as if she knows what he is talking about.

An hour later, vermouth splooshing about her bladder, Lexie thanks Dimitri. They agree to meet later in the week once the ball and chain has been consulted. They laugh at their inside joke. Lexie thinks she might hurl. She is not sure who scares her more, Nik Pappas or his son.

***

It's late afternoon. Too early for supper, too late for lunch. Woo Woo suggests they have afternoon tea. Charlene thinks it's a great idea. She offers to make sandwiches and munchies, while Woo Woo and Lexie make their way from downtown Halifax. Everyone agrees to meet in an hour.

"Terrell needs to hear this," says Lexie. "Woo Woo, you should text him."

The text is non-committal. Terrell doesn't know what to read into it, and he doesn't know what the hell afternoon tea is.

***

There are English cucumber sandwiches with mayonnaise and cream cheese on white bread; egg salad with diced onion and Dijon on whole grain; and ham and cheese on rye. (Charlene made a quick trip to the grocery store.) Everything is cut into fingers, crusts removed. (Madoff got a few crusts, but he's holding out for the ham and cheese.) Pickles, chow, and chutney are spread out on the table along with the sandwiches. Tea is on.

Charlene is impressed with herself. She realizes when her friends arrive and ooh and aww that what she is feeling is not self-satisfaction but contentment. She has fun with her friends. They sit down and reach for

74

the sandwiches. Terrell arrives a few minutes later. He can hear the Angels—nope, still not right—talking and laughing. He yells out hello as a four-legged cream puff hurtles himself at the detective. There are licks and nudges and jumps and cuddles. And there is a chew stick. Madoff loves Uncle Terrell.

It's taken 55 years, but Michael Terrell now knows what afternoon tea is. He could get used to this. Even the cucumber things are great. He sends a quick text to Boone to let her know how the other half lives.

Once bellies are full, pleasantries exchanged, and Terrell and Woo Woo have completed their awkward dance, it's down to business. Bottom line: in two days the three women have learned a lot and learned absolutely nothing to help Luke.

Charlene relives her meeting with Nik Pappas. He did not confess to being a drug trafficker. He did not admit that Luke Castle is innocent. On the plus side, Charlene has a follow-up meeting, and he serves great coffee.

Similar reports come from Lexie and Woo Woo. They had longer, more personal conversations but nothing that got them any closer to understanding what has happened with Luke or even if their respective targets (Charlene saw that in *Hung Out to Die*, the mystery she is currently reading) are involved in the drug business or the specific incident.

You can feel the women's disappointment. They all knew not to expect much going into these meetings. Still, they all expected great things. Even Terrell is disheartened—for Luke Castle and for the three women.

"Let's do a lateral arabesque," he says. Three women and one dog look at him in surprise. "It's a ballet thing."

"We know it's a ballet thing," says Lexie. "How the hell do you know that?"

"Boone. Apparently, her parents enrolled her in dance classes when she was little."

"Bet that went over well," says Charlene with a grin. Everyone grins back. "So what position are we shifting to?"

Terrell suggests they focus not on the details they learned about the business or the "assignment." (He has given in on the use of this word.) "Let's zero in on the people themselves. What did you learn about them? Nice? Nasty? Pushover? What impressions are you left with?"

Lexie goes first. She tells them about Dimitri and the booze. Does this indicate a problem or posturing? Then there are the floodgates, admittedly small gates, that opened about the chain around his neck. "Dimitri does not seem to like his father. At the very least, he does not like having to report to his father."

"We could use that," says Terrell. "We could also use the booze thing."

"How?" Woo Woo asks. She's not sure she wants to know the answer.

"The only way to get information, if you don't have physical evidence, is to have someone tell you. Dimitri is starting to sound like someone who likes to talk. When people talk, they let things slip. Sometimes they even tell you outright." The detective is being forthright, but gentle. He understands without ever having to ask that using people does not sit well with Woo Woo.

"There is another advantage to connecting with Dimitri," Terrell adds. "He works out of Enigma and Kimolos. Bit of a go-between it would appear."

"Or dogsbody," says Charlene.

"I do get the feeling Kostas is the favorite child, but there is nothing but my gut to support this," Terrell says. He turns to Lexie. "Do you think this guy is smart?"

Lexie considers this. It's a good question and one she has asked herself. "Dimitri is full of swagger, and it's easy to dismiss him as a serious contender. I think that would be a mistake."

Woo Woo paints a much different picture of Sofia: open, gracious, friendly, burdened. It's the last description that gets everyone's attention. "Maybe dogsbody applies here as well. I get the sense Sofia runs Suite and Savory under Nik Pappas's thumb. She doesn't own this business, but for all intents and purposes, it is hers. She has made it what it is. Successful."

"We can use that too," says Terrell. He does not look at Woo Woo. "Discontent is always to our advantage. It nudges people to share information they might otherwise not share. It encourages them to do things they might otherwise not do."

"Don't forget, though, there is a buffer between Sofia and Pappas. Her husband," says Woo Woo.

"Did you get a sense if the marriage was happy?"

"I didn't get the sense it wasn't," says Woo Woo.

"Of course, men are such strange creatures when it comes to affairs of the heart," says Charlene. Terrell (and everyone else for that matter, including Madoff) knows she is no longer talking about Sofia Makri and her husband.

"I think Nik Pappas has a weak spot," says Charlene switching gears. "Pride. Certainly for anything Greek. But perhaps that also extends to family, stature in the community, personal reputation. Threaten any of those and this man just might make a mistake."

Terrell is impressed. In hindsight, he shouldn't be. Charlene has said on numerous occasions that the cornerstone of being a successful auditor is knowing how to read people even better than financial statements.

It's agreed the three women will, carefully, continue to meet with their newly formed contacts. They also inform Terrell they'll be reaching out to Stephanie Kellor. "You're good on that front. Luke's lawyer has silently agreed to go along with the 'enhanced investigation.'"

"How do you silently agree?" Lexie wants to know. Terrell stares at her and smiles. "Ahh, that's how you do it."

"There is one more person you might want to meet with," Terrell says quietly just as it appears they are coming to an end. "There has been a small development." He reaches inside the file in front of him and takes out three pieces of paper. He gives one to each woman. "This is a summary of what's on Luke Castle's phone. Anything stand out?"

Woo Woo and Charlene are still scanning the page. Lexie is grinning. "I'll be damned."

Terrell laughs. "Nice to be famous, eh."

"It is indeed," agrees Lexie.

"Would someone like to tell us what's going on?" says Charlene. Madoff raises his head. He doesn't like Mama C to be left out.

"Line 24," says Terrell. And there it is. Among the apps on Luke Castle's phone is one for podcasts, among his favorite podcasts, Punchlines.

"It's great that Luke like's Lexie's podcast, but how does that get us in to see him?" Woo Woo asks.

"One of two ways," says Terrell. "Lexie can go to visit him under the pretext of helping to make his day brighter, like celebrities do during hospital visits. Or she can go with his mother and the offer of help is on the table for everyone to see. The best option will likely be obvious once you've met with Stephanie Kellor."

"I could even do a podcast from there," says Lexie. "If you think we could get permission."

"How does that fit in with the theme of Punchlines?" Charlene wants to know.

"It's a new podcast I'm thinking of starting up," says Lexie. "Working title: Polygraph: Truth be Told."

"Good grief," says Charlene at the same time Woo Woo says, "That's wonderful."

Terrell thinks they're both right.

Madoff farts.

It was the ham and cheese sandwich.

Chapter 10.

It's nearly midnight. Nik Pappas is done for the day. He hangs up his phone, the phone his wife doesn't know about and the one the cops can't tap. There will be more calls about this particular problem tomorrow, but it's late and Pappas is tired. He does not make decisions when he is tired. That's when you make mistakes. Pappas does not make mistakes.

He sips the last few mouthfuls of his Metaxa, stands up and stretches. He has one final ritual to perform. He goes to the bedroom. Angela is asleep. She has been asleep for hours. Neither a late-night person nor a light sleeper, Angela is not disturbed by the schedule Pappas keeps, physically or otherwise. That's his business.

Pappas gives his wife's forehead a gentle caress. She doesn't stir. He admires her ability to shut down. Tomorrow is Friday. They will have a family and friends' dinner. It's a weekly event. It will be loud, it will be filled with laughter, someone (probably Dimitri) will drink too much, there will be at least one disagreement and one put down, likely between brothers although Sofia can be difficult when she puts her mind to it. It will not matter. This is about coming together.

Family is on Nik Pappas's mind. He knows his youngest son is frustrated. With him. He knows his daughter-in-law is chafing under his thumb—and this will turn to anger when she understands his plans for Suite and Savory. His store. This anger will force a wedge between him and Kostas. In the end, Kostas will pick blood over some woman, even some woman he loves.

First though, Pappas must talk with Angela. She must be on side. He cannot imagine she won't be. Together they will talk to Mirabelle. Mirabelle may not be on side, and that will break Pappas's heart.

Washed, undressed, teeth brushed, Pappas is ready to call it a night. He has one more ritual to perform. He pads softly to Mirabelle's room. She is fast asleep, covers kicked back and in a ball. Pappas quietly straightens the covers. He makes sure not to disturb his daughter. He leans in and kisses the top of her head. God, he loves this little one.

The day is done. Pappas is about to turn off his bedside lamp when he gets a notification on his phone—the one the cops can tap. It's a simple text: Charlene Kurtz. Done.

***

The face in the bathroom mirror smiles back at Sofia Makri. The manager of Suite and Savory has had a good day and is looking forward to a repeat performance tomorrow. She takes the jade roller and moves it lightly over her temples, her cheeks, her jawline, and, as Woo Woo Aeron would say, her third eye.

Woo Woo is part of the reason Makri is smiling. Well, Aeron is part of the reason why Sofia feels she has the world by the tail. If she leaves Suite and Savory behind—and her father-in-law with it—it would be good to have another partner. The daughter of an aerospace billionaire would make a great partner. Sofia has plans to cement that partnership.

She makes her way to the king-size bed she shares most nights with her husband, now dead to the world. He worked late, ate quickly, and dropped off almost immediately. Something is up with this kid in juvie, but Sofia didn't get the details. She'll get them tomorrow. Kostas is about as closed as his father when it comes to business and bumps, but Sofia is his exception. He trusts her implicitly. In part, because he knows she is outside the business. In part, because she is his wife and family is everything. In part, because Sofia has spent 12 years cultivating this openness.

It is never Sofia's intention to hurt Kostas, but if she moves forward with her plans that is exactly what she will do. She wonders how much she should tell Kostas and decides what she has decided all along: absolutely nothing. Kostas is daddy's boy. He will not be pleased with his wife, the one person in the world he trusts implicitly.

***

Dimitri Pappas is on his third bourbon. He's feeling the melting effects. He'll sleep well tonight. He looks at the blonde woman in the bed beside him and tries to remember her name. He fails. It doesn't matter. She's not Greek, which would piss his father off, so she is perfect. Perhaps he'll bring her to dinner on Friday. Dimitri laughs. The blond stirs for a moment then melts back into the shadows of the bed.

Perhaps he could do comedy, Dimitri thinks. That would also piss his father off. But it might be something he would be good at. He certainly had Lexie Hill laughing. If you can make a comedian laugh, you must have talent. It doesn't occur to Dimitri that Lexie was laughing to be polite. She has similar problems with her mother. That's what brought them together. Dimitri would have made a pass, but he knows she's gay. Lexie is open about her sexuality. Fact is, it's

nice to have that out of the way. He needs
someone he can confide in, someone who is
not joined at the hip to his father. Someone
who doesn't deal drugs. And let's face it,
someone that isn't blond.

Chapter 11.

Nathan answers the phone on the second ring. "Vitality+. How can I help?" A man Nathan is sure he doesn't know asks to speak with Charlene Kurtz. "One moment," he says and puts the man on hold. Telling Charlene she is wanted on the phone also means saying hello to Lexie. They both go to the office after yoga, after coffee.

It's not that Nathan doesn't want to say hi to Lexie, he's just not sure what to say, "Hiya Mom." Nathan is not a "hiya" kind of guy, and Lexie is not his mother. That would be the woman who adopted him 38 years ago. Maybe Nathan could say, "Hello bio-Mom." He knows that won't work either, just as he knows at some point they have to move beyond whatever the hell this is right now. It then occurs to Nathan that Christmas is coming. "Dear god, do I have to buy her a gift?"

After a few awkward seconds that Charlene does not want to live through again, Nathan manages to squeak out that she has a call on hold. Charlene settles into her business stance. "Charlene speaking."

She instantly recognizes the voice on the other end of the line. What she doesn't know is why Nik Pappas is calling her. He gets right down to it. "I need an accountant." Charlene smiles. She gets asked this a lot. "I have several people I'd recommend." Nik Pappas laughs. "Sorry. I wasn't clear. I need an accountant, and I'd like you to take the job."

***

This is how things were supposed to have gone. Charlene would set a time with Zoe for a follow-up appointment. That's when Pappas and the gym co-owner would sign any papers, shake hands, and enjoy another delicious cup of coffee.

Things did not go that way. To Charlene's amazement—and it can be heard in her voice—Pappas wants her to do the books for a business he owns. There will be a change in ownership.

Part of Charlene is impressed with herself and the impact she has made, a job offer after only one meeting. Another part of Charlene is insulted. She is a certified internal auditor. She doesn't "do books." Usually she would let the offeror down softly with only a little huff. This is a different situation. Charlene wants to learn more about Pappas and his operations. She does

87

not, however, want to be involved in money laundering.

She thanks Pappas for the offer and expresses her interest. "I don't feel I can take on any new work without first discussing it with my co-owners. Would it be all right if I got back to you early next week?"

Pappas assures her this will be fine. Charlene thanks him for the offer. Mostly she thanks him silently to herself for giving her some breathing room. There is something going on here that she can't quite put her finger on.

***

Madoff senses Mama C's consternation. He gets up from his doggy bed and licks her leg. He wants Charlene to know he loves her. He is also aware that in times of consternation his mother often absently reaches for dog treats. Madoff can always eat treats. He tells himself Mama C feels better when he does.

There is no feeling better today. Charlene weighs the pros and cons of saying yes, relives her meeting with Pappas, goes over in her mind what could have led to this unusual request. (The man surely cannot do business this way.) Then she repeats the process, going nowhere and to Madoff's dismay going nowhere near the treat cupboard.

88

It's time for action. Charlene does something she has never done before. She texts Terrell and asks if he can meet for coffee tomorrow. She includes Lexie and Woo Woo on the text, but everyone knows protocol has been broken. This may be distraction or it may be that Charlene is tired of mincing around Woo Woo and the detective as they play out their own Hallmark holiday movie.

Terrell reads the text. He pours himself a beer and sits in front of the television. The TV is not turned on. Woo Woo moves to her meditation room. She sits on her cushion and stares at nothing.

Lexie laughs. She laughs so hard tears stream down her cheeks. Lexie is not a Hallmark fan.

Chapter 12.

Luke has a nickname. He knew it would happen. Everyone in here has a nickname. It's about boredom, it's about domination, it's about tradition. It is inevitable.

Some names are based on physical attributes (Beast, for example). Some are based on personality traits (Beast, for example). Some are based on crime committed (Beast, for example). It doesn't matter. Once the name has been given, it sticks. Luke hates his nickname. Hates it because it isn't true. Hates it because it is. Hates it because his mother will hear it. Hates it because his mother won't hear it if she can't visit.

Some part of Luke, the part that he brings out at night when the lights go off and the darkness is so thick you can spread it like peanut butter on fresh white bread, knows that his nickname is a badge of honor. He has earned respect, respect he never asked for, respect he doesn't want, but respect he savors, nonetheless. Another part of Luke, the part that follows him through juvie every day, during school, doing chores, watching

TV for the allotted 60 minutes, knows the nickname doesn't matter. It's a juvie nickname. Luke is going to federal prison. Chances are Luke will never get out of prison no matter what you call him.

It may be that stark reality, it may be that Luke is still a kid, it may be that Beast is above him snorting and farting, but Luke misses his mother. He wants to see her. And Brandon. But he's in Waterville, about 90 minutes from Halifax by car. Luke's mom does not have a car. She can't afford to rent one. She might be able to borrow one, but that is not as easy as it sounds. It would mean asking an acquaintance, likely someone from work, or asking her old boyfriend. Luke does not want his mother going anywhere near that trash.

Ironically, perhaps, Luke had been looking forward to going to the Abbie Lane. Not that he wanted to be in a mental hospital, but he wanted to be in Halifax. His Mom could visit. Brandon could visit. Today he was told by a guard that he's not going to the city. No beds. "Healthcare in this province is fucked." Luke feels a little like the healthcare system.

Ironically, perhaps, Luke may be in the safest place he could possibly be. Beast has taken a liking to him. Or at least he doesn't dislike him. When others approach, others Beast doesn't approve of or Luke doesn't know, Beast stands up. That's all it takes. Luke gets to eat his meals in peace, he gets to relax during break without fear of being swarmed, he does his chores knowing any bruises he gets will be of his own making. Luke may not know what "ironically" means, but he knows he has a friend in a boy named Beast. Luke listens to the snorting and the farting, and he breathes a little easier. It means Beast is alive.

His lawyer will arrange for his mother to visit, and maybe Brandon. Luke will insist on it. He's not sure what he has to bargain with, what it is that will give his insistence any weight, but he will think of something. He has his insurance policy, of course, but that is a desperate measure for much more desperate times.

Now he has to learn to sleep in this place, to find some comfort in knowing the people he loves are safe because he is here. That is a choice he has made, and he would make again in a heartbeat.

His nickname is not a choice. His mother will hear it. It will crush her.

Kingpin.

Chapter 13.

A blend coffee from Timor, Sumatra, and Papua New Guinea sits in the French press. Five kinds of herbal tea, including echinacea and hibiscus, peek out of a small bowl on the lunchroom counter. A tumble of morning glory muffins is on a plate beside a small stack of napkins. Lexie arrives first. She pours herself a coffee, grabs the muffins, and walks into the office. Charlene is working on a PPT. Within a few minutes, Terrell and Woo Woo arrive. Separately. They're both carrying steaming mugs: coffee and tea. Maybe that says everything, Lexie thinks.

No one is sure why they are here. Charlene is not drawing out the suspense. She's uncertain about the PPT. Madoff finds a fingerful of muffin passed his way absently. Charlene decides not to open the slide show now, but it may be needed later. She looks at her friends.

"Guess who called me last night?" This is not on the PPT.

"Nik Pappas," says Woo Woo. Charlene sighs. Really that woman can be a pain.

Terrell grins. Lexie hoots. Madoff accepts another mouthful of muffin. (Not his favorite, but this is for Mama C.)

"He wants to hire me." Charlene waits. Everyone sits up. Perhaps she has a future in comedy, Lexie thinks. "As an accountant?"

"What the fuck," says Terrell. Three women sit back. Madoff sits up.

"I have a PowerPoint," Charlene says. Everyone agrees they should see the slides. They are no further ahead at the end of the presentation, which was very well done, Woo Woo assures her friend.

"Why you?" Lexie wants to know.

"Why now?" Woo Woo asks.

"Why me?" Terrell says. To himself.

***

It's agreed Charlene will meet with Pappas to learn more about the job offer. She'll let him know she has the blessing of her business partners but needs to be certain she is a good fit for the job. She'll try to sound excited but cautious. "All accountants are not the same. They come with different backgrounds. She needs to be sure her experience will benefit Pappas." Charlene puts that key message on a PPT slide.

"I will not help anyone launder money," Charlene says. She is adamant. Madoff thinks Mama C may be distracted. He looks for a piece of muffin. Nothing.

94

"Do you know how to launder money?" Woo Woo asks.

"Of course I know how to launder money," says Charlene. "It's accounting 101."

"Will you be on my new podcast?" Lexie asks.

Terrell wonders if Charlene has any rum.

***

As he leaves Vitality+, Terrell texts Boone. "Arrow."

Boone knows what this means. Something is up. Something that concerns her senior detective.

***

As Terrell's text lands in Boone's phone, another lands in his. It's from Luke's lawyer. "Good to go with Stephanie Kellor. I've given her a head's up. I've also cleared everyone with Waterville."

Terrell turns around. He texts Boone. "Will have to be a late lunch. I'll text you."

The Triad has scattered throughout the gym, but no one has left. Lexie is the first to see Terrell's about-face. She gathers up Woo Woo and Charlene. They all head to the office. Terrell is waiting when they get there.

He wastes no time. "Stephanie Kellor will meet with you." He pushes a piece of paper across Charlene's desk. It has Stephanie's phone number.

"Now?"

"No time like the present," says Terrell.

Charlene's penchant is to plan things out carefully. Lexie likes to rush in headlong. Woo Woo prefers to feel what the universe is trying to tell her. Today, Lexie wins.

"Are you coming?" Woo Woo looks at Terrell.

That's the million-dollar question. Will his presence scare off Luke's mother or reassure her. It's decided Terrell will have lunch with Boone, and the women will text him if they feel his presence will be helpful. If not, they'll meet up with him and Boone at the Silver Arrow afterwards.

First though, Terrell has to call the Silver Arrow to see if it's okay to bring a dog with him.

***

The two-bedroom apartment the Castles call home is in Spryfield, a community that spans the class spectrum. Stephanie Kellor lives on Lemon Walk, in public housing. Small units that show the neglect of a beleaguered government and weary renters. Less than a kilometer up the road there are homes with ballrooms in them. Those owners are neither beleaguered nor weary.

Stephanie Kellor is waiting for her guests. She has tea ready and a plate of cookies sits on the coffee table in the living room next to a stack of papers and a book,

The Thong Principle. Stephanie sees Lexie shoot Charlene a quick look. She gives a tired grin. Stephanie has spent much of her life defending her existence. "Not mine. It's Brandon's communications textbook."

There is no time for small talk. Stephanie has to be at Tim Hortons, her second job, by three o'clock. "I'm not sure why you're here."

Charlene and Lexie look at Woo Woo. This requires an empathetic touch. "We're not sure why we are here either. We've been asked to help Luke. There is widespread concern he has confessed to something he did not do."

Stephanie Kellor looks at Woo Woo. She turns to Charlene, then to Lexie. She turns back to Woo Woo. It would seem this is a moment of decision, although the three guests are not sure what that decision might be. Stephanie needs to be certain. There is only so much you can do on your own, only so much you can contain in one body. There are also threats that come bearing gifts. This is her child's life at stake here.

Woo Woo reaches out her hand. She rests it gently on Stephanie's. The exchange lasts less than two seconds. Stephanie has decided. She puts her mug down. She looks beyond the three women sitting in her tired living room. She looks beyond the peeling paint and the leaking roof. She pushes past her fear of letting people in.

She puts her head in her hands and sobs.

***

Charlene and Lexie make an involuntary movement forward. Woo Woo raises a finger, and they stop mid-bend. Stephanie continues to cry, loud, wracking sobs that come from somewhere buried deep within. Woo Woo leans forward quietly and pours her a cup of tea. Everyone waits. Stephanie takes her time. She moves from bawling to blubbering to barely making a sound. She takes the tissue Woo Woo has somehow placed in her hand and dries her face. She reaches for her tea, takes a sip. "What happens now?"

This is Charlene's territory, strategic planning. "We'd like to learn more about Luke, about yourself and Brandon. We'll better understand how we can help."

"My son is in jail because he works for a drug dealer. He works for a drug dealer because I am poor. I am poor because I am a single mother with a grade 12 education who has a shit for an ex-husband. Anything else you need to know?"

"No," says Lexie. "That about sums it up."

Stephanie shoots her a look. Suddenly, she puts down her cup and laughs. And laughs. The sound starts in her bowels and works its way through abdominal organs and chest until it rolls out her mouth. Lexie joins in. Then Woo Woo. Lastly, Charlene. Four women are sitting sprawled over sofas and chairs and pillows and a plate of cookies when Brandon Castle walks in the door. He looks at his mother. He looks at the faces of three women he doesn't know. He grabs *The Thong Principle* and his papers. Between snorts his mother answers his unasked question. "I'm okay."

She finds her breath. "They're here to help Luke."

That stops Brandon cold. He sees three old women (anyone over 40 is old) with money. He knows this because rich people perch in the presence of poverty. Poor people sit back, kick back, and relax. It's a different way of being. Brandon knows what his life is, he knows why. What he doesn't know is how these women can help his brother. He grabs a cookie and sits in the recliner next to the TV. He sits in the middle of the chair.

At this point, Stephanie has relinquished her grasp on doubt. She is willing to trust the three strange women perched in her living room. Brandon is still clinging to skepticism. It's a safety mechanism. None of the old women try to dissuade him. He lies back, and listens.

Luke's life sounds like most of the teenagers Woo Woo, Charlene, and Lexie have ever known or ever been: good heart, rebellious streak, yearning to fit in. Where Luke's story varies is cocaine. Stephanie is up front. Her oldest child has $400 sneakers. He has a cell phone that rings at odd hours. Once she heard him say, "Yes, sir." She also knows her rent is paid three months in advance.

"Luke has never told me he is dealing. I never asked." Stephanie looks at her youngest son. "I should have. There are some things more important that having your rent paid in advance."

Stephanie takes a slow sip of tea. "Here's what I know about Luke. He's not stupid. He's certainly not stupid enough to drive 150 flour sacks stuffed with cocaine and not check that each bag is secure. He's also not stupid enough to jeopardize the life of anyone he loves. If he thinks that is a possibility, Luke will say he's guilty until the day he dies."

"You don't think Luke is involved in the current charge?" Lexie asks. Brandon snorts.

"Lady, look around. Does this look like the mansion of a major drug trafficker." Brandon doesn't wait for an answer. "It looks like the apartment of a guy who thinks he has it made when he can buy $400 skunks."

"Maybe he's smart enough not to flaunt his money," Lexie shoots back.

"Yeah, that's what you learn in grade eleven. How to traffic coke without getting caught."

She can't help herself. Lexie grins. Gotta give the kid points for balls. "Would you like to be on my podcast?"

***

As the three friends settle into seats at the Silver Arrow, a server arrives with one Annapolis Cider (Woo Woo), one Corona with lime (Lexie), one cabernet (Charlene), and one small bowl of water with two ice cubes (Madoff). (He found the hamburger a little salty.) Terrell and Boone are already fed and watered. They're trying not to push for details. The server thinks they're failing.

"Went well," says Lexie. She reaches for a leftover nacho on the plate in front of Boone and tries to hide a grin. Lexie is having a good time. Terrell is not.

"Ha, ha," he says.

That sets everyone off. They needed to laugh out loud and at length. Without realizing it, the weight of the situation has been bearing down, driving home the price of privilege. Boone dries her eyes. "Glad to hear it went well."

Charlene enjoys a good laugh, but business is business. She thinks she'll prepare a summary PPT for everyone. "Stephanie Kellor is giving us access to Luke, to herself, to whatever we need. She's at wit's end, and she needs friends."

"Brandon is even on side," says Woo Woo. She speaks quietly but clearly. No one has any trouble hearing her over the din of pub crawlers looking to let loose on a Saturday afternoon. Terrell thinks she has the most wonderful voice: firm yet soothing.

"What's next?" Boone wants to know.

"We need to see Luke," says Charlene.

"That is not a problem," says Terrell. He pauses. "I think it should be Lexie who goes. With Stephanie."

There is a small stabbing pain in Woo Woo's heart. Charlene's mouth opens almost involuntarily. Terrell doesn't give anyone any time to interject. "Luke knows Lexie through her podcast. She'll be a minor celebrity. He might open up more."

That makes sense. Pain and objection evaporate. "What do you mean 'minor'?" Lexie asks.

The laughter is back, but not for long. This is serious business, and everyone knows the risks even if they don't believe they will materialize. "Do you think I should ask the warden if they would like me to perform for the boys?"

Boone and Terrell exchange glances. After two decades working together that's all it takes for them to communicate. They're in agreement. "The more you can be around Luke, the better," Boone says. "But you need to be careful. If Dimitri finds out, he will connect the dots."

No one is laughing.

Daily Thoughts–
Shondra (Woo Woo) Aeron

Saturday, December 10th

I'm finding it hard having money. So much money. I've always found it hard. You know that. But today it was particularly tough. Stephanie Kellor is raising two teenage boys and working two jobs to barely make ends meet. My car costs more than she makes in a year—and it was a birthday gift from my father.

It feels good to be helping (if we are helping), but it is a band aid. Even if we are lucky enough to get Luke off on the charges, he is dealing drugs. If he doesn't face jail time now, he will at some point. I'd like to talk to Michael about this, but we don't seem to be talking. I don't know why. Maybe we should settle for friendship. Right now, I feel like even that is slipping away. I'm feeling sorry for myself (didn't meditate today).

On the plus side, Charlene wasn't the only one to get an invitation from the other side. Sofia called today. She invited me to brunch tomorrow. That's nice. I think. Frankly, not sure how to interpret this. Does she want to build on the connection we made this week—as friends? Partners? Is she on to me? Most likely she wants to get as close to my father's billions as possible. I hate money.

I said yes. To Sofia. It doesn't matter why she wants to meet. I told Charlene it could even be good for Vitality+. She liked that.

Dimitri also texted Lexie. To everyone's surprise. Surely he knows she's gay. Maybe he wants to be close to a minor celebrity. Inside joke. He asked Lexie if she'd like to come for drinks tomorrow night and hear the open mic performers. Thought it might help with her event. We're hoping it will do more than that, although what specifically I can't say.

I'm looking forward to the restorative yoga on Monday. But that's a day away.

I'd really like to talk to Michael.

Sincerely,

Shondra Aeron

Chapter 14.

Suite and Savory is bustling. With roughly three weeks until Santa arrives, shoppers are out in full swing, and they are willing to spend money. Sofia loves Christmas. Customers are in a good mood, their wallets are flexible, and merchandise that has sat on shelves for months is flying into reusable shopping bags.

She's ringing up a customer who needs three bags for her purchases when she spies Woo Woo. Sofia gives her the five-minute sign. That's okay with Woo Woo. She likes to shop, and Suite and Savory has lots of fun, frivolous, and fabulous options. That reminds Woo Woo she'll need gifts for her friends. She didn't need to worry about that last year. This Christmas is so much better.

There are bright scarves and elegant notebooks and mandala bracelets and snuggly slippers. All of which are lovely. None of which are right. Tucked on the lower shelf of a glass cabinet are three miniature pewter figures in yoga poses: lotus, shoulder stand, plow. They're perfect, Woo Woo thinks as she bends down. Woo Woo straightens up. They are perfect, for her. She's shopping for her friends. And Michael. She wishes she could talk to Michael.

Woo Woo turns away from the shelf and the three perfectly posed pewter figurines. She turns into Sofia. The two women laugh. Sofia takes her elbow. "I've reserved a table for us."

Over eggs benedict with a spring salad, Woo Woo and Sofia talk about the store's booming business, holiday plans, gift shopping ideas, and family traditions. "It's been me and my dad for so many years now," says Woo Woo. "It sounds sort of lonely. But it isn't. We have an old-fashioned dinner with all the fixings. There's a fire in the fireplace, a real one. We have champagne and later apple cider. It's comfortable and comforting."

Woo Woo can feel Sofia's eyes on her. She sees the lift at the corner of her mouth. She starts to turn a deep magenta, but there is nothing to be embarrassed about. "It sounds lovely," says Sofia. She focuses her gaze on some spot in the distance. Woo Woo knows this technique, knows sadness when she sees it. "Our Christmas is so different. It's jammed with people. It's loud and chaotic. Food and gifts everywhere. Kids out of control. I hate it."

Without being aware of what she's doing, well, maybe a little aware, Woo Woo reaches over and pats Sofia's hand. The lift is back on Sofia's lips. "Did you find anything you want to buy?"

The two women spend the next 20 minutes making plans for the reflexology/reiki offer. The big debate is timing: throw it in the holiday mix when people are spending money and stressed or wait until the new year when self-care, resolutions, and boredom drive people to gyms and bargains. Sofia glances around the store. She sees women and men (but mostly women) looking for original ideas and a little fun. Woo Woo follows her eyes. She feels the energy in the room. It's warm, pleasant, upbeat.

Before Christmas it is. That doesn't give a lot of time for promotion, but signage can be kept simple and social media used to full advantage. Sofia and Woo Woo will tap into their respective customer lists. It's agreed they'll get together on Tuesday—Woo Woo suggests some more of that hot chocolate tea—to finalize plans.

Sofia waves Woo Woo away when she reaches for her purse. "Please, brunch is on me. I'm so glad we got to spend some time together."

Woo Woo thinks Sofia may actually mean it. The magenta bloom is back.

***

Sofia is back tending to customers. Woo Woo is weaving her way around shoppers and bags and kids and the occasional dog. On the second floor, where the crush is in full force, Woo Woo makes her way to a corner display case. Here she finds two great gifts for Lexie: relevant, funny, usable. One will require personalization. One floor down Woo Woo finds a gift for Charlene, although she wonders if she is overdoing her theme. To her delight, on another bottom shelf, she finds another gift for Charlene that is sure to find a spot on her desk at Vitality+. It, too, will need some personalization.

Somewhere in this throng is Sofia and the answer to Woo Woo's personalization needs. Woo Woo spies her on the third floor in front of the counter and the cash register. Sofia is being more than helpful and assures Woo Woo her gifts—personalized professionally—will be ready in plenty of time for Santa to put them under the tree. Woo Woo can't thank her enough. Sofia reaches out and gives her a hug. Woo Woo likes hugs. This one is a little tight though. And it's getting tighter.

***

The reason for that tightness is 6' with black hair. There is a six o'clock shadow that took skill with an electric shaver. A slate turtleneck offsets dark pants and what Woo Woo swears are deck shoes. Sofia drops Woo Woo and forces a smile.

108

"Nik, how wonderful to see you. I wasn't expecting you today."

"Purely personal," says Nik Pappas. "Mirabelle and I are shopping."

Sofia's forced smile is back. Woo Woo wonders if the drug lord can see it. Or sense it. Mirabelle seems oblivious. Pappas turns his glance to Woo Woo, then back to Sofia. She shakes her head as if she has made some small faux pas. "Please, let me introduce you to my friend. Woo Woo, this is Nik Pappas, my father-in-law."

Woo Woo sees the confusion in Pappas's face, and the curiosity in Mirabelle's. "It's a nickname."

"You may know Shondra's father," Sofia says. She is reluctant to play this card, to potentially expose her hand, but senses she has no choice. Her father-in-law always does this to her. "Benjamin Aeron."

The change in Nik Pappas is swift and subtle. Woo Woo has seen it a million times. She knows what it means, and she knows the kind of man that makes this move. "Of course," says Pappas. "Your father and I have sat on a number of committees together. Please tell him I said hello."

As Woo Woo assures Pappas she will give her father his regards, Mirabelle wanders off. She stops at a display of slow fashion sweaters. Pappas skips the merest of beats as he scans the room for his daughter. Woo Woo feels his momentary alarm. So, the big man has another weak spot.

"I never know what to get her for Christmas," Pappas says. Woo Woo is uncertain if this is a door opening or brush strokes painting the picture of a good father.

Woo Woo opens the door. She's usually more reticent, but there are factors at play that supersede her own comfort level. "Teenagers are so hard to buy for. I know my niece is into all things environmental. The One Young World conference is being held in Montreal next year. Perhaps you could register her. You could all go together. A mini vacation with heart."

Pappas peers at Woo Woo like she has two heads. It is an expression Woo Woo has seen much of her life. The first time Michael looked at her that was the look. Mirabelle has selected two sweaters from the sustainable display and is making her way back to them through the crowd. *In for a penny, in for a pound,* Woo Woo thinks. "Of course, if travel isn't possible, you can always get her a Cavalier King Charles puppy."

Woo Woo fully expects Pappas to look at her now like she has three heads. She knows the playbook. Pappas does not play by the rules. He doesn't look at Woo Woo. He sees her. Woo Woo understands how this man came to run an empire. Illegal and otherwise. "That's impressive. How did you know?"

Woo Woo will shrug this off. She'll say something about how teenagers love puppies and aren't cavaliers the cutest. There are only seconds now until Mirabelle is back with them. Sofia has been momentarily distracted by a question from a customer. It's now or never. "Of course, you know what she really wants." She can feel the strength in Pappas's stare. He nods, the slightest of nods. Woo Woo plows ahead. "She wants what every young girl wants." Pappas doesn't move. "She wants a family that loves her."

Mirabelle is with them now. Sofia's attention has returned to the small group rooted to this singular spot. For a second, they sense the intrusion, understand at some level they have interrupted an important conversation. But Nik Pappas has returned. He gives Mirabelle a squeeze and admires her purchases. Sofia says she'll ring them up. It's time to disperse. As Woo Woo turns to leave, Pappas touches her arm. "I'm wondering if you'd like to join us for dinner on Friday. It's something we do each week with family and friends."

***

Lexie and Stephanie Kellor have finalized plans for a trip to Waterville tomorrow. There is no way to let Luke know they are coming. The warden's office is closed. (And they really have to stop using cops to get them access; it will draw attention to Luke). No calls are allowed on Sunday, so they can't reach out to Luke directly. It's a quiet day at the center. A time for youth to reflect and settle into themselves. No calls are allowed on Monday morning. All residents are in school until noon. Lexie and Stephanie will be there by then. Luke will be in the dark.

"It doesn't matter," Stephanie says. "I'm going to see my son."

***

Charlene and Madoff go for a long walk. Madoff loves his walks with Mama C. If there is no one else around, they sometimes sing "Hound Dog" by Elvis Presley. It's great fun. Today, Mama C is preoccupied. Madoff doesn't know this word, but he knows he doesn't have his owner's full attention. She's somewhere else. He thinks she is worried about the laundry.

Charlene bends down to pick up a small, round mound of moist warm poop. As she turns to straighten, she looks directly into the big brown eyes of her dog, and she apologizes. This is their walk. Charlene breaks into song. Madoff cocks a leg. There is a tree he missed.

***

Terrell is Christmas shopping. He finds himself at Suite and Savory. He's not sure

112

this is a good idea. He does not want to run into Sofia Makri or, god forbid, her husband, father-in-law, or brother-in-law. But this is like casing the joint. The Drug Unit has no evidence that anything illegal is happening at the store, including money laundering. The assumption is Pappas is looking for legitimate businesses. Still, Terrell wants to sniff things out. He walks all three floors and sees nothing out of the ordinary except for a water bottle that cleans itself and sweaters that are slow. When he picks up a $500 candle—and quickly puts it back down—he knows it is time to leave.

Chapter 15.

The house is quiet. Angela is out for the afternoon. Some poetry reading or something. Mirabelle has made a bolt for her room. She wants to unwrap her packages and relive the excitement. Pappas is happy for his daughter—and happy to have some time alone. He wants to relive his own afternoon. What the hell was that?

Pappas doesn't doubt that fate puts people in your path. He wonders if Shondra Aeron is one of those people. That woman knew things. Not things like a cop knows. Not things a competitor knows. Not even things family knows. Things only Mirabelle knows. Things only Pappas knows.

The drug lord makes the sign of the cross. He hasn't done that in years. His mother did it almost hourly. It was a way to ask for forgiveness. Nik Pappas isn't looking for forgiveness. He's content in himself and with himself. It's not often Pappas is thrown. Today, he was thrown.

He goes through the meeting with Woo Woo. He doubts it lasted even five minutes and she had more impact on him in those five minutes than most people do in five years. There was no threat. Pappas knows threats. There was hesitancy. He doubts it is because this woman thinks she's wrong. Probably Nova Scotia politeness.

So, this woman he met for five minutes was politely telling him what to get his daughter for Christmas—one gift he already knew (and reluctant to get), the other out of the blue and spot on. It was her last suggestion, though, that has Pappas fixated. He knows what she meant. He knows she knows he knows what she meant. And so on.

Pappas has realized this for some time. He has not yet realized what to do about it. But he must do something. He will talk with Angela today.

He will also talk with Kostas. It's time he dealt with the issue at hand. No one likes to disappoint family, to disappoint those we love. But you cannot avoid the inevitable. Pappas has made it clear he is not going to change his mind. His son will have to do something. Today.

Pappas picks up his phone.

Chapter 16.

Blocks. Blankets. Knee pads. Head rests. Woo Woo goes through the list of props in her mind and checks each one off as she brings them from the storage unit onto the studio floor. Restorative yoga requires a lot of props. The three women are helping Kristi, their yoga instructor and partner in Vitality+, prepare for the class and tuck participants into poses as needed.

Woo Woo savors this time of day. She savors this task. Both are full of hope. Hope for what is about to come—a fabulous day, a fabulous yoga class. Woo Woo is quintessentially hopeful. Except perhaps when it comes to Michael.

Kristi comes up behind Woo Woo. She brings with her gratitude. Unfortunately, the fit, graceful yoga instructor moves like a cat. She scares the bejesus out of Woo Woo. Once the initial shock abates, the two women collapse on the floor in a fit of giggles. This is how the first of the participants find them. It bodes well for the next 60 minutes.

Kristi is starting each class this month with a restorative pose and ending with buried savasana, another restorative pose. One new pose is introduced in each class, and the yogis work on the pose of the month: melting heart.

Today, the new pose is reclining princess. Woo Woo thinks it sounds lovely. Lexie finds it mildly offensive. Terrell is suspicious. But everyone is a fan. Blocks and bolsters are arranged behind their backs, another bolster is nestled under their knees, blankets are wrapped around their feet and draped over their reclining bodies. Eye pillows are gently placed on their third eye. Life is good. It gets even better when Terrell learns the other name for this pose is Barcalounger.

Terrell should know better. Just when you think you have this yoga thing aced, Kristi has everyone move into adept's pose, a recommended sitting pose for meditation. One knee and heel move in toward the groin, nudging the inner thigh. The other knee and foot move in the same direction. The ultimate goal: both knees on the ground, both feet seemingly interlocked. So goes the theory. Bodhi and Woo Woo are the only ones in the class who can do this. Bhodi is in significant discomfort, but he refuses to let on. Woo Woo knows this. She smiles.

Buried savasana is fun. Bodies are protected by pillows and bolsters and weights. Everyone collapses into themselves. Kristi goes around the room and rests a small, scented pillow on everyone's eyes. They breathe in a bit of heaven.

Heaven's gates open at the sound of the closing bell. Everyone sighs and starts gathering up props. There is a hint of reluctance, an unwillingness to let go of sanctuary and step into the world outside the studio doors. *"Anyone for coffee?"* Eight hands go up. Coffee makes the real world much more bearable.

***

Some idiot walked on a lake without checking the ice safety first. In he goes, and his dog jumps in after him. A passing RCMP officer comes to the rescue. The coffee crew is scanning iPhones to make sure the dog is okay.

"The little one is fine," says Charlene. She feels herself tearing up. Unacceptable for a professional auditor, but she is thinking of Madoff who is sound asleep upstairs in his doggy bed. Nathan is watching him. Charlene suggested Lexie ask Nathan for this favor. She never saw Lexie exit a room so quickly. She really has to get a grip, Charlene thinks. She ignores the issue she is avoiding, telling herself it's not relevant. No point going down an unnecessary path. It's what any good auditor would do.

Slowly people begin to move back into their routine. Archina and Bonnie are the first to leave. Kristi checks her phone for the third time and lets everyone know she'll be in the studio for the rest of the day. Terrell and the three women are waiting for Honey to leave. There will be a quick update before Lexie gets on the road. Honey makes no move to leave.

"Don't mind me," she says. "Pretend I'm not here."

***

There are two issues to address. One will come as a surprise. The first is relatively straightforward. It's a non-issue, Lexie thinks. "I went to Enigma. I had a drink. I talked with Dimitri, who had several drinks. He derided his father. He had another drink. I left."

"You don't think he suspects anything?" Terrell asks. Woo Woo hears the concern in his voice.

"I really don't," Lexie says. "He's focused on the bar. He thinks I bring the bar—and himself—cred."

"Did he mention the pizza joint?" Terrell wants to know.

"Only thing he said was he had to be at work there today. What a waste of his time. And that is a direct quote. I may get more out of him on Wednesday. We're doing the run-through then."

Charlene reaches for a napkin and crumples it, a signal the debrief is over. Woo Woo leans in. "I do have one small thing."

119

She feels everyone's eyes on her. Everyone's except Honey, who seems mesmerized by something on her phone. "Nik Pappas invited me to dinner on Friday."

Terrell chokes on his last mouthful of coffee. Charlene pitches the napkin across the café. Honey is no longer pretending to stare at her phone.

***

Stephanie Kellor is too nervous to eat. She made herself toast and a cup of tea. She's sipping the tea, but the toast is sitting on her plate untouched. Stephanie is trying to figure out why she is so nervous. Is it worry about Luke? About this new woman Lexie? About what she'll find out when they get to the detention center?

It's everything, and more. Brandon is off to school. So he says. *The Thong Principle* is sitting on top of his binder. Her son is pissed that he can't go to Waterville with his mom. She promised him next time. That means there will be a next time. Stephanie wonders how many next times there will be. How many years.

Now she knows what is really worrying her.

***

Charlene took some time with her appearance. She wants to look casual, as if

120

she is just popping into Pappas's office. But the pretext is that she is visiting other downtown businesses, so she needs to look marketing professional. (This is distinct from auditor professional.) She opts for a pair of taupe checkered pants with a black crew neck sweater. It's the dark brown leather belt that clinches the ensemble, Charlene thinks.

Zoe, looking elegant in a black one-piece jumpsuit with a burgundy blazer, welcomes Charlene like an old friend. Charlene makes a mental note to run this behavior by Terrell. Then she reminds herself she is not here as an auditor. "I apologize for stopping by. I was downtown and thought since I'm here Mr. Pappas might be available for a few minutes."

Mr. Pappas is available. In fact, he's standing in the doorway, hand outstretched. "And please, call me Nik."

Zoe is on her way to make some of that delicious coffee. Charlene is not sure how she knows this, but she does. Charlene is also not sure how the hell she ended up here. She sends a silent message heavenward. *Thank you, God.*

***

It is about an hour and a half drive from Halifax to Waterville, straight along the 101, although there is nothing straight about the east-west highway that runs from Bedford to

121

Yarmouth. Lexie worried about conversation, specifically, the lack of it, but Stephanie is an adroit conversationalist. Lexie point blank asks her about this. "Working retail you learn to make small talk," says Stephanie. "What I'm more worried about is what I'll say to my son."

Answering this question takes up most of the drive.

***

Beast is restless. It's never a good thing when Beast is restless. Or bored. Or frustrated. Or annoyed. Well, you get the idea. It's history class. Some days Beast likes history. He particularly likes World War II. Beast feels he would make a good soldier, particularly back then when it wasn't all stealth missiles and computer-aided drones. Beast likes a good tank. He would make a good tank driver. Beast wonders if the army would hire him. If he ever gets through this class, he could get his grade nine.

The instructor, Beast can never remember his name, suggests they take the remainder of class to identify the factors that led to the start of the Second World War. Beast raises his hand. "It was Hitler."

The instructor agrees but suggests it might be more nuanced than that. The instructor quickly rephrases. "It's about more than Hitler. What else was at play?"

Beast's hand goes up. "Fascism."

The unnamed instructor is impressed. He reminds himself not to stereotype these kids, to look beyond where they are and why they are here. He scans the class. "What is fascism?"

Beast is tired of playing this silly game. "Fascism is Hitler's middle name."

He doesn't wait for the nameless teacher to respond. "That's the lunch bell."

The teacher starts to hold up a hand to stop the exodus from the cramped classroom. The lunch bell rings.

***

The coffee is as delicious as Charlene remembered. Nik Pappas is as charming. He waves away her apology. "My door is always open." Charlene almost believes him.

She has not rehearsed what she is going to say. Charlene is not a rehearser. The main character in her latest mystery, *Hung Out to Die*, would have written down word for word what he was going to say and committed it to memory. But then, he is a psychopath.

The auditor's discomfort is apparent. Pappas prepares himself for a no—and to transform that rejection into acceptance. What has him momentarily confused is the in-person visit. A "no thank you" is usually delivered by phone. Even text. Pappas is not fond of anything that leaves a paper trail.

"I assume you have made a decision." Pappas smiles. It is warm. It may even be real.

Charlene matches his smile, and Pappas knows he has been wrong about the rejection. Pappas is rarely wrong. He knows there is more here than mere acceptance.

And here it is. The caveat that follows: "I'd be delighted to review the books for your company." Charlene points out she is a licensed CPA and is required to prepare a report on her findings. "I'm obligated to make that report available if requested."

Pappas takes a long, slow sip of coffee. The smile never leaves his face. Is this an implied threat? A way to get out of the job offer? What does this woman know?

Charlene has not rehearsed what she was going to say, but she did prepare for the questions Pappas would have, spoken or unspoken. Foremost among them: Do you know what I really do for a living?

She shuts down that line of thinking. "I bring this up because if you are changing a business's ownership, one of the buyer's requirements will be for any financial reports."

Pappas sighs. It is relief. It is also contentment. Things are going his way. Things usually go his way. With only a hint of dramatic flair, Pappas reaches into his pocket and takes out a loonie. He slaps the coin gently on his desk. "You're hired."

Charlene's confusion is obvious. Pappas finds it both reassuring and a little endearing. "Is this not what lawyers do when they want a conversation to be confidential?"

The auditor in Charlene gets it now. She's still offended, but she understands Pappas is about to tell her something he doesn't want anyone else to know. Oh well. His mistake.

"I'll certainly sign a non-disclosure. That's standard," says Charlene. "It's important you feel free to share information."

Pappas is waving again. It's unclear whether he doesn't feel the need for an NDA or if this will be dealt with at a later date. He leans forward. Takes another sip. "I am not selling a business. I am giving one to my daughter, Mirabelle, a gift for her eighteenth birthday next year."

"What an amazing gift," Charlene says. She means it. She also knows the odds of an 18-year-old successfully running an established business are slim. What could tip those scales—a damn good accountant. *Dear God, what have I gotten myself into?*

***

It's Two-Meatball Monday. That's what everyone calls the spaghetti lunch ladled out at the detention center at the start of every week with, you guessed it, two meatballs. (Beast gets at least four.) Luke doesn't mind the meal. It's usually made that morning. It has real meat, and salt can disguise any flavor you don't like.

He is halfway through his pasta mound when a CO walks up to a guy two tables over. The CO nods, and a kid about 14 follows him out of the dining hall. This pattern will be repeated over the next 45 minutes as family and friends arrive. It's visitation time, what the correctional officers call VT and the residents call get out of jail free.

The pasta on Luke's plate is getting cold. He shoves the last three forkfuls into his mouth and reaches for his bun. Luke is in no hurry. He has no family coming. He sees the CO heading to his table. He looks to see who is getting out of jail free. The CO makes eye contact with him and nods.

***

The December air is crisp. It's cool on the lungs, but not cold. A bright sun embraces Argyle Street in a golden glow. There is even some warmth to the sunshine despite the winter temperatures and the tilt of the earth's axis. Charlene takes a moment to breathe in gratitude and exhale what she no longer needs. It's a thing they do in yoga. One more breath.

Charlene heads to the Italian Market. She's going to have company tonight although this was not her plan for the day. As she makes her way to the car, she texts Lexie,

Woo Woo, and Terrell. "I have news. Dinner at 6."

***

Luke sees his mother as soon as he turns from the hallway into the visiting area. It is a grey room: grey walls, grey metal tables, grey plastic chairs. There is even a picture of a grey jay on one wall. Luke thinks it is the most beautiful room he has ever been in.

The seventeen-year-old makes his way to the table where his mother is waiting. He would bolt if the CO would let him. The CO wouldn't. Stephanie is in tears. They are flowing freely and fiercely. This is joy. This is fear. This is sadness. Some woman Luke has never seen has her arms around his mother. After what seems like a million years, but is less than four seconds in reality, Stephanie Kellor is hugging her son. Tightly.

Hugs are allowed in Waterville. These are kids after all. They are also kids with a record. Luke hears the CO clear his throat and steps back from his mother. They sit down, holding hands. Holding hands across the table is allowed. Everyone was searched before they were permitted inside the grey room.

Stephanie is trying to ask her son a hundred questions—Are you okay? Are you eating? Are you safe?—at the same time her son is firing his own round of inquiries—Is Brandon all right? Do you need money? Is something wrong? Mother and son burst out laughing. They have forgotten where they are, they have forgotten about the woman sitting at the table with them, they have forgotten a CO is watching their every move.

Someone in the grey room does move. Beast gets up from the table where his grandmother is telling him about the importance of getting his grade 12 and that she loves him. He walks across the room toward Luke and his mother. Stephanie looks up, and up. She feels nothing but fear, for herself and her child. The COs in the room are on full alert. Some back and forthing is permitted during VT. Roommates often introduce themselves to each other's family, some become family. But this is a first for Beast. Firsts for Beast are not always pleasant experiences.

They aren't for the woman sitting with Stephanie Kellor and her son. Before a CO and a side-handled baton can intervene, Beast leans over and hugs the woman. "I can't believe it's you." A CO is inches from Beast now, his baton even closer. He hesitates. Sounds like Beast might know this woman.

Luke Castle does. For the first time, Luke looks at the woman at the table with him and his mother. He knows this woman. "You're Lexie Hill."

Lexie nods. She is not sure her lungs are working. Maybe it's her heart. The big guy hugs really, really tightly. The CO is not taking a chance he has misread the situation. He steps forward. "Down, inmate." Beast doesn't move. It's not that he is refusing to obey, but he's too busy looking at Lexie. Lexie and Stephanie are not certain what is going on, what to do. Luke knows the answer to both. He stands up quickly and says loudly, "It's okay. This is a friend of ours—both of ours."

By now the CO has company. There are four officers, including a sergeant assessing the situation. Somewhat miraculously, Lexie finds she can speak. "I'm fine officer. Just getting a hug from a fan."

The sergeant doesn't know why Lexie is famous (or if she even is) but he's not taking any chances with social media blowback. "Visitors and inmates must be seated at all times during visitation." This is not true, but no one is going to argue. The moment has passed. Beast is thrilled to be here with Lexie Hill (he listens to her podcasts on Luke's iPad), Luke is glad no one is hurt, Lexie is trying to ascertain if there is any permanent damage to her chest. Stephanie Kellor has heard for the first time what they call kids here. *Inmate*. She can't breathe.

Chapter 17.

The menu is simple and appropriately hardy for a winter dinner: Italian wedding soup and deli sandwiches, prosciutto, basil and bocconcini on sourdough panini buns, and smoked turkey breast, roasted red peppers, and Swiss cheese on focaccia. The ready-to-eat menu also means less prep time for Charlene and Madoff (he is the taste tester), and it doesn't matter when everyone arrives. The meal can be dished up in minutes.

Terrell is the first to ring the bell. He usually is. He walks Madoff before they eat. Sometimes it also gives him a chance to have a quiet moment with Woo Woo. Not tonight. Woo Woo hasn't arrived yet, but Madoff is happy to see the detective. There are lots of licks, and Madoff picks the right pocket to find the hidden treat. (There are treats in both pockets.)

Lexie walks through the front door holding out an Italian red. She looks for Madoff and realizes Terrell must have been the first to get here. Lexie makes her way to the kitchen. Charlene is stacking sandwiches on a plate. "Do you have any Voltaren?"

"Where does it hurt?" Woo Woo asks. Charlene and Lexie whirl around.

"You're like a shapeshifter," Lexie says. "And all over my chest."

Woo Woo is doing reiki on Lexie when Terrell and Madoff walk back through the door. Madoff doesn't understand why Woo Woo is leaning over Aunt Lexie, but it looks nice. *Maybe she'll do that to me*, he thinks. Terrell thinks the same thing.

***

There is a rhythm to meals when everyone gathers to discuss "business." There is wine or beer, banter, and tidbits for Madoff. Then there is coffee, dessert, and getting down to it. Woo Woo isn't sure if the routine they have created is to remind them they are friends first or to delay what can be difficult conversations. In her case, it also gives her more time with Michael. And her friends, of course.

Woo Woo has brought a lovely ginger orange tea to settle the stomach and tease the nostrils. She also brought a Kivu Congo Reserve from Just Us! She thinks Michael will like it, and she gets to support two co-ops in the process, one in Nova Scotia and one in the Eastern Democratic Republic of the Congo. For dessert, there are pecan tarts compliments of Lexie.

"No ribs are broken," Lexie says. This garners her both concern and raised eyebrows. Lexie tells them about her visit to the detention center, about Luke, about Beast, about what little she has learned.

"On the plus side, Luke seems to be doing okay in juvie. Beast has taken to him, and there is no better safety mechanism."

"There is a downside, I assume."

Lexie gives Terrell a look. It's not her squash-a-heckler look. She's weighing what she is about to say. "Luke did not say much about his situation. I don't know if that's because his mother was there or because he is not going to say anything regardless."

"You need to go back. Without Stephanie." Woo Woo reaches to pat Lexie's hand. Lexie isn't fast enough to move it beyond reach. Her friend's intuition or acumen or whatever the hell it is never fails to amaze her. It's a gift—and maybe a gift she could use to draw Luke out. Woo Woo should come with her.

"Yes," says Woo Woo. She can feel Michael and Charlene's confusion. "I'm going to juvie with Lexie."

"Of course, you are," says Terrell. He feels a sharp stab in his chest. Must be indigestion. "What's the pretext for returning?"

As it turns out, no pretext is necessary. One of the COs got word to the superintendent about someone "famous" being onsite. Glenn Best made an impromptu walk through. He shook hands, he made polite chitchat, he worked his way nonchalantly around to the table with the somewhat shortish, somewhat round woman, and the big man-boy. Glenn Best had never heard of Lexie Hill (the internet soon changed that), but he was experienced enough and savvy enough to know she was no threat to his operation and might be an asset.

"He invited me to do a show for the kids. I also suggested we do a workshop. I'll use the workshop on my podcast."

"When?" Terrell wants to know.

"Thursday," says Woo Woo.

***

Terrell congratulates the women on their progress. He also cautions them. Again. Inside, he is breathing a sigh of relief. Making friends is fine. There is no danger here.

Charlene brings in a fresh pot of tea. "I do have some news. I've been invited to dinner at Nik Pappas's on Friday." The pain in Terrell's chest is back.

Woo Woo is delighted she'll have company. Lexie is a little annoyed to be left out. Terrell points out the issue everyone has been avoiding: How do you keep the hackles from rising on Pappas's neck?

"I really don't think it will be a big deal," says Charlene.

"No, a man who is by nature suspicious will find it perfectly normal that two women he has never met before suddenly turn up in his life at the same time he has lost $6 million in cocaine."

Terrell has a point. It is the point Charlene has been pushing into some compartment in her mind all day. It is the reason for dinner. It is the river they must cross before she can get to the other side.

Charlene looks at her friends. She is a little dismayed with herself and the mess she has landed them in. "It is a bit of a chunderfuck."

Now her friends are looking at her with surprise. Charlene feels a ripple of heat spread throughout her neck and her face. She is not a curser by nature, but this seemed to fit the situation. "It's a word in a new mystery I'm reading. *Hung Out to Die.*"

Lexie hoots. Woo Woo giggles. Terrell massages his heart.

Interestingly, it is Terrell—going against every fiber in his body—who finds the way out of the dilemma. "You need to approach other businesses downtown and elsewhere. You need to offer discounts, workshops, onsite yoga courses, whatever you can. You need to be visible. Pappas needs to know the Vitality+ owners are making the rounds and meeting with local merchants."

Everyone dives in. Charlene starts a spreadsheet and together they come up with a list of likely businesses. They get contact info and divide the list up. This is what the women will do for much of the week. They'll even get Kristi involved. They may even pull it off.

***

Tuesday dawns dull. There is more dullness than dawn. The thermostat has dipped below zero and moisture clings to the air. The Bedford Basin is shrouded in sea mist. The triad goes to yoga class and try to remain buried in savasana for as long as possible. Kristi rouses them with a soft mantra and the gentle tinkle of a bell. Then it's off to coffee and a day of phone calls, appointment-making, and teeth gritting. No one is looking forward to this; no one can see any way around it.

The three women have filled Kristi in on the marketing campaign, just not it's reason for being launched. As usual, the agreeable yoga instructor has offered to help out. She is given a list of companies and promises to report back by the end of the day. She also offers to come up with some more organizations to contact. Lexie can't believe their good fortune.

Three of the four women are on the phone and sending emails. Woo Woo has decided to head downtown. This will give her an excuse to pop in on Sofia. Perhaps they'll have a cup of coffee.

135

***

Sofia is on the floor of Suite and Savory. Woo Woo waves and walks over. "We're approaching businesses and organizations in the downtown, and since I was here, I thought I'd drop by."

The businesswoman seems pleased to see Woo Woo. In fact, she offers to draw up a list of businesses Woo Woo and her co-owners can approach. "Feel free to say I referred you. First though, a hot beverage. We need that today."

Sofia clearly wants someone to talk to. She certainly couldn't talk to her family about some of the things she says to Woo Woo. Her father-in-law is the main source of despair and discomfort, but there is also something going on with her husband. Woo Woo gets the feeling it's about the store. She makes a soft jab.

"You've been running Suite and Savory for a long time now. You father-in-law must be proud of your success."

"You'd think," says Sofia. "To be fair, he knows the store is doing well. What he doesn't understand is that it is doing well because I am running it. He thinks anyone can run a store."

"That surprises me. He is a shrewd businessman. He knows what it takes to be successful."

Sofia shoots Woo Woo a look. She's not sure if it is suspicious or conspiratorial. "You'd be surprised what my father-in-law would do to ensure his success."

Woo Woo waits a beat. Sofia does not move in to fill the silence. Woo Woo pushes forward, like jello against the side of a glass dish. "I understand ambition. Well, you know who my father is." Woo Woo silently apologizes to her father.

"There are lines your father would never cross that Nik Pappas doesn't even realize are there."

Woo Woo feigns surprise. Sofia moves in to fill the silence. "I'm sure you've heard the rumors. Well, they aren't rumors."

"Are you okay?" Woo Woo thinks this is good. She isn't prying directly into Pappas, she's showing concern for her friend, and the question is open-ended enough to be open to interpretation. Sofia interprets both personally and professionally.

"Thank you for asking. I'm fine. But ..." Sofia looks around the café and leans in. "I'm making plans to be better than okay." She scans the floor again. "I'd like to tell you, but not here. Let's grab lunch later this week."

***

The ketchup in the packet is moving in tandem with Terrell's fingers. After the third push and release, Boone reaches over and takes the packet from him. "We've been down this road before. I believe you ended up with ketchup all over your shirt.”

Terrell cedes the packet to his boss. He doesn’t look pleased. Boone knows this has nothing to do with condiments. “Woo Woo and Charlene have been invited to supper at Nik Pappas’s this Friday.”

“Jesus,” says Boone. She presses down hard on the ketchup packet. Red tomato paste flies through the air and lands. On Terrell’s shirt. The detective resigns himself to his fate, and heads for the washroom. He ignores Boone’s laughter as he walks across the pub floor. What he can’t ignore is the nagging feeling this is an omen.

Once the ketchup has been wiped away (Terrell now carries his own Tide To Go pen), Boone and the detective first class get down to business. Two questions need to be answered. The first: Is it time to pull the plug on Operation Citadel, as the op is known in HPD files? The second: Does the associate chief justice need to be pulled into the loop?

To Terrell’s dismay, the answer to both questions is “No.”

***

The gym is hopping. That’s unusual for a weekday afternoon. Most people are at the office, juggling kids, or running errands before they have to juggle kids. “It’s likely Christmas guilt,” says Nathan. Lexie looks at him in surprise. He doesn’t know whether this is because he spoke to her without Lexie asking a question or whether she's amazed at his clairvoyance. Turns out, it's neither.

"What the hell is Christmas guilt?"

"The knowledge you are about to eat too much, likely too much junk food, and put on unwanted pounds."

"Isn't that what happens in January?"

"Most of our members are Type A."

Lexie bursts out laughing. It feels good to contract her diaphragm and circulate more blood to her heart. It feels good to feel good. Especially with Nathan. "I've come to ask a favor." The words are out of her mouth before she realizes she is even speaking.

Nathan is moved, and wary. His biological mother has never asked him for a favor before. "We're doing some marketing for the gym. Calling local businesses. Would you like to help?"

Ahh, so this isn't biological mom talking. This is the boss. Then again, it's talking. Nathan nods. He's not sure he can speak— and he's not sure why.

Lexie is having trouble herself. She starts to turn away. "Let's grab a coffee."

***

There are three columns on the spreadsheet: contact, response, outcome. Most of the businesses have this beside their name: message left. One or two say, "Not interested." There are several, however, that

139

include scheduled appointments. One says, "Will offer employees a discounted membership." (This organization has an asterisk beside it indicating follow-up is required.)

Charlene is impressed with the results. She saw the exercise as part of the assignment, not an actual business-development initiative. Turns out it's both. She decides to start a PPT deck to document the results.

What the PPT won't include, of course, is whether this foray into pretense will work on a man who can usually see through pretense, who is by nature or lived experience highly suspicious, and who certainly does not believe in coincidence.

"You need to be a damn psychologist to figure this out."

"Figure what out?" Kristi asks.

Charlene didn't realize she'd spoken out loud. "Whether this will work in the market." Charlene is pleased with her answer. She believes she is fast on her feet. She isn't that fast. Kristi doesn't buy this answer for one minute, but she trusts her friend and her partner, and that is saying something given the fiasco with her last partner.

Kristi isn't quite sure how to say this to her friend and her partner, so she just says it. "You do know a psychologist."

Dammit.

Chapter 18.

Cell phones are not allowed in juvie. One, they don't want you calling your drug dealer. Two, they don't want you calling in favors. Three, they don't want you planning. Anything. It's also about isolation and control. Juvie works, when it does, because the only life you get inside is the life some uniform says you are entitled to. Everyone wants to get the hell out of juvie.

Until then, that means no cell phones. Yet, here it is, two o'clock in the morning, and Beast is leaning over the top bunk, hanging on to the bottom rail of Luke's bed. He has a flip phone in his outstretched hand. "We've got to get rid of it before the shift change."

Shift changes at eight. Breakfast is at 5:30. They'll do a head count at 5:15. Luke figures he has at least an hour, maybe more. He calls the one person he never wants to see him in this place. The phone is picked up on the second ring. Luke worries that the call was screened. He's so glad it wasn't.

The next 50 minutes are joyous, and heartbreaking. They are precious. "I don't know when I can call again. I love you," Luke says before he hangs up.

Beast jumps down from the top bunk. He moves like a cat, Luke thinks. Not a sound. Beast holds up both hands. Luke has 10 minutes. He calls his brother. It takes three attempts before a groggy Brandon answers. "Jesus, this better be good."

"It's your brother." Luke can't keep the glee out of his voice.

Brandon is wide awake now. The grog is gone. He spends nine minutes on the phone with the man who means the most to him in this world. It is a blessing. Brandon doesn't call it that. He doesn't think like that. But he promises his brother no illegal shit until Luke is out and they can talk face to face.

Luke sits up in bed. He wipes the tears from his eyes. He stands up and moves toward Beast. Beast doesn't budge. There is a natural confidence in being the biggest lion in the savanna. No one is going to take him on, and Luke is his friend. His friend walks up to Beast and puts his arms around him. Who knew there was joy in juvie.

"How do we get rid of it?" Luke points to the phone.

Beast takes the phone and crushes it in one hand; he then demolishes it into a hundred small pieces. The pieces are put in a baggy. The baggy is put inside Beast's underwear. Luke doesn't ask what will happen with the baggy.

Chapter 19.

It's planning day. Charlene loves planning day. Any plan. Any day. Woo Woo tackles such tasks as she would the dishes. Meditatively. Lexie barrels on through willing the work to be finished.

For Charlene and Woo Woo, planning day starts in the office. Charlene draws up a timeline for reviewing the books at Suite and Savory. (She refuses to call it an audit.) Nothing will start formally until the new year, but Charlene would like copies in advance. She has a list of documents that she needs: balance sheets, income statements, cash-flow statements, and statements of shareholders' equity. She is preparing a file for Pappas. Normally she would email this information to the client and there would be an online back and forth until she had everything she needed. In this case, Charlene will drop off the file in person later this morning. Pappas's request.

Woo Woo has created some posters that can be used to promote the reflexology day. They will be put up throughout Suite and Savory and Vitality+. The event itself will take place on Saturday. Most stores are only open for half a day on Sunday in Nova Scotia, and there is usually a flurry to get ready for work and school the next day. Errands usually get done on Saturday; and a little self-care will be welcome. It's a good day to test the waters.

It's decided the three women will head downtown together and meet up with Terrell after for a drink. Woo Woo can feel his concern even when he is not in the room.

***

The coffee, as expected, is delicious. What wasn't expected was the coffee itself. Charlene isn't sure what it is that Pappas wants to tell her but hasn't. She has seen this behavior in clients on many occasions. There is some small, sometimes large, issue they want to raise. They aren't quite sure how.

It's the auditor's job to make clients feel comfortable sharing (or fearful what will happen if they don't). Charlene takes a sip of her coffee. "I realize the review doesn't officially start until the new year, but it's always helpful to have the documents in advance. I can organize them, even identify if there is anything more I might need."

Nik Pappas smiles. It's as smooth as the coffee. "I'll be sure to get the documents to you, but I will need just a little time to gather them together."

"If you need me to facilitate the process, I'd be more than happy to help." This is not an offer Charlene would normally make.

It doesn't surprise Pappas. He is used to people going above and beyond for him. "There is something I must tell you."

Charlene waits. She tries to look unconcerned. "I've told you I'm transferring ownership of a business to my daughter. I haven't told you the name of that business. I think it's time you know that."

Now Charlene does.

***

Woo Woo's planned "unplanned" visit with Sofia is not nearly as interesting. In fact, it's a non-visit. Sofia is not in the store. She's at the warehouse and not expected back this afternoon. Woo Woo thanks the clerk and leaves the posters. She texts Sofia to let her know she has dropped them off.

***

Dimitri is ready for Lexie Hill's visit. He has a great craft beer on tap and Voss bottled water chilling in the cooler. He put out cashews, mustard pretzels, and donair chips. Not his first rodeo.

Lexie is right on time. She has a ton of gear. Dimitri grabs a couple of the guys from behind the bar, and they haul it in. Lexie starts with set up. Dimitri lends a hand. He can feel the comedian's energy. This is what professional feels like.

The event is on Tuesday night. Dimitri hopes it will be the first of many. His father isn't quite as enthusiastic, but he did sign off on the idea. Perhaps it's an early Christmas gift. Then again, the event is being billed as a fundraiser for ElderDog Canada. Hard to say no to furry friends and seniors at the holidays.

After about two hours, the equipment is set up. It's time for the sound check. Dimitri suggests they take a break. Lexie opts for another water. She sits down and scans the stage. She shifts her gaze to Dimitri. "Thanks for this."

He shrugs off the compliment, but he's beaming inside. "I'm hoping this could become a regular thing."

"Me too," says Lexie. She's not sure she's lying. "Do you think you can convince your father?"

"Money convinces my father. And accolades. He likes being the big man about town."

Lexie would like to pursue this train of thought, but she stops short. A good-looking man and an equally good-looking teenager are making their way across the floor. About halfway to the table the girl breaks into a run. She stops inches from Lexie's chin. "You're Lexie Hill!"

Lexie grins. Who doesn't like to be adored. "I am."

"My friend loves you."

"And I love your friend."

By now, the man has arrived at the table. He extends a hand. Confident. Assured. "Nik Pappas."

Lexie introduces herself and thanks him for the opportunity. He waves the praise away. "Sorry to intrude. My daughter wanted to meet you."

"We're just about to do the sound check." Lexie turns to the girl. "Would you like to help?"

The girl looks at her father. He smiles and nods. Mirabelle jumps up and hugs her dad, then Lexie. Even Dimitri gets a hug. He doesn't hug back.

***

Sound check goes smoothly. Dimitri oversees the mains, the mix for the audience; Lexie and Mirabelle are on stage with the monitors making sure there is no feedback. Dimitri feeds them instructions. Loud and clear. Dimitri needs to balance the sound, so Lexie and Mirabelle break into song. Abba's "Dancing Queen." Mirabelle does the refrains; they both do the bridge. Mirabelle has a great voice. Lexie does not.

Somewhere between the young night and the tambourine beat, they are quietly joined by Nik Pappas. Mirabelle spies him first. She waves. Her joy is palpable. Now, so is his.

Lexie is not sure why that surprises her. Why she assumed this man would be cold and uncaring. Because he sells drugs? Because this is a stepdaughter? Because she has read too much James Patterson?

***

The gear has been left on the stage. An abbreviated version of the sound check will be done before the set on Tuesday. In fact, today's sound check could have been skipped, but Lexie wanted to get comfortable with the acoustics in the room, and she wanted an excuse to spend time with Dimitri. Pappas's presence is a bonus, although he has said only two words to her.

Until now.

"Let me walk you out." Pappas extends an arm in the direction of the front doors. Lexie is a little frightened—drug lord, and all—and part of her, the part that thinks she is a descendant of Sherlock Holmes, is thrilled.

Turns out, the drug lord is polite. "I want to thank you for letting Mirabelle join you. She had the time of her life."

"She was actually a great help. And obviously, a great singer."

"Do not tell her that, please. She'll want to join a band next. I'm still trying to dissuade her from getting a tattoo." He stops briefly and looks at Lexie. "Do you have a tattoo?"

"I do." Lexie is not sure whether she should be proud or reticent.

"What does it say?"

"Nathan."

What impresses Lexie most is that Pappas doesn't ask any questions. Most people would want to know who Nathan is, why Lexie has inked his name among all others on her ankle. He can't know who Nathan is, of course, but he seems to know that this is deeply personal, and it is not his place to pry. That ability to read the room and the people in it must be a great asset when your job requires you to routinely break the law, Lexie thinks. The compassion behind it, whether real or contrived, is also a great way to win friends and influence people. Lexie counts herself, if only slightly, among those. That feeling is about to intensify.

"I wondered if you would like to join us for dinner on Friday. It's casual and loud. It would mean the world to Mirabelle."

Lexie hesitates for the merest of seconds. She's not wondering what Sherlock Holmes would do, but Michael Terrell. And she's out of time. "You are too kind. I'd be delighted to come."

***

The Propeller ESB sitting in front of Terrell is still cold, but the level in the glass is diminishing. Rapidly. Terrell would like to

149

order another one, but he's trying to keep an eye on his weight. Seems everything to do with this case, and with the triad, in particular, involves food. It also involves his nerves. Surely, that calls for another beer.

And one appears. With it arrives Jennifer Boone. She takes a sip of her Alexander Keith's pale ale and makes a face. "Should have had a chardonnay."

"Why do you do that?" It's not the first time Terrell has asked his boss why she persists in buying beer when she is a wine drinker.

"Seems to be the drink of choice among cops. I am a cop. Ergo..."

"How's that working out for you?"

Boone shoves her beer toward Terrell. She searches the room for the waitress. There is no need. She appears behind Boone, a glass of white wine on her tray. There is also a bowl of peanuts and another one of pretzels. Terrell gives up, finishes his ESB and reaches for the Keith's.

"Lexie got invited to dinner on Friday."

Boone chokes on her wine, which Terrell kinda enjoys. Boone thinks it's a waste of wine. "What the hell do these women do? Emit gamma rays that make people invite them into their homes."

"Yes." Terrell thinks it's as reasonable an answer as any other.

"What's the plan."

"To keep them alive." Terrell thinks that is getting harder and harder.

Daily Thoughts–
Charlene Kurtz

Wednesday, December 14th

I have dilemmas. Specifically, three dilemmas. Dilemmas are not my favorite thing, although I am beginning to think I like the word "dilemma."

I'm rambling. Auditors are not ramblers. Rambling is not second nature to me professionally or personally. (Apparently, I also like the word "ramble.") I am outside my comfort zone. I even used the word "chunderfuck." I don't know what it means. It startled Madoff, and my friends, and me, I must admit.

Here goes. Dilemma one. As an accountant, and certainly as an auditor, I must keep information confidential. I have no intention of doing that with the Pappas assignment. (I do like that word.) Is that a conflict? Could my license be stripped? Could I be suspended?

On the plus side, I did not sign an NDA. I'm not sure why Pappas didn't insist. I should have insisted, and I would have if this were business as usual, which it isn't. I'm assuming the lack of an NDA gives me some wiggle room legally, if not ethically.

The ethical issue: what to tell the team. When this started, we were looking for an in, some way to get information that the police couldn't. None of us envisioned that I would end up doing the books for a drug lord. (Surely to god, there is another word for what this man does.) Yet here I am. Here we are. Does my obligation to share information, even information that is seemingly irrelevant, extend to et al? (I don't know what the hell to call them. Perhaps I am a curser.)

I need to discuss this with everyone. I know what they'll say. I need to see how I react when they say it. In the meantime, I'm getting all the info together to start the review after the holidays. It's quite a gift. Some people have more money than they know what to do with.

Dilemma two. Sam. Sam is a dilemma. What to do about my newly discovered half-brother is a dilemma. How to tell my daughters about Sam is a dilemma. And now I am getting tired of the word "dilemma." I'm also getting tired of dilemmas.

Sam and I have agreed we'll talk once a week. Eight o'clock Tuesday night is the appointed hour. We really don't have much to say to each other but we're trying. I'm going to give it one more try, and then I'll call

Dora and Billie. How wonderful, my two daughters have a new uncle for the holidays.

And that is dilemma three. Dora and Billie have both invited me for the holidays. I generally bounce back and forth. I don't play favorites. This year I think I'd like to stay home. Madoff would like it if I stayed home, although this year there are more places for him to stay while I'm away.

The business is booming. The stuff we're doing for Honey is actually bringing in new members and creating a bit of a buzz. I should stick around to keep an eye on things.

That is silly, of course. A week or so away is not going to make a hoot of a bit of difference, and Vitality+ is fine. Truth is, I don't want to go away for Christmas. I want to stay here with my friends, with my dog, with my stuff. I have things to do. Things I want to do.

Does that make me a bad mother?

Sincerely,

Charlene Kurtz

Chapter 20.

Thursday, December 15th is overcast. The sun darts behind clouds and grins out every once in a while, a sardonic reminder that warmth and brightness will come again. But not today. Lexie makes her way into the detention center and is instantly aware that however grey the world is outside these doors, it is much greyer inside.

Despite efforts to lighten and freshen and invigorate this world, reality prevails. This is a jail regardless of what moniker you give it. The people inside these walls are grappling with bars and rules and restrictions that tell them when to move, where to move, what to eat, where to sleep. Lexie feels the weight and wonders how weary these kids must be.

She forgot to account for Beast. Lexie is frisked, patted, zapped (with a metal detector). It all pales in comparison to the hulk of a man-boy hurtling at her, arms spread, calling her name like they are long lost friends. Lexie feels bad for her chest. She is also surprised hurtling is allowed in a detention center. Then again, who is going to argue with Beast.

Her chest does protest somewhat, although this hug is gentler than its predecessor. Beast seems content just to be in her vicinity. That's fine with Lexie. This is one reality she knows: nothing will happen to her if Beast is nearby. She also knows nothing will happen to Luke if Beast is in the vicinity, and where the former goes you'll find the latter. Like now.

Woo Woo steps forward. She introduces herself to Luke, extends a hand. Luke shakes her hand. This is what grown-ups do. She turns to Beast, steps forward, and wraps him in her arms. Beast doesn't move. No one moves. Woo Woo unravels herself from the man-boy. The CO standing guard by the front door stiffens. He makes the slightest movement. Luke shakes his head, "No."

There are a half-dozen boys in the room setting up chairs for the podcast. They look at Beast; they look at the woman who is about to die at the hands of a man-boy. Beast tilts his chin down. It is the smallest of movements. Every kid in the room sees it as if it were displayed on a 72" screen. They resume unstacking chairs and placing them around the room.

"What just happened?" Lexie asks Luke amid the noise of metal chair legs hitting a concrete floor.

"Beast just told them your friend is off limits. No one will hurt her, inside these walls or outside."

Lexie doesn't want to know how kids in juvie get to control what goes on outside this walled world, she just knows they do.

Beast and Woo Woo are setting up the podcast table. Beast seems to know a fair bit about mics and filters and sound boards. Woo Woo does not. Lexie swears at one point she hears a giggle. She's not sure if it is Woo Woo or Beast.

There are 125 teenagers in Waterville, too many for the podcast. The COs asked each person in all five cottages, as detention housing is called, who would like to attend. Twenty names were then drawn from a hat. Two of the kids drew the names, so there was no outcry. Everyone will attend the show later this afternoon.

Lexie has prepared 50 questions. Each boy will draw two questions and answer them as part of the podcast. If time allows, there may be a third question, and some can be repeated if necessary. Most of the questions are lighthearted, a few are not.

A cocky young man called Colin raises his hand to be the first to the mic. He swaggers enroute from audience to hot seat. His first question: What's the best thing about juvie?

He doesn't hesitate. "Getting out." Everyone laughs. The boys give him a round of applause. *This is good stuff,* Lexie thinks.

The morning moves along quickly. Some of the kids are obviously nervous, some clam up in front of the mic. Some are articulate, some are not. Lexie assures everyone not to worry. She can edit out any hiccups. They will all sound good. She gets a rousing round of applause.

Luke's turn at the mic comes mid-way through the group. By now everyone is relaxed, and everyone is on the edge of their seats. They don't know what the questions will be, or their answers. This is like their life. There is no way to prepare.

Luke pulls a question out of the box Woo Woo is holding. He hands it to Lexie. She looks at the question; she ignores it. She has her own question for Luke. "Many young men in here swear they are innocent, but they plead guilty anyway. Why would someone do this?"

The seventeen-year-old boy in the seat across from Lexie shoots her a look. It is the look of a man who is not a fool. "Lots of reasons," Luke says with an ease that seems to surprise everyone in the room, including the CO still standing guard at the front door. "Money. Family. Love."

Lexie probes what Luke means by each answer. *One.* Families don't have the funds to fight a lengthy court battle. *Two.* The boy is stepping up to protect a parent or a sibling. *Three.* They are shielding someone they love from a world of hurt. *There are no surprises here*, Lexie thinks.

She is wrong.

***

Sofia is waiting for Woo Woo when she arrives at the restaurant for dinner. Urchin is a trendy new eatery in downtown Halifax. The color scheme is slate and azure. Woo Woo feels like she is floating in the French Riviera with the mountain peaks reflecting off the water.

Sofia matches the décor. She looks casually put together in a sky blue turtleneck and deep grey pants, but Woo Woo knows this took thought and planning. Sofia is always stylish, like her store, but this feels more deliberate to Woo Woo. Extra attention often means a favor is about to be asked. She hates it when she feels this way, and she feels this way a lot. A lifetime of being the daughter of the man whose company owns 32 percent of the global aerospace market has taught her to trust her feelings.

Before Woo Woo can sit down, Sofia is out of her chair and giving her a hug. Something is definitely up. The meal starts with caviar toast and small talk. Sofia asks Woo Woo about her day. Woo Woo decides to take a risk.

"It was great. I was at the Waterville Youth Center."

The piece of toast making its way to Sofia's mouth stops mid-journey. "I'm not

158

sure if I'm more intrigued that you were at a detention center or that your day was great."

Woo Woo tells Sofia she has a friend, a comedian, who was conducting a workshop for the kids. Woo Woo was there to help.

"Did you?" Sofia asks.

It's a great question. Woo Woo isn't sure of the answer. She helped to set up the gear, she helped to move the kids through the podcast process, and she helped tear down. The kids could have done that. She spent a little time with Luke, enough to know he has secrets he isn't sharing with a woman he met six minutes ago. Lexie would have better luck getting into the vault that is his mind, body, spirit.

No, the reason today was great and the reason Woo Woo was helpful can be summed up in one word: Beast. Whatever their connection, it was immediate, and it is real. At least to Woo Woo. She has been doubting her third eye lately. The Terrell thing and all.

One thing Woo Woo has learned from the detective: the fine art of deflection. She puts that knowledge to use. "How was your day?" she asks Sofia and chomps down on a toast wedge heaped with roe.

This is the opening Sofia was waiting for. Woo Woo braces between bites. "I had a great day. I made a decision. It is the right decision for me."

The waiter glides up with a platter— turbot, shallots, zucchini, boiled parsley potatoes. The women load up their plates. They focus on the food and sigh in contentment.

It isn't until the walnut whiskey ice cream arrives that they wind their way back to Sofia's decision. Woo Woo feels the timing is exactly as intended. She thanks her third eye.

"I've been avoiding this," Sofia says. "My decision. I know it's the right decision for me, but I also know it will create some havoc in my life."

"Sometimes upheaval is a good thing." Woo Woo does not believe this, but she is skilled at conversations like this one. She is waiting for the shoe to drop.

"I'm going to buy Suite and Savory."

Woo Woo tenses. How much will this cost her? Nothing as it turns out.

Sofia unburdens mind, body, spirit. She has been holding this back and holding this in for a long time. She tells Woo Woo about her father-in-law's iron fist, his old ways, his ingrained belief women are not really good at business. She does not tell Woo Woo about the drug business although she might if asked. Woo Woo wonders if she should ask.

"You think your father-in-law will say no." It isn't a question.

"I think he will be annoyed I asked him at all. This is something that should come from my husband."

"Your husband doesn't think you should buy the store?"

"Honestly, I have no idea why Kostas is so reluctant to talk to his father. It's a business decision. They discuss business all the time."

"This is family," Woo Woo points out.

"And I'm not."

"Of course, you are."

"No, I'm family adjacent. Don't get me wrong. As long as I am married to Kostas, I will be treated like a member of the family, but unlike sons, daughters, and cousins, I am disposable."

"But you are a member of the family now. Shouldn't that bode well for your father-in-law to sell the store to you."

"It doesn't matter." Sofia sounds like she means it. Perhaps for the first time.

Woo Woo decides to take advantage of Sofia's good mood and peace of mind. "I've been thinking about your staffing problem."

"Looking for a job?" Sofia smiles at her own joke.

"I have a friend of a friend who works two jobs—both in retail. Single mom, trying to make ends meet. I thought she'd make a great assistant for you."

Sofia is intrigued. Both by the possibility of having a designated other to take things off her plate and by the offer itself. Is Woo Woo asking a personal favor? Is there an expectation here that Sofia will comply? Or better yet, if Sofia says yes, is there a quid pro quo?

Sofia says yes.

Chapter 21.

Terrell does not want to come out from under the haven that is buried savasana. He is bundled in blankets, supported by blocks, melting under an eye pillow. This is so much better than the real world where he will have to make decisions, question why he has not made decisions, and try to keep some stubborn-ass kid out of jail. Terrell loves buried savasana.

Even utopia has a time limit. Terrell hears the chime and rouses himself from the warmth of stillness. He picks up the remnants of his recent joy and puts them back in the prop closet. Respectfully.

Coffee brings him firmly and thoroughly back to the here and now. A few yogis hang around for a post-class beverage, but everyone seems to have somewhere they need to scurry off to. Woo Woo suggests the four of them go to their office in the gym. Lexie and Charlene agree.

Terrell wonders what the hell is going on now. Utopia is so long ago and so far away.

***

Everyone has news. Lexie updates the group on the Waterville workshop. No big revelations but a clear indication that Luke knows exactly what he is doing and why. They debate the pros and cons of the three reasons Luke gave for denying one's innocence. Money is clearly an issue, but a lifelong issue. Luke and his family know how to live with the shackles of poverty. They understand legal aid, they understand pro bono, they understand the system works against them so get what you can when you can. Money would not appear to be the tipping point.

Family is a more likely reason. Mom can be ruled out. Brother Brandon cannot. Terrell has a file on the fifteen-year-old. It is not reassuring. It is unsettling. "Kid is headed for big trouble. So far, he's managed to keep himself out of juvie."

"That's likely Luke," Lexie says, an expert now in all things Luke Castle.

"It might be," Terrell agrees. "You know what that means." The detective gives the women a few minutes to think this through. Woo Woo makes it to the finish line first.

"If Brandon is involved in this, Luke will never give him up. And with his confession, the court is unlikely to take any accusation against Brandon seriously."

"Would we want them to?" Charlene asks.

There is a mixed reaction to this. On the one hand, Terrell wants the guilty party to go to jail. On the other hand, Charlene wants to protect the younger brother. She wonders where this family-first commitment is coming from. *Dear god.*

Love is a winning reason to go to jail for someone the crew concludes. But Luke has no love interest, at least as far as anyone knows. If he does, he's kept it hush-hush. The question then becomes "Why?"

Terrell makes a note to bring Brandon in for an interview and review all Luke's socials for the magic appearance of Aphrodite. He does not share his notes with the three women. Lexie says she'll nudge Luke and Stephanie about Brandon and girlfriends. She might even be able to get Beast to open up. Woo Woo offers to go with her the next time she takes Stephanie to the center.

Charlene tentatively raises her conflict-of-interest issue. To her delight, and proudly, everyone—including Terrell—says she should not cross any line she is uncomfortable with and certainly no one needs to know Pappas's business if it doesn't relate to the assignment. Charlene is relieved. Madoff is delighted. He gets three belly rubs.

Woo Woo has news although she is not sure how it relates to what is happening with Luke. Chances are it doesn't. She tells them about her lunch with Sofia. "She's going to approach her father-in-law with a business offer. She's not sure he'll bite."

"Sounds like life with Nik Pappas," Lexie says. "Dimitri is always complaining his father won't give him more responsibility and let him fly on his own. It's an issue of trust."

"And arrogance," says Terrell.

"For Sofia, it may also mean her marriage." Now Woo Woo has everyone's full attention. "She wants her husband to fight for her. So far, he hasn't."

"What do you think will happen?" Charlene asks.

"Sofia wants to run her own company her own way. If her husband isn't behind her, I fear he's history."

Terrell is rapidly making notes. This doesn't have much to do with Luke Castle, but any family upheaval is good news for the good guys. Sofia just might talk. "When are you seeing her again?" That would be tomorrow. It's reflexology day at the store. "Can you ask more about her proposed new venture?"

Woo Woo is a little perplexed. She and Terrell are usually on the same page. "I doubt anything will have changed, but I could be wrong." Woo Woo is getting that added dose of attention again.

"What are you talking about?" Lexie asks.

Woo Woo states the obvious. "Sofia wants to buy Suite and Savory."

"Oh dear god," says Charlene.

***

There is a small mountain of paper on Boone's desk. She looks at it with dismay. Somewhere in here is a coffee she got earlier this morning from Tim Hortons. A voice from the doorway solves her problem. "It's behind the stack on your left. Close to the edge, I might add."

Boone waves Terrell in as she gingerly reaches for the cup. He has croissants. Boone wishes the public could see this. Kill the donut cliché. Her mouth is full when Terrell tells her about Suite and Savory. He should have waited until she swallowed.

Once Boone can breathe again, she reaches for the phone. The Drug Unit needs to know about this. While they're waiting for the inspector on duty to arrive, Terrell says he wants to bring Brandon in for an interview. He says why. Boone reaches for another croissant. "Good idea. Scare the shit out of the little bastard."

***

It's been decided the three women will show up together at Nik Pappas's house. Charlene has been tasked with finding a nice bottle of wine to bring, and Woo Woo is getting flowers for Angela Pappas. Lexie has signed posters for Mirabelle. They've run

167

through scenarios about how they will tell Pappas they know one another and have concluded the only thing they could do is wing it and sound natural.

Turns out that was enough. For Nik Pappas anyway.

***

The Pappas mansion is, well, large. And lovely. But mostly large. It is in Glen Arbour Estates, known for its panoramic views and its pristine golf club. Most of the 12,000 square feet that comprise the Pappas family home overlook Little Sandy Lake, although the winter frost and chilly winds have stripped the trees and the water of their summer vibrancy. Now it just looks cold.

Pappas opens the door when the women ring the bell. Mirabelle is close behind. She nods at Charlene and Woo Woo and reaches for Lexie dragging her inside. "Come see my room."

Pappas is standing still. It is a stillness Charlene doesn't know how to read, but she understands how this man successfully runs a drug-trafficking enterprise. It is about control, internal and external. Woo Woo understands what it takes to run any kind of business—and how to disarm potential threats to the business. "We realized on the way here that you may not be aware you invited three of the four Vitality+ owners."

168

"I was not," says Pappas. He looks from one woman to the other.

Charlene steps in. "We've been hitting so many businesses downtown with promotion ideas we couldn't remember who has met whom."

"Sofia gave us such wonderful ideas. They've already paid off."

The ice is starting to thaw. Pappas welcomes them in with a smile. He reaches for their coats. It's all over in a matter of seconds. Sofia has arrived now. Woo Woo turns to give her a hug. "I was just telling your father-in-law how helpful you have been giving us contact info for our promotion."

Sofia shrugs off the praise. Charlene suspects she is pleased. Pappas knows she is. They move into the living room. It is open and light. The default color is cream. Charlene is glad Madoff is home. Sometimes he has dirty paws.

This is small talk time. Pappas seems to have accepted that three women he did not know were connected have landed on his front doorstep and are now drinking pinot grigio in his living room. He is a consummate host: attentive, pleasant, charming. Charlene and Woo Woo start to relax. Maybe they can pull this off.

Maybe.

***

Lexie has been transported back 40 years. Mirabelle's room is warm and cozy. Salmon hues make it feminine; a climbing wall makes it clear there is an edge and an independence to the room's owner and chief decorator.

"I can't believe you're here."

Lexie can't either. "This is a great room." She motions to the walls and décor around her. "Is this all you?"

Mirabelle blushes with delight. She nods. "Mom said I could hire a designer, but I didn't want one."

"You didn't need one." Lexie means it. She wonders if Mirabelle would decorate her place.

"I'm going to your show at the club on Tuesday. Dad said I could. He's coming with me. Mom is too."

"Nice." Lexie grins. "It will be good to have a receptive crowd."

"I wish my boyfriend could be there." Mirabelle sounds wistful. Lexie remembers young love.

"I didn't know you had a boyfriend."

"He's kind of a secret. Mom is protective. Dad is worse."

"Bet you have a picture though."

Mirabelle makes a grab for her phone. "He's a big fan of yours."

Indeed, he is.

***

Dinner goes smoothly. Not that Charlene thought it wouldn't, but there are lulls and dips in conversation that are often interpreted as awkward silences. She likes to avoid those. Pappas is adept at guiding conversation. So is Woo Woo. Kostas is on his best behaviour. His wife and Dimitri are not quite as well behaved, but this is more barbs than bad conduct. Mirabelle is glowing. Sometimes secrets are best shared.

They move into the library for coffee and Metaxa. Woo Woo offers to help clear the table, but Angela waves her away with a smile. Mirabelle absconds with Lexie to the media room, and Charlene makes her way to the washroom. She could do yoga in here.

Kostas is waiting for her when she exits. Zen-like state is shattered. "I'll be quick. Don't tell Sofia."

The conversation might be cryptic, but Charlene knows how to decode it. "I'm not saying I have any idea what you're talking about, but hypothetically, if I did, I am bound by client privilege to keep what I know to myself."

Kostas gives Charlene a penetrating look. Message received. By both of them.

***

Nik Pappas is not a risk taker. That might sound strange for someone in his line

171

of work, well, his primary line of work, but being cautious is central to survival. When you take your time sharing decisions and accepting people into your world, you live longer and you live larger. Yet risk-averse Nik Pappas is currently weighing the pros and cons of going out on a limb. He swirls the brandy in his glass and contemplates the satisfaction he would feel when this whole issue is put to bed. Once and for all.

He wonders if he should quietly ask Angela what she thinks. That would be a first. Then again, if he goes ahead with this plan, it would be a night of firsts. The anticipation of going where he usually doesn't go has Pappas thinking he should tell Mirabelle his plans. He would like that over with as well. But better parenting surfaces. That is a personal issue. He and Angela need to sit down with their daughter in private.

Isn't the other issue personal as well? Yes. And no. Pappas takes a sip of brandy. By the time he puts his snifter down he has decided it is more "no" than "yes."

He has reached a decision.

***

A fresh pot of coffee, including decaf, has arrived. Angela pours. Pappas nods at his oldest son. Kostas stands up and offers another round of brandy to his family and their guests. Woo Woo is still on her first. Dimitri is on his third.

Small conversations have sprung up throughout the room. Woo Woo and Sofia are discussing plans for the reflexology promo on Saturday. Angela says she'll drop by. Woo Woo says that would be lovely. Sofia says nothing.

Dimitri is talking to his brother about something business-y, but mostly he is looking at the door. The guest he really wants to chat with is somewhere else in this house. With a kid. Pappas and Charlene are discussing the state of the business community post-pandemic. Kostas overhears, leans back, and interjects. "Fortunately, everyone still wants pizza." Dimitri laughs. Too loudly.

Pappas takes that as his cue. It is time to wrap things up. Most men would stand up to make an announcement of this magnitude. Nik Pappas does not need to rise to command attention. Somehow silence descends. Everyone turns.

"Thank you all for being here tonight. It has been such a lovely evening. Family and friends."

There is a murmur of agreement, of thanks. Woo Woo pats Sofia's hand. Angela gives her husband a warm smile. Dimitri looks toward the door.

"I'm not one for making announcements, and I am certainly not one for fanfare, but this has been such a lovely evening, I would like to be someone else for just a moment. Someone who has something to say that is very near and dear to my heart."

Everyone looks up in surprise. Angela has no idea what is coming but she is not concerned. She knows the relationship she has with her husband. It is secure. Sofia is also in the dark about what is about to come out of her father-in-law's mouth, but she is indifferent about most of what he has to say. Kostas feels his heart pound. He is his father's son. He does not like surprises.

Surprise is an understatement.

***

In the silence—you can almost feel breath being held in breastbones—Nik Pappas looks up and raises his glass. "I would like to acknowledge the hard work and dedication of my daughter-in-law. She has overseen the operation of Suite and Savory for five years. In that time, it has thrived."

Everyone turns to Sofia and applauds. Woo Woo is thrilled for her friend. And terrified what might be about to come next. Kostas thinks his heart will erupt from his chest. He makes the slightest movement. His father stops him with the merest of gestures. Sofia is not aware of her friend's concern or her husband's pending heart attack. She is focused on her father-in-law. She knew this day would come. She knew if she stuck to her guns she would prevail. She tries not to gloat.

Perhaps Kostas talked to Nik after all, perhaps he stood up for his wife and to his father. In the seconds since Pappas raised a glass to his lips, Sofia turns to her husband. She loves this man. Her look lets him know that. She worries slightly though. He looks grey.

The applause has died down. Pappas let it linger. He will give this moment to his daughter-in-law. "Business is about moving forward and moving on. Sofia has done that for Suite and Savory, and now it is time for the next generation to be given an opportunity to excel." Pappas is looking at a spot on the wall in front of him. *We call that a Drishti in yoga*, Charlene thinks. Then, *what a silly thing to think about.*

Everyone is waiting for the shoe. To drop.

Chapter 22.

Three dessert plates, two wine glasses, four forks. Nik Pappas is helping to bring in dishes from the dining room to the kitchen. He wouldn't normally do this. He's not one for domestic chores, and there is a cleaning team coming in the morning. This is not, however, a typical evening.

He passes the dishes in his hand and the forks in his pocket to Angela. His wife would not usually be doing the dishes. She isn't one for … Well, you get it.

Pappas is trying not to look pleased with himself. He is a gloater at heart, but he has enough awareness and ego not to be seen as boastful. Applause is most satisfying when it isn't asked for. He wonders if the comedian—the one Mirabelle is so taken with—feels the same way. Perhaps one day soon he will ask her.

Right now, he is trying his best not to ask Angela what she thought of his announcement. He decides to lead subtly to the topic. "This was a very pleasant evening. I thought the women from Vitality+ were lovely. Funny, intelligent, gracious."

Angela Pappas knows her husband as well as she knows each of the sixty-seven pairs of shoes in her walk-in closet. She knows he is not nearly as subtle as he thinks he is. She knows his attempts at humility fail more often than they succeed. Angela doesn't care. She loves this man. The fact that he is filthy rich is a bonus. She'd be with him regardless.

His greatest asset, in her mind, is his devotion to her daughter. Angela is well aware Pappas has a family of his own, a complex, fractured family admittedly, but one he adores nonetheless. It is that family-first tenet that initially had Angela worried. She wasn't sure how Mirabelle would fit in. Would she be family, or family adjacent? Or worse, Angela's daughter.

To Pappas, she is none of these things. She is his daughter, and Angela loves him all the more because of it. When you love someone, you don't want to hurt them or see them hurt. You also want to protect them from further hurt and embarrassment.

As Angela squirts more Dawn detergent into the sink (Mirabelle insists they buy this brand to save oiled ducks), she weighs her next move. Honesty or deflection?

Before she can decide what direction to take, her mouth opens of its own accord. "Our guests were wonderful. I am so glad you invited them."

Now, she can take the path of least resistance, make a comment about the gym.

Perhaps suggest she'll join. That will lead them into the work the women are doing to promote their business, a discussion about the comedy fundraiser on Tuesday.

Or Angela can take the road less travelled.

***

Kostas would like to stop at the pizza storehouse on his way home and pick up his Kevlar vest. He's going to need it. Sofia will come at him with both barrels. He can't blame her. What the hell was his father thinking?

The eldest son of Nik Pappas knows at least part of the answer to that question, even if he doesn't want to admit it to himself. This was about making an announcement. It was also about reminding his offspring who runs the business, who makes the decisions, and whose orders have to be followed.

Kostas did not follow orders. He was told point blank and on more than one occasion that he had to tell Sofia her time at Suite and Savory was coming to an end. There would be another business venture for her, another impressive title, of that Kostas was sure. His wife, however, had other plans. Plans to own Suite and Savory outright. Tonight, her father-in-law imploded those plans.

That would not be what bothers Sofia most. It would drive her nuts that some old man was trying to dictate her future, but

178

Pappas had always insisted on ruling his domain with an iron fist. What would hit her in places her father-in-law could never reach was the fact that her husband had not confided in her about his father's plans, had not trusted her with that information, had allowed her to dream.

Those dreams died at 9:46 tonight.

***

At this moment, and perhaps for many more moments to come, Sofia Makri hates men. Two, in particular. She may even add Dimitri to that list. Simply for being a twit. On the other hand, he was a twit with the backbone to look at her first when her father-in-law dropped his bombshell. Her husband and his sperm donor did not have that courage.

Courage is important to Sofia. It's what has got her to where she is today, and she has gotten somewhere—despite her husband and his papa. (Sofia decides these two men, no longer welcome in her life, need new names. Perhaps Dumb and Dumber? She'll think on it.)

Sofia feels the key in her hand, unaware she had even reached in her purse. Maybe even unaware of the drive that brought her to the front door. That's not good. She needs to be mindful. Survival depends on paying attention.

There are two men she'll no longer attend to. She's glad to cut Pappas out of her life. It's time. And time to make her move. She's sad though to have to leave Kostas behind. He's a good man. Was a good man.

The door opens and Sofia steps inside, reaches for the light. She'd like to throw her coat on the floor and bury herself under the covers. She forces herself to follow her nightly routine. She hangs up her clothes, puts on her pjs, cleans and moisturizes her face. Not quite ready for bed, Sofia heads to the kitchen. The marble and metal island gleams under the overhead light. Sofia opens a cupboard (rustic alder, the designer was right) and scans the herbal teas, settles on a lavender coconut blend. Only at Suite and Savory.

Well, those days are done. Sofia has made her peace with this day and the endings inherent in it. She heads back to the bedroom. She grabs a book, *Hung Out to Die* (everyone is raving about it), on her way. She stops at the entranceway to her bedroom and looks down on the living room, the vestibule, the dining room. She loves this place. As she turns, she notices a line of dust on the banister.

She has been neglectful. It's time to clean house.

*****

Dimitri pours himself a large brandy. The good stuff. Metaxa Private Reserve. He took it from his father's place. Least the old man could do. Dimitri is not close to his sister-in-law, and he is a fan of drama, but really, the old man went above and beyond tonight. *Asshole*, Dimitri thinks. He thinks this a lot.

Now it is time to think about what this latest upset means for him. On the surface, it means very little. However, Dimitri has learned to look beneath the surface when it comes to his father. What they were told tonight: Suite and Savory will be a hush-hush 18th birthday gift for Mirabelle. Until then, Sofia will take Mirabelle under her wing and teach her the ropes. (Dimitri wonders how many ropes there can be.)

Part of Dimitri thinks his father can never pull this off. The other part doesn't care. All of him, though, recognizes the significance of the gift. A gift neither he nor Kostas has ever been offered. Yes, he and his brother are big cogs in the Nik Pappas empire, but cogs, nonetheless. Dimitri wonders how Kostas, stalwart Kostas, is taking the news.

Chances are brother dearest is more concerned with how his wife is taking the news. That could not have gone over well. Not that Sofia will be left rudderless, but the message is clear. In the family hierarchy, Sofia is on the bottom rung.

And there it is, the thing that has been nagging at the back of Dimitri's mind. Dear old dad is cleaning house. Favorite family members will be rewarded; those in disfavor will be demoted. Question is: Where does Dimitri stand on the list of loved ones?

He should be in the middle at the very least, and maybe close to the top. That could change, however, if his father finds out what happened with the kid. So far, the kid has kept his mouth shut. So has big brother.

It better stay that way.

***

Call. Please call. Mirabelle is hoping that wishing will make it so. Wishing does not. Her phone sits silently on her bedside table. An admonishment to foolish thinking. Mirabelle wishes—yet one more wish—that Lexie was here. Lexie would make her feel better. Lexie would make her laugh.

She'd like to tell him that. If only, he'd call. If only he could call.

At seventeen, Mirabelle embodies all the longing and optimism of youth. At seventeen, she also feels adulthood intruding in her being and slowly taking over more and more cells. Something happened tonight. Something wonderful. She shared her news—her wonderful news—with Lexie. That is a lot of wonder.

Something else happened tonight. Something that did not fill her family with wonder. Dad was happy certainly, but he was a minority of one. And Mirabelle couldn't ask Lexie 'cause Lexie was with her. Mirabelle has a 50/50 chance her mother will tell her. Sometimes they are conspiratorial, sharing secrets and hugs. Sometimes Mom is in lockstep with Dad, and no amount of prying will open the vault.

There is no doubt Sofia and Kostas looked upset, although they did not look at each other. Dimitri seemed to be hovering somewhere between disapproval and delight. Mom was playing perfect hostess to guests who were masking awkwardness with forced smiles.

Lexie threw Mirabelle a look. It was not the same look she threw her friends.

Call. Please call.

***

Angela takes the road less travelled. She turns to her husband, she smiles. "Come have a coffee with me. Decaf."

Pappas smiles back. The smile comes from love, and he does love this woman. It is also the smile of self-satisfaction, although he is trying to yearn less for applause and basking in the glow.

Husband and wife are sitting in the aftermath of dinner with family and friends. Crumbs are scattered across the gold linen tablecloth. Small stains dot the fabric, a testament perhaps to a meal savored. Angela reaches for her husband's hand. He squeezes. And basks.

This will not be easy, Angela thinks. Correctly. She looks up at her husband, at his hopeful eyes. What she is about to say will thrust a thorn in his heart. She will say it anyway. Albeit gently.

"Do you think Sofia is all right?"

"What do you mean? Why wouldn't she be all right?"

"You did toss a grenade into the conversation tonight. I doubt she was wearing body armor."

Pappas feels the glow fading. His first reaction: defensiveness. He breathes in/out and continues to look at his wife. She has helped him to understand the importance of honesty, at least in relationships. He will not react with his knees jerking. "I'm not sure I see the issue. I think I should, but I must admit, I don't."

Still gently, Angela guides Pappas down the path she thinks Sofia might have taken when she found out her livelihood, and a tremendous source of pride, was being stripped from her. Not for non-performance, not for misbehavior, but because a more favored family member was waiting in the wings.

Pappas has the grace to be ashamed. Not deeply, but still, ashamed. He had been thinking of himself, of being centerstage. He had not considered Sofia with more than a passing thought.

"Good god, Kostas."

Angela nods. "I doubt his life will be an easy one over the next few weeks."

"He should have dealt with this." The defensiveness straining to make an appearance breaks through. "I have been talking with him for months about this. He has done nothing."

"Now, all he can do is pick up the pieces."

Angela is right. Kostas got caught up in his father's search for the spotlight. Now he is hurting as a result. As is his daughter-in-law.

"How can I make this right?"

"You might want to start with an apology."

That is a good idea. Pappas thanks his wife. He means it. He sweeps a few crumbs from the tablecloth and rises.

There is no way in hell he is apologizing to the hired help and a son who didn't do what he was told.

***

The lights are out. That is a good sign. And a bad sign. Kostas turns into the driveway of his home and presses the garage door opener. He has debated this move. The noise might wake Sofia or at the very least alert her to his presence. On the other hand,

185

he doesn't want his BMW X6 getting pummeled with snow or sleet.

Kostas takes his time getting out of the SUV. He's in no hurry to face the wrath of his wife or, potentially worse, her cold shoulder. He wonders whether this moment could have been avoided. Could he have handled the situation better? He knows the answer is yes.

There was no way his father was going to sell Suite and Savory to Sofia. He knew this in his heart, his mind, and his body. He is not sure why Sofia did not know it. Perhaps she did at some level, nestled somewhere in a recessive gene or mired in bone marrow. But her lack of acknowledgement does not excuse his father's behavior. Now that he thinks about it, perhaps her desire to buy the business was a test of his loyalty as a husband. He failed.

That failure permeates Kostas's muscles. Climbing the two stairs to the back door is an effort. His legs feel like Douglas firs. Massive. Immovable. This is not reluctance. This is shame. Whatever Sofia wants to throw at him, he is ready. He deserves to be punished. He has let his wife down.

She is not alone in feeling betrayed. Kostas knew his father would never sell the business to Sofia. He never expected in a trillion years though that his father would whip it out from under her and give it to someone else. Kostas's surety rested in his belief that his father would never bring someone into the business who was not blood. Selling Suite and Savory to Sofia would do just that, and it would open the door to the empire.

Sofia knows what Nik Pappas does for a living. Hell, half the city likely knows. Still, his father keeps up the pretense within the family. The stories we tell others and maybe even ourselves: Entrepreneur. Businessman. Rags to riches. Bootstraps and other myths.

Family first. That's the Pappas motto, and Sofia is not family. Neither is Mirabelle. That is what was so shocking—and disturbing—about tonight. His father's grand gesture. The love of a parent for a child for all to see. Yet this child is not blood. Kostas cannot fathom why his father is doing this.

Is Angela delivering an ultimatum? Unlikely. Kostas saw the look on her face when his father pronounced. It was not self-satisfaction. This was all his father. His father wants Mirabelle to have the business. And that is a greater dismissal of Sofia. It is rejection of her and the son who married her.

It is time to be punished. Kostas has managed to move both legs up the steps, he has opened the door, he is standing in the kitchen. In darkness.

Cold shoulder it is. In some ways this is disappointing. A loud, angry fight full of accusations, tears, and perhaps the odd broken vase is intense—and immediate. Then it is over. There is often an intimacy that comes from the ashes of intensity. The cold shoulder lasts longer, and resolution is less satisfying, an awkward return to routine.

There is no need to walk quietly or pretend all is right with the world, and this home in particular. Kostas pours himself a shot of ouzo. This may be a delaying tactic; living in an ice castle is not enjoyable, but it is more about finding some peace for a few seconds. Kostas's world is unsettled. The things he knew for certain are no longer known. There is no certainty.

He yearns for his wife. To take her in his arms, to hold her, to apologize, to own her hurt and fill his body with it so she might find the peace he seeks in this glass of liquid licorice. Now there is sadness. Kostas can't comfort his wife. She will be resolute in her rejection of him, his cowardice, and the father that sired such weakness.

The bedroom is in darkness, as expected. Kostas undresses in the shadows and climbs quietly into bed. Sofia doesn't move. After a minute, he reaches tentatively to touch his wife. There is no response. Sofia is not there.

She is not anywhere in the house.

Daily Thoughts–Lexie Hill

Friday, December 16th

I missed the excitement. While I was upstairs talking about boys with Mirabelle (can you believe it!), the drug lord was downstairs spilling his guts. That may be a little dramatic, but it appears Pappas's news took everyone in the room by surprise: wife, sons, daughter-in-law, undercover guests. Didn't surprise me. I wasn't in the room.

I'm okay with missing out. I had news of my own, which I spilled as soon as we were on our way home. I should have waited for their news first. Always best to have the punchline.

We texted Terrell once we were in the car and out of sight. He was at Woo Woo's by the time we pulled up to drop her off. That meant more coffee and conversation. Actually, it was some magnolia tea thing Woo Woo said would help us sleep. (It's 2 a.m., and I'm wide awake.)

Our detective seems to think the evening was eventful. I think my news took top billing, not that it is a contest. It is, however, more directly related to the case. It is interesting that Pappas is giving a business, an apparently legitimate business, to his stepdaughter, but what does that have to do with drug trafficking and Luke Castle? Terrell isn't sure there is a connection, and neither am I.

Still, the announcement says something about Pappas (although I'm not quite sure what). Terrell pointed out it also says a lot about how we have engrained ourselves in the Pappas family. He didn't seem pleased when he said it.

He's right. Why the hell would a man who barely knows us drop a bomb on his family with us (well most of us) in the room? Charlene says he was showing off. Woo Woo says it was safer this way. No one would make a scene with them in the room. Terrell says they are probably both right.

So now we know more about Pappas the man. How does that help us? Terrell says we know more than that. We know how important Mirabelle is to Pappas. More important than his sons it would seem and certainly more important than his daughter-in-law.

"We can use this," Terrell said. He sounded pleased. Charlene and Woo Woo were not pleased. Mirabelle is not a pawn. Terrell says getting to checkmate is what matters. We agreed to disagree. (Somehow Woo Woo ended up defending Terrell, and he said her point of view mattered. Get a room.)

The emphasis on Mirabelle, of course, took a decided turn when Terrell heard my news.

I'd love to share that news with Nathan. Talk over what we're doing and why. Get his insight. Ask his advice. Listen to him listening. Then again, I'd like to talk over anything with Nathan. Somehow everything has gone quiet. No more coffees, no quick chats in the gym. Only nods, waves, smiles. Nothing lasts more than 2.2 seconds.

This is on me. I should be the one stepping up. Suggest coffee, or lunch. Just the two of us. I think about that every time I see him at the gym, at the café, in the parking lot. I have learned thinking and doing are two very different things.

That is a challenge for another day. The current challenge is the comedy sketch. It's been a while. Rehearsal went well. I didn't trip. I was comfortable. I got laughs admittedly from people who likely felt obliged to laugh.

I know I'll do well. I've been doing this for 30 years, and it is for charity. People always like you better when their money is going for a good cause. I won't do another rehearsal before the show. I'll do a read-through just to get in the zone, but I need to be fresh.

What I don't need is sleep. Performing for me is adrenaline. Being well rested is something that happens after a show. I'm not worried it's now 3 a.m. I am worried about Mirabelle. She is being thrust in the middle of a family fracturing at the seams, and she doesn't know it. My guess: she'll feel it soon enough.

She told me something in confidence, and I immediately violated that confidence. Doesn't seem right. Terrell says it's not about right; it's about finding out the truth. What we found out puts Mirabelle right in the middle of Nik Pappas's drug business and the case against Luke Castle.

Terrell says that's what happens when you are head over heels. You lose perspective. You don't think clearly. You tell the court you are a drug kingpin to protect the girl you love.

But what exactly is Luke protecting Mirabelle from?

That is a question that will not be answered tonight. Or perhaps ever. But we'll keep trying. Jail is a nasty place to live out your days.

LH

Intention: Invite Nathan to lunch. Or dinner. Or coffee, just the two of us. It doesn't matter. Just invite your son to something. (I copied this from my last Daily Thoughts. Evidently, I have this intention thing down pat. It's execution that eludes me.)

Chapter 23.

The water is intense, not quite scalding but so close any difference is nuance. Terrell wonders if he is trying to separate skin from bone, to feel anything but fear. He now knows why Luke Castle pleaded guilty. At least the foundation for that decision: He is in love.

Terrell and Boone were up running scenarios until the moon called it quits. It's still not clear why being in love with Mirabelle Fortin would compel Luke to lie about running drugs. He could have pleaded not guilty, and the case would have progressed. Sure, the spotlight would have been on Pappas, but it is anyway. The truck is owned by Kimolos Pizza, and Pappas owns Kimolos. There is no way cops don't speak with Pappas, don't investigate the company. Of course, that investigation is more perfunctory than profound when you have a signed confession.

So, is the kid protecting the father figure in Mirabelle's life? Keeping her from the harsh reality of what Pappas really does for a living? Unlikely. On paper at least, Kostas and Dimitri run Kimolos, president and VP, respectively. If there's any suspicion, it will land on them. Do you spend twenty years of your life in jail for your girlfriend's stepbrothers? Terrell can't imagine why. Neither could Boone.

We're missing something.

Whatever it is, it is not going to be found in the shower.

***

The dominos have dropped. Terrell has called Clayton Manning who called Stephanie Kellor who spoke with her youngest son. There was no way Brandon was going to admit to being scared to talk to a cop without an adult present. He's all swagger and no common sense. Terrell was counting on this.

It's agreed. Brandon will come to the station. Terrell offered to meet him at the apartment, but Brandon made it quite clear he didn't want anyone seeing him with cops. Terrell was counting on this.

He's also counting on Brandon knowing more than he has said to date or knowing more than he thinks he knows. Getting past "go" and collecting the payout, however, will be a game of balance. Terrell heads to Bellissimo and gets a latte, a black coffee, and a hot chocolate. He gets a peppermint tea for himself. It reminds him of Woo Woo.

By the time Terrell is back at the station Brandon has arrived. He's waiting in an interview room. Not patiently.

The bluster boils over as soon as Terrell enters the room. Terrell lets the kid rant. Lets him think his testicles are bigger than those of a detective with thirty years on the job. Finally, Brandon has to breathe. Terrell takes this opportunity to move the conversation in the direction he wants.

"Hot chocolate?" He's guessed wrong. Brandon sneers. Babies drink hot c. Terrell offers up a coffee and a latte. He's not sure Brandon knows what a latte is. The choice is coffee. Terrell exits the room and grabs the coffee from the cardboard carrier. He's tempted to spit in it. Instead, he puts it in a mug and zaps it.

Brandon sips the coffee slowly. He's pretending to size up the detective. He doesn't know what the hell he is doing, but Terrell plays along with the pretense. "Thanks for coming in."

"Didn't have much choice."

Terrell could let this slide. He doesn't. "The choice is all yours. This is an interview, not an interrogation. You are not being charged with anything. You are not being accused of anything."

The fifteen-year-old fashions a look of disbelief. This is what you do when you're cool. Terrell has seen this a thousand times. Most of those times he has wanted to squash the kid like a bug. This is not one of those times.

"Your brother has a girlfriend."

Brandon shrugs. It's a practiced move that could mean "yep" or "I had no idea" or "get out of town."

Terrell pushes his chair back and looks directly at Brandon. It is a practiced move. "Kid, I don't care how cool you are or how much you hate cops or when you last got laid. I care about your brother, and right now it looks like I'm the only one in this room that does."

The bluster is back. Brandon is spewing something about Terrell not knowing him or his family or his brother or what in the hell he is talking about. Terrell heads for the door. "Here's what I know Brandon. One, your brother has pleaded guilty to a crime he didn't commit, and he will go to jail. Two, you're not helping."

Terrell's hand is on the doorknob. "Thanks for coming in."

The detective is through the door watching his last hope of a conversation closing behind him, when Brandon says, petulantly, "What do you want to know?"

Terrell returns to his seat, sips his peppermint tea. "Tell me about the girlfriend."

"It's a girl."

"Have you met her?"

Brandon hesitates. "Yes."

"Where? When?" So, this will be an exercise in pulling teeth.

"Couple of times. We went to the movies once and McDonald's afterward. Once she came to the house with pizza from the same joint where Luke works. Mom wasn't home."

"What's her name?"

"Bella. Something."

"Do you like her?"

"What's not to like. She's a girl. She's kinda quiet. I don't think she drinks." The latter is an afterthought, and apparently a demerit.

"How come your mom hasn't met her?"

Brandon shoots Terrell a look. He's not sure how the detective knows this, doesn't realize he just told him. "Look man, there's something about the girl's parents. Her dad is real strict or something, so they're keeping it on the DL."

"How do you feel about that?"

Another look. "Not my problem."

Fair enough. "Does your brother love Bella?"

Brandon sits straighter, easier to muster the bravado that he thinks makes him cool and one day will get him in serious trouble. Halfway to perfect posture, however, he pauses. Switches lanes, from swagger to acceptance. "Can you really help my brother?"

"I may be the only one who can." Terrell has a little swagger of his own. "I can't help him without more info."

"Luke is whipped."

Technically, a little more info. Terrell waits. Brandon is opening up. It's a mistake to push. "He was buying a ring. The ring. That's why he wanted the money."

"What money?"

Brandon realizes his slip. He also realizes he is in too deep now. "From dealing."

"Are you saying the drugs in that truck were your brother's?"

"Shit no. Luke don't got that kinda money."

"What kind does he have?"

"Man, the kind you get from selling flake to guys who order pizza."

***

The deal works like this. Customers call Kimolos and order a pizza dusted with parmesan. That means they want to buy an eight ball. Double the order and you get double the drugs. The delivery guys, like Luke, tuck the coke inside the doughball that sits in the middle of the pizza. Anyone watching sees a pizza guy delivering food and getting paid.

"It's brilliant," says Boone. "We'd never suspect."

"And now we know," says Terrell. "Question is, what do we do with that knowledge?"

198

***

Saturday at Waterville is what the guys call a snow day. No school. No chores. No expectations they will do anything but what they want (and what the system allows). The TV room is always crowded, a few of the tougher boys are in the exercise room, a few of the not-so-tough kids are in the library. Luke is in his room with Beast. (He is trying not to use the word "cell.") They're talking about what they'll do when they get out. It's make believe. Luke knows he's not getting out; Beast knows he'll be going right back in.

A CO bangs on the bars. "Castle, you have an appointment in twenty."

Luke sits up. He has no appointment. "What do you mean?"

"What I said. Get ready to move."

Beast is sitting up in his bunk now. Luke can feel the CO stiffen. "Move it, Castle."

Luke gets off the bed. He brushes his hair and his teeth. The CO checks his watch and bangs his billy on the bars. Luke heads for the door. He gives Beast the thumbs up. It's false assurance.

As Luke makes his way across the compound with the guard, he pumps for additional information. There isn't any to be had. The CO knows nothing more than what he's already told Luke.

199

The guard takes the seventeen-year-old to one of the interview rooms. He asks him if he'd like water. Luke says yes. Thank you. For a second, the guard feels bad for the kid. "I don't think it's anything serious. We weren't given any heads up about possible trouble."

About ten minutes later, a small man with round tortoise-shell glasses walks in. He's carrying a small brown case. He extends his hand. "I'm Dr. Brian Sitra."

"I'm not sick."

Sitra sighs. He should have expected this. Communication in juvie is bad at best. "Not that kind of doctor."

It takes Luke less than ten seconds to figure out what is going on. This is his psychiatric evaluation. "It's Saturday."

"Backlog." Sitra wonders if the whole conversation will be in code. "We get to patients when we can."

"Now it's my turn." Luke doesn't know whether to be happy to get this over with or terrified it's about to be over with.

Sitra waits. It's a shrink technique to get patients talking. Sitra hasn't met Luke Castle. After one very long and awkward minute, the psychiatrist raises his hands in defeat. "You win."

It's almost imperceptible but Sitra's patient relaxes. "How does this work?"

"However you want it to."

"Yeah, right." Luke gives a hoot. It's a deep belly laugh, and it's genuine. Sitra likes this kid.

"My job is to figure out if you're sane. The legal definition of sane."

"I am."

"I can see that."

"So, we're done."

***

Turns out they were not done. Brian Sitra is good at his job, and Luke Castle is bored. A winning combination for competency reviews.

Luke wants to know how Sitra knows he's sane. "You're aware of your surroundings and your situation. You respond appropriately to both."

"That means I can be sentenced."

"It does." Sitra waits a beat. "Are you worried about that?"

"Is that what shrinks do? Ask questions?"

"It is."

"Why?"

"To get answers."

"Smart ass."

Now it is the doctor's turn to belly laugh. "We ask questions to get you thinking about the answers."

"So, ask me a real question."

"Why did you plead guilty to a crime you didn't commit?" To Sitra's surprise, Luke answers the question.

***

Competency evaluations are tricky. Sitra's loyalty is divided. He has a legal obligation to the court to determine if the defendant is sane. That's the easy part. It gets tricky when a doctor is asked to defend that position. To reveal what has been said in the interview that leads to a determination of sanity. Luke Castle is in big trouble. Brian Sitra is not sure how he can help him without violating doctor-patient confidentiality or without stepping outside the confines of his role as a court-appointed psychiatrist.

Sitra doesn't know what to do. He knows he needs to do something.

***

Beast is waiting for Luke when he gets back to the room. He gives his friend a hug. Then he gives his friend a phone. Beast leans in the doorframe of the cell while Luke calls Mirabelle. He tells her he loves her. Then he calls Brandon, but he doesn't get any answer. He leaves a message. "I love you. You have to stay out of jail. For Mom. For me."

Chapter 24.

Suite and Savory is wall-to-wall people. There is little more than a week until Santa and his reindeer arrive, and last-minute buyers are out in full force. Those savvy shoppers who made their purchases early have also descended in droves driven to stores by relentless advertising, parental guilt, and sheer adrenaline. Sofia loves this time of year. In particular, she loves the ring of the cash register and the rustle of shopping bags as satisfied customers leave a little poorer than when they arrived.

Sofia grabbed a bowl of butternut sage soup from kitchen and is spooning it rapidly into her mouth. This will have to be lunch. No time to relax even though she has a new assistant manager to help her, and she is helping. Sofia already feels the relief of having a second in command, even a distant second. She scrapes the last hearty spoonful of soup from the bowl and turns to head back to the melee.

She walks into her husband.

"Camila let me through," Kostas says by way of explanation for his presence in the back of the shop. He realizes he has never had to justify being in his wife's office before. He is not filled with holiday cheer.

"Did you need something?" Sofia's tone is professional, cool, dismissive. "I have to get back out."

"I wondered if we could talk."

"We have nothing to talk about."

"Sofia, please."

"Kostas, you had months to talk to me. You're out of time."

This is a new Sofia. She is formed from the woman he loves, but she is harder. She wears resentment like body lotion. It is everywhere. Kostas tries again, knowing he will fail before he even opens his mouth.

"You made your choice Kostas. You picked Daddy." Sofia walks around her husband as if he is a piece of detritus in her path. "It's time to live with your choice. I am content to live with mine."

Kostas watches his wife's back as she makes her way into the front of the store. There is something different about this fight. Something definitive. A decision that can't be undone. Kostas feels immense sadness. Then, and he hates himself for this, he wonders what his father is going to say.

***

Sofia is only a few feet into the jewelry section when Stephanie Kellor comes up to her. Sofia is not thankful for the distraction. She doesn't need one. Kostas is her past. She is moving forward. It's business as usual.

"There's a pricing error on the Constantine pendants. I have removed the tags for now."

This is going well, Sofia thinks. "I'll have Camila adjust the pricing in the system, and we can put a little handwritten sign beside the necklaces for now."

Stephanie nods. "Did you need any help with the reflexology room?"

Why not.

***

Woo Woo opens the door to Suite and Savory and the throb of the crowd pushes her back for a second. She had expected busy. This is beyond busy. She puts her tote over her shoulder and heads for the large dressing room on the second floor that has been converted for today into a reflexology refuge. Lexie and Woo Woo have transformed a white-walled box into a sanctuary. There is a massage table in the center with a fringed taupe blanket and a snow-white head pillow. Chakra banners hang from the walls; battery-lit candles flicker from four corners; a diffuser emits sweet orange essential oil.

The room welcomes Woo Woo like a second home. This is her space if only for a few hours. She breathes in deeply and closes her eyes. She imagines a pale light slowly filling the room. This is gratitude. It is also a healing light.

Woo Woo opens her eyes. She reaches into her bag and removes balm, corn starch, and eucalyptus cream. She also removes three jade gua sha pieces and two acupuncture pens. As she is organizing everything neatly in the basket beside her stool, Sofia arrives. A center of quiet amid the chaos. She is smiling. Woo Woo thinks this is what a Cheshire cat looks like.

Sofia gives Woo Woo a big hug. "We have a full house."

Woo Woo is delighted, for Sofia and for herself. The woman behind Sofia (Woo Woo almost missed her in the muted light) steps forward with a clipboard. "Here is the list of customers who have signed up. If anyone doesn't show, you can take a walk-in."

There are fourteen names on the list. Woo Woo starts to do the math in her head. At ten minutes a session, with five for clean-up ... She doesn't get too far before there is a swirl of energy moving through the room, and Woo Woo is caught up in another embrace. This one is enthusiastic and carefree. Mirabelle has arrived.

There is no awkwardness. Woo Woo is not sure whether to attribute this to the call she made to Sofia alerting her to the invitation she had extended to Mirabelle before Pappas dropped his bomb. Mirabelle was keen to help, to learn reflexology, to have a role in the run-up to the holidays and to be with a friend of Lexie's. Mirabelle is smitten with Lexie. *Aren't we all.*

To Sofia's credit, she didn't bat an eye when Woo Woo called. This may be her professionalism, her desire not to drag a teenage girl into adult family drama, or her indifference to all things Pappas and Pappas adjacent. Now Sofia is being embraced. Her response is not enthusiastic or heartfelt, but it is also not dismissive. *So, this is Switzerland.*

Mirabelle comes out from under her aunt's breastbone and realizes there is another woman in the room. She apologizes for intruding. Explains she will be greeting customers, helping with clean-up, assisting in dismantling the room.

"Mirabelle, this is Stephanie Kellor. Our new assistant manager."

Stephanie extends a hand. It takes Mirabelle a few seconds to respond. She is too busy staring. Woo Woo coughs gently.

"I am so sorry. I don't mean to be rude." Mirabelle hesitates. "You're Luke's mom."

"I am. How do you know Luke?"

Mirabelle turns to look at Woo Woo. She is seeking permission. She knows if Lexie knows about her boyfriend so does Woo Woo. There is the slightest nod from Woo Woo. Mirabelle isn't sure whether it is real or imagined, but it is all she needs.

"Luke is my boyfriend."

Stephanie Kellor should be the most-surprised person in the room. She isn't.

It is a full afternoon. The registered shoppers show up at the appointed hour, for the most part. There are a few latecomers and lots of drop-ins hoping to find a vacant spot. Woo Woo is giving, as Woo Woo does, one hundred percent to each client even if it is only for ten minutes. Mirabelle is also giving it her all. She makes customers feel welcome, and if there is a delay, she chats with them about the season, reflexology, and Vitality+. This is unplanned, but not unappreciated. *Luke is lucky*, Woo Woo thinks.

The last customer of the day is a woman in her thirties. Two young toddlers, twins perhaps, have been passed along to grandma so mom can have a few minutes of peace to herself. Mirabelle dims the lights a little further and adds extra drops of neroli oil to the diffuser. Music is playing softly in the background, a melodic mantra: Om Shanti Shanti Shanti.

Woo Woo takes her time with the woman. She applies gentle pressure to the ten zones along the feet. She hears a slight moan, and smiles. Reflexology is good for the heart in more ways than one. After twenty minutes, Woo Woo sits back. Her client rises slowly from the massage table.

"That was absolutely wonderful."

Mirabelle grins as if the compliment was hers. In a way, it is. A loud wail can be heard from the other side of the door. "Reality beckons," the woman says, but she does not begrudge the call.

Woo Woo and Mirabelle are partway through clean-up and tear down when Sofia pops her head in. "How did it go?"

"Wonderfully," Woo Woo and Mirabelle say in unison.

Sofia laughs. "That's what we're hearing. I think we need to make this a regular thing." She turns to Woo Woo. "It's nuts out there— which is a good thing. Why don't you and I connect later this week to debrief and plan next steps."

Clean-up over, Woo Woo and Mirabelle begin the trek toward the front door of the store lost amid bags, backpacks, and mountain-high carts. *This is what Everest must feel like*, Woo Woo thinks. Halfway to the summit, Stephanie hurries over to lend a hand. There are no protestations when she grabs bags and equipment.

"Thank you," Woo Woo and Mirabelle say. The unison thing again.

"We're hearing fabulous feedback from customers."

"It was a great afternoon," Mirabelle says. She hesitates. "Have you seen Luke?"

In the center of the storm that is holiday shopping—bags rustling, babies crying, boots clacking, Bing Crosby predicting a white Christmas—there is suddenly no one in the room, no sound in the background. Stephanie looks closely at this girl she met for the first time today, this girl who says she is her son's girlfriend. She sees the truth in that pronouncement. She feels the ache of loneliness and the stabbing fear reflected back at her from this seventeen-year-old. *So, this is love.*

Stephanie is gentle. "I have seen Luke." She doesn't wait for the next question or its follow-up. "He is doing well. Safe. He has a friend. Beast. Not as bad as it sounds. Woo Woo can tell you about Beast, about our visit. Or we could grab a hot chocolate later this week if you'd like."

Mirabelle most certainly would like. Impulsively she steps forward and wraps her arms around Stephanie. "Tell him I'm okay."

"I'll be going to see him this week. If your parents agree, you can come with me. Lexie is coming as well. And Woo Woo."

Tears have gathered in the corners of Mirabelle's eyes. They can't be contained. They flow down her cheeks, over her chin, and drip softly on her winter coat. Stephanie leans forward and brushes them away.

Woo Woo feels her own eyes welling. This was a good day. She turns to the front door but turns back. Sofia is standing at the other end of the store. She waves. Even at this distance, Woo Woo can't miss the huge smile on her face. This really was a good day.

***

A man, lean, lanky, dark haired, anchor beard, is leaning against a white minivan. He's looking at his phone. *Like every other man waiting for their wife or daughter or mother*, Woo Woo thinks.

The man looks up as she and Mirabelle exit the store and begin walking to their car. He moves away from the van. Woo Woo thinks he might be going to offer to help them. Christmas spirit in the flesh.

Lean and lanky steps in front of Mirabelle. She sees what she thinks is kindness. Woo Woo sees what she knows is a gun.

***

The room is dark and cold. Not so dark your eyes can't make out shapes and form. Not so cold you shiver or ache. Woo Woo waits for her eyes to adjust then begins to look around the room. Carefully. It appears to be grey, cement. Functional. There are boxes piled high. A small forklift stands idle in one corner. Styrofoam buttons litter the floor. There are no windows, but light hovers at the bottom of a rolling rock door.

Woo Woo waits. She needs to assess her surroundings. She needs to think. Clearly. When you are the daughter of a billionaire, kidnapping is well within the realm of possibility. She has trained for this. Admittedly it has been years, decades, truth be told, but Woo Woo was well trained. She was a good student. She will get out of this. When she does, someone will suffer the wrath of her father. She does not want to be that person.

***

The lean, lanky, bearded man is back. This time he is holding bottles of water. *The gun must be holstered*, Woo Woo thinks. She checks for a bulge. No bulges. *Is he that confident we can't get out of here?*

Lean and lanky thrusts two bottles of water at Woo Woo and Mirabelle. It is a reflexive gesture. And useless. Duct tape covers their mouths. Their hands are each tied around the back of a chair. Their ankles also bound. Lanky withdraws his offer of hydration. Makes a move toward the woman, thinks better of it.

"Here's how this is going to work. I'm going to untie you. I'm going to remove the duct tape. You're going to sit there quietly." He raises his hand as if to ward off protestations. There are none. "Drink your water. I'll be back later with food."

He does as promised. When he gets to their ankles, he stops. He looks up at both women. "I'll undo the ankle straps. You can stretch, walk around. Use the bucket in the corner." He points. "What you can't do is get out of here. There is only one door, and I am right outside."

Finished with his tasks and his pronouncements, lean and lanky rises and starts toward the door. Still no bulge. "Can you tell us why we're here?" Woo Woo asks. She hopes she sounds calm and respectful.

She gets another long look in return. "No."

Woo Woo persists, calmly and respectfully. She has been trained. "Is there anything you can tell us?"

Lean and lanky considers the request. "You will be treated well if you follow the rules. Tomorrow someone will be here to speak with you."

"Thank you," Woo Woo says. She nudges Mirabelle. "Thank you," says Mirabelle. She does not sound calm.

***

The training proves true. As the rolling rock door hits the floor and closes, Mirabelle breaks into sobs. They take over her body. Shivers set in quickly. Woo Woo looks for blankets and finds some packing quilts. She wraps them around Mirabelle and offers her

213

water. Mirabelle shakes her head "no." "You need to stay hydrated," Woo Woo says. Mirabelle takes a few small sips.

"Have you been trained?" Woo Woo knows the answer before she asks the question, but she asks anyway. Mirabelle is clearly puzzled. "Captivity survival."

The words are harsh. They need to be. Both women need to be alert to the situation they are in. "You need to speak with your father about that when we get out of here."

Mirabelle is about to ask "why," but thinks better of it. Instead, she focuses on Woo Woo's last words. *When we get out of here.*

***

Escape will not be easy. It often isn't, according to Woo Woo's abduction trainer. She walks the entire length of the room. It's a square. Boxes, large and small packing boxes, line two sides of the room; the door consumes most of the third. The remaining wall is littered with some excess packing material and remnants from boxes. Their two chairs take center stage.

Lean and lanky has turned on an overhead light, so they can see where they are and where they are going, a few feet in any one direction. Woo Woo repeats her surveillance. There are no other doors, no windows, no ceiling vents. Woo Woo pictures the space with the door open. It takes up most of one wall. *We're in a warehouse.*

That insight does not get the women any closer to getting out of there, but every piece of information is important Woo Woo knows. She starts searching in corners. Sometimes people drop things that can be used as a weapon: a jackknife, a pen, scissors.

"What are you doing?"

Woo Woo could lie. That might make Mirabelle feel better. But this is not about reassurance; it's about survival. "We need to get out of here. We need a weapon."

Mirabelle is a fast learner. She joins in the search. After thirty minutes, they have come up empty. "What do we do now?"

"We sit down. We drink some water. We talk about what we know and what we might know." Woo Woo follows her own advice. "Then we'll rip the shit out of these boxes."

Chapter 25.

Terrell is about to tear into a medium-rare sirloin. His plate is perfect. He's loaded his fries with gravy. Beef gravy. He's got a splotch of ketchup nestled in the left quadrant. He's salted the steak even though it doesn't need it. The Midtown always has the salt-to-blood ratio just right.

Steak at the Midtown Tavern on Grafton Street in downtown Halifax is a long-standing tradition for Terrell and several long-time friends. Tonight, those friends have bailed, a situation that has become all too common over time as kids and spouses make demands—on time and attention. Still tradition is tradition, and a man's gotta eat. So, Terrell invited Boone. She has about as much of a personal life as he does.

He lifts his steak knife, poised to savor the first slice and the first tasty morsel. But the cut Terrell feels is not on his plate. It's in his chest. He leans forward over the table and tries to breathe. Boone pushes beer and napkins and plates out of the way. She grabs her friend's arm. "Are you okay?"

"Fuck no," Terrell manages to say.

Boone is reaching for her phone. She's about to dial 911. Terrell lifts his right hand off the table a few inches. "I don't think this is a heart attack."

"It's something."

Whatever it is, it hurts. Terrell tries breathing in for a count of four, holding for a count of seven, and exhaling for a count of eight. Woo Woo taught him this. He thinks of Woo Woo. The pain gets worse.

"Something's wrong with Woo Woo."

***

Terrell is still hunched over the table. Breathing is a little easier now. Boone has Charlene and Lexie on speaker. "She's fine," they both say. Terrell shakes his head. Boone relays the message.

"She texted us earlier," Lexie says. "Has gone cross-country skiing at a friend's cottage. Will be spending the night. Internet spotty."

Terrell shakes his head "no" and doubles over the table. By now a small crowd has gathered asking if they can help. Boone assures them everything is okay. She takes the phone off speaker. "You better get down here now. And bring Tums."

***

Lexie and Charlene take one car. It will be easier to park and there is comfort in numbers. "What the hell is going on with Terrell?" Lexie wonders.

"It's guilt and remorse and fear. Love will do that to you."

Lexie laughs. It feels good. Despite her belief Terrell is simply losing it, he has scared her. This is out of character for him, and she hates to admit, it is out of character for Woo Woo.

***

There is a white wine and craft beer on the table when the women arrive. Terrell has managed to upright himself. Lexie and Charlene hug him first. Then they drink.

"Sorry," Terrell mumbles. "I may have overreacted."

"You don't overreact," Boone points out. "You're trained not to."

Lexie and Charlene agree. "What the frig happened?" Charlene asks. She gets looks from the table. It's the word "frig." Charlene was thinking she'd try it out.

"I don't know what the hell happened," says Terrell. "Felt a pain in my chest and all I could hear in my head were the words 'Woo Woo'."

"Now he's psychic," says Boone. That gets a weak smile from Terrell and grins from the other women.

They agree, collectively, that Woo Woo is likely okay, and Terrell is just lovesick. He would have objected to this description if his chest didn't ache so badly. They also agree Woo Woo's sudden absence is unusual. The likelihood of something having gone wrong is debated while Boone finishes her steak and Lexie and Charlene share a donair pizza.

"There is a possible solution," Boone says between bites. "Text Woo Woo. You just might get an answer."

Everyone looks at Terrell. He reaches for another Tums, then his phone. His fingers thump away. "Just checking in to make sure everything is okay."

Everyone hears the whoosh of the note being delivered. Then all they hear is silence.

***

Inside the warehouse, Woo Woo's phone pings. Lean and lanky picks it up and reads the message. He calls his boss. "We may have a problem."

***

Lean and lanky is back. He's carrying a cell phone in front of him like it has venereal disease. Woo Woo recognizes the phone. She understands instantly what is going on. Mirabelle does not. She throws Woo Woo a

219

worried look. Almost imperceptibly, Woo Woo smiles and nods.

"Answer," lean and lanky says thrusting the phone at her. "Do not send."

It's a message from Terrell. He's checking in. Terrell has no reason to check in on her on a Saturday night. I mean, it's not like the man is ever going to ask her out. But perhaps now is not the time to go down that road. This is a good sign.

"All okay. Just out of easy cell range. Spur-of-the-moment plans with yoga gang."

Lean and lanky leaves. He returns a few minutes later. "Nice try. Now do it right."

So, this is someone who knows Woo Woo. Maybe even Mirabelle. Woo Woo types in a new message. "All okay. Just out of easy cell range. Spur-of-the-moment plans with Maidoff."

The strong, silent type returns in less than a minute. "Who the fuck is Maidoff?"

Woo Woo is ready for this. "My meditation coach. We do nature retreats. Friends are more likely to believe that than cross-country skiing. You may have fucked up."

***

It's decided there is nothing to be done but have a sleepover. Boone is not convinced Terrell is not having a heart attack, but he refuses to go to the hospital. Charlene is not convinced Terrell isn't getting some subliminal message from Woo Woo. Lexie is convinced the guy is never going to ask Woo Woo out. Straight people.

***

They land at Charlene's. She has lots of room, and Madoff has been left alone long enough. There are extra toothbrushes and t-shirts to get them through the night. "I have almond cookies and herbal tea. From Woo Woo. We might just get some sleep."

***

No one believes that. Still the pear infusion proves calming, and the cookies are tasty—Terrell has yet to eat anything. Just as they are about to call it a night, Terrell's phone pings. It's a message from Woo Woo. "All okay. Just out of easy cell range. Spur-of-the-moment plans with Maidoff."

Charlene gets up and fills the kettle. Lexie digs the ice cream out of the freezer. Boone calls the station to get a trace on Woo Woo's phone. Madoff wonders if there will be a bowl of ice cream for him.

***

Lean and lanky has a name. Giannis. Mirabelle asks when he brings them dinner: hamburgers, fries, cola. Woo Woo is both impressed with Mirabelle's aplomb and concerned by its origin. She isn't sure if this is cleverness—a way to get him talking, to build alliances—or working through fear. Both good. There is a third possibility: acceptance. Not good.

Woo Woo doesn't pick up the conversation thread. Perhaps she should, but she is too busy interpreting Giannis's response to the question. Indifferent. *So, he doesn't care if we see him. He doesn't care if we know his name.* Not good.

It's time for them to make a move. Woo Woo isn't sure how, when, or where, but she doesn't like where things are heading. Mirabelle is saying something. Woo Woo tries to focus. Her request is obviously reasonable. Giannis puts the food down on the ground. He scans the three box-covered walls and heads to the furthest wall. Takes out a jackknife and opens one of the boxes. He returns with two small accent tables, small, bullet grey but large enough to hold their plates.

Mirabelle is saying thank you. She sounds like she means it. Giannis remains indifferent although he is a little surprised that the older one seems so interested in the grey blobs. The older one is very interested. She has seen these before.

Woo Woo knows where they are. She knows who has brought them here.

***

There are no forks, knives, stir sticks. Nothing that could potentially be weaponized. But there is food. Woo Woo says they need to eat first, need to wait until Giannis clears out the plates before they do anything.

Mirabelle dives in. She eats with the appetite of a teenager. Woo Woo has no appetite, but her training has taught her to keep her energy level up. To make things appear normal. Things are not normal. She wants to pump Mirabelle for information, but she does not want to scare her further. Apparently, imminent death trumps scared girl.

"I think I know where we are."

Mirabelle is thrilled at this progress. Intrigued to find out. Amazed at Woo Woo's smarts. Determined she will get capture training.

Woo Woo takes her time waiting to see if Mirabelle follows her thinking. "It's a warehouse."

Admittedly, Mirabelle is disappointed. This is not a eureka conclusion. "I think you may have been here before."

223

Mirabelle is no longer disappointed, and Woo Woo is back on the pedestal. The teenager looks around the room with renewed interest, less fear, less searching. She takes her time. Woo Woo doesn't push. "If I've been here before I don't remember," says Mirabelle after a few minutes. "Of course, it could be the circumstances."

"Let's come at this another way." Woo Woo makes it sound like this is typical dinner conversation. To Mirabelle's credit, she doesn't demand to know where Woo Woo thinks they are, doesn't try to decipher why Woo Woo is taking the long way around to what is surely a simple answer.

"Think of all the warehouses you've been in."

"It will be a short list."

"That's good."

"Well, obviously, I've been in my father's warehouse, for Enigma." As soon as the words are out of her mouth, Mirabelle turns to Woo Woo. Eyes wide. Horrified. "You think my father is doing this."

Woo Woo leans forward. She puts a hand on Mirabelle's thigh. Softly. "No, I do not think your father is doing this. Not for one minute."

Mirabelle is in tears. Woo Woo is not sure if this is relief or shame. Shame that for one minute she could ever have believed that was true. Woo Woo takes her time. She reassures Mirabelle that her father loves her, that when he finds out she is missing, his world will fall apart. Mirabelle knows this is true. She is easily comforted.

They finish their supper in silence. Woo Woo will bide her time. She will bring Mirabelle to the conclusion she knows is true without uprooting the girl's entire world in one fell swoop. They will dip a toe into toxic water, haul it back, dip it in again. Until they are ready to immerse themselves in the ugly truth.

***

There is a cold round pressure on the back of Terrell's neck. He opens his eyes and tries not to panic. His first thought: Gun. His second thought: Guns aren't moist. The detective, not at his sharpest first thing in the morning, doesn't have time for a third thought. Madoff has scrambled over sheets, pillows, and body parts to lick Terrell's face. It's mostly love, but Madoff would like to pee.

In the few minutes it takes to get dressed and make his way to Charlene's kitchen, Terrell's detective training has kicked in. He can smell bacon and coffee. This would be heavenly if it weren't for the circumstances. On the other hand, nothing dreadful has been learned since he unexpectedly slept so soundly, or breakfast would not be the boisterous aromatic affair it is. Terrell has also discovered that when a dog needs to pee there is nothing to do but take the dog for a walk. Right away.

Lexie is waiting for Terrell at the bottom of the stairs, leash in hand. She shakes her head no. "Nothing new."

Terrell feels the sharp pain in his chest. He has learned in the last 24 hours that this is not a heart attack. Madoff waits a respectful 12 seconds for the pain to subside, then nudges the detective's calf with his nose.

"Breakfast will be ready when you're back." Lexie covertly hands Terrell a small bag of dog treats. Madoff sees every movement. He loves company.

By the time dog and walker are back—two grateful beings—eggs, bacon, toast, and hashbrowns are ready and everyone is gathered around the breakfast nook. They'd usually sit in the dining room, but it is too painful without Woo Woo.

Boone gives Terrell the signal. Madoff barks. "Might as well tell us all," says Charlene.

"Can't get a trace on either Mirabelle's phone or Woo Woo's. That means the sim card has been removed or they are somewhere there is a jammer."

"But we got texts," Lexie points out. "You said you could trace the phone the instant it is turned on."

"We can. Last text to Terrell was made from the middle of Halifax Harbor."

"What the f***," says Lexie at the same time Charlene says, "They were on the ferry."

"It would appear they were," says Boone. "My guess. Someone hopped the ferry from Halifax to Dartmouth or vice versa, sent the text, then chucked both phones into the water. It's getting too risky to use them now."

"What does that mean?" Charlene sounds nervous. Madoff is on full alert, a piece of bacon uneaten on the floor.

"The kidnappers bought themselves some time, but anyone this smart is smart enough to know we'll be on to them soon if not already." It hurts Terrell to speak. "They might figure on a few more hours, but they'll go dark to protect their location."

"If this is about money," Boone adds, "we should hear from someone soon."

"What do you mean 'if'?" Charlene asks. Lexie doesn't hear the question. She hasn't heard anything since the word "kidnappers."

***

Madoff is uncertain what is happening, but he knows it isn't good. Everyone at the table, all these people he loves, are upset. They are not petting him. They are not laughing. These people are laughers. Madoff absently eats the bacon on the floor.

A sharp piercing sound cuts through everyone's concern. There's someone at the door. Charlene is up and out of her chair in seconds. The rest are close behind. A tall, thin man is standing on the step. His posture is erect, his face composed, his stance controlled. Charlene has no idea who this is. Neither does anyone else.

"I'm so sorry to interrupt," the man says before anyone else can speak. "Something has happened to Woo Woo." With those six words, the man suddenly slumps, his face crumples, he stumbles. Terrell grabs his elbow.

"Please, come in Mr. Aeron."

***

Losing control is not something that happens often to Benjamin Aeron. In his world, he can't afford it. But he feels safe here. He understands why Woo Woo has invited these people into her life. They are kind. They are genuine. They think beyond themselves. They love his daughter.

Charlene has poured him a fresh cup of coffee. Boone has thrust a plate of toast in front of him. Lexie insists he eats something. Madoff licks his leg. Aeron is not a man who likes dogs, but his leg feels warm. He relaxes for a nanosecond.

"My daughter and I call each other every night before bed and first thing in the

228

morning. It's because we love each other. It's also safety protocols."

No one asks what this means. Everyone knows now. "I was prepared to let last night go. There is a man in her life." He looks closely at Terrell for the first time. "But two missed calls is not merely unusual. It is a warning sign."

Lexie has a hand on one of Benjamin Aeron's arms, Charlene is patting the other. Somehow there is a dog on his lap. Terrell introduces himself. Name, rank.

"So, you're the one," says Benjamin. Lexie swears Terrell blushes. She finds a smile on her face for the first time in hours.

Terrell doesn't know how to respond to the forthright man sitting in front of him. It's clear though that Woo Woo is his daughter. "We haven't heard from Woo Woo since yesterday afternoon. And that text was likely fake. Last call was made from the harbor."

"The ferry," Benjamin says, mostly to himself. Madoff sits up. Licks his face.

Boone enters the room. No one was really aware she'd left. "I have two detectives on their way to Suite and Savory. That's the last place for sure we know Woo Woo and Mirabelle were supposed to be. They'll talk with Sofia and get any camera footage they can." She turns to Aeron. "We'll set up a relay at your home, but command central will be at the Pappas residence."

"You don't think this is about Woo Woo," Benjamin says.

"I don't know," says Boone. "Two high-profile targets. Could go either way."

"But you think Woo Woo is an easier target on her own. Why take the child unless the child is whom you really want."

Boone nods. *Smart man.* Terrell is heading for the closet and his coat. Movement feels good. Charlene is scurrying around putting files and her laptop in a carrying case. She has no idea why. Everyone heads in a flurry for the front door. There is an unspoken understanding: We must get to Nik Pappas's house.

Benjamin is walking out the door. Every fiber wants to yell, to run, to jump up and down. He forces himself to walk, evenly, calmly. He has his hand on his car door. Boone points to her SUV. They will go together. Charlene gives him a hug. Lexie thrusts something in his hand.

It's a leash.

***

Pappas looks at his phone as if it is an exotic animal he has never encountered before. Angela raises both eyebrows. "Everything okay?"

"I'm not sure." Pappas continues to look at the phone. "That was Charlene. Says she is on her way over. We should put coffee on."

The front doorbell rings just as the aroma of freshly brewed ibrik coffee is

230

wafting through the kitchen, the living room, the den. Charlene is not alone. "Sorry to interrupt your Sunday, but we need to speak with you." She waves her hands to include the people on either side of her. Two of those people are cops.

Angela is at the front door now. "Please come in."

The small crowd steps into the hallway. Nik Pappas continues to stare at Boone and Terrell. He can smell cop a mile away.

No one has said anything more than a few words but clearly something is wrong. Pappas stiffens. Cops can't come into his house without a warrant. Unless invited in. Dammit, they were invited in. This is not the place Angela goes to in her mind—although it is equally frightening. People have descended on her home without invitation or warning. At least two of them are cops. (Angela can smell cop a mile away, too.) It hits her like a ton of bricks.

"Oh my god, something's happened to Mirabelle." She feels her knees buckle under her. Terrell steps forward quickly and grabs her elbow.

"Perhaps we should sit down," says Boone. *So, this is the top dog*, Pappas thinks.

By the time Lexie and Charlene return, uninvited, from the kitchen with coffee, Pappas and his wife have been introduced to everyone, and they have been briefed. Angela is in tears, but she is composed.

"Why are we here?" Pappas asks. He looks at Benjamin by way of further explaining his question.

"Woo Woo is the easier to grab. More often on her own. Lives alone. Mirabelle is a bigger challenge. Our guess is that they took her when they could. Woo Woo happened to be with her." Terrell isn't quite sure what is wrong with his voice, why it is so difficult to speak.

Boone shoots him a look, uncertain if he should be here. "We have a team at Benjamin's house. If a call comes in it will be relayed here—with your permission."

Before Pappas can answer, before he can think, Angela says, "Do whatever you need to do."

Boone draws a radio from some corner of her being that Pappas never saw. "Unload and enter."

Within seconds there are more cops on the front step. They're weighed down with surveillance equipment. Angela clears the dining room table. Lexie gets up to make more coffee. Benjamin moves next to Pappas. He smiles, sadly, and places a hand on the man's shoulder. From some place Pappas did not know he had in him, he begins to cry. He cries and he cries and he cries.

Cops have seen this before. It is as commonplace to them as handcuffs and doughnut jokes. They move quietly and respectfully around Pappas. Most of them are parents. They cannot imagine what he is going through. Parenthood trumps drug trafficking.

Lexie is back with coffee for everyone. The surveillance equipment is set up. Digital still and video cameras take center stage. There is also GPS for tracking, computer surveillance, phone-tapping monitors. It looks like the scene from the bridge of *Star Trek*. Angela finds it comforting. Pappas is terrified.

Two of the police officers look at Boone and get the unspoken okay to leave. One remains behind. Someone will always be here until Mirabelle is home. Or otherwise.

Without anyone really knowing how, they find themselves sitting in the living room. (Boone is good at her job.) "We need to talk."

Everyone nods. This is the easy answer. Boone is not looking for easy answers. "It is going to be an uncomfortable conversation." She sees Pappas tense. "It is also an off-the-record conversation for anything that does not pertain to the kidnapping."

It is the first time Angela has heard this word. She rolls it over in her mind, on her tongue. Terrell makes it to her just as she throws up into the outstretched garbage tin. (Terrell is good at his job.) Pappas knows he should comfort Angela, but he can't move. He feels a hand back on his shoulder. Lexie has wrapped an arm around Angela. Charlene has disappeared.

Angela is following Terrell's instructions: breathe in for a count of four, hold for a count of seven, breathe out for a count of eight. She begins to relax. Then she feels guilty for doing anything but thinking about Mirabelle.

"The best thing you can do for your daughter is to be present, be calm. Think clearly." The room looks at Benjamin. They're seeing Woo Woo. "Capture training," Benjamin says as if this explains everything. He looks at Angela and Pappas. "We'll need to talk about that later."

Now the attention turns to Boone. And on cue, the front doorbell rings.

Kostas and Dimitri are ushered in by Charlene, drawn from somewhere in the house. She takes them to join the group. No explanation is needed for them to know something is wrong. Something is seriously wrong. There are two cops sitting in the living room.

Now it is Pappas's turn to take control. "It's Mirabelle. She's been taken." He stops for the merest of seconds. "Woo Woo is with her."

"How do you know?" Kostas asks.

It's a question that surprises his father and his stepmother because it is a question they didn't think to ask. They took the police and these new friends at their word. Pappas can feel himself stiffen once more.

"It's a question we asked ourselves," says Boone. Her tone is neutral, but she would really like to spend more time with this smart son who can take control of a room and send a seventeen-year-old kid to jail without apparent reservation.

Terrell takes out an iPad from some pocket or crevice Pappas failed to see. He really needs to get his eyes checked. "We have footage from outside Suite and Savory. It's the last place we could confirm Woo Woo's presence." He hesitates. "You may not want to see this."

Pappas reaches for the iPad. Terrell hits "play." The clip is over in less than thirty seconds. That's how long it takes to stop two women outside a store, show them the handgun clipped to your belt, and shove them in the back of a van. Terrell puts out a hand to steady Pappas. He realizes he is not so steady himself, and he has seen this clip more than a dozen times.

Pappas does not want Angela to see this. Angela does not care. She watches the clip. Every fiber of her being wants to wail. She feels the room looking at her. She seeks out the one person who can steady her. She locks eyes with Benjamin Aeron and breathes in for a count of four, holds for a count of ....

***

Silence is deafening. Lexie finally understands what this means. She feels the world imploding, weighing on her, dragging her to a conclusion she does not want to reach. The marrow in her bones hurts. No one says a word.

The front doorbell rings. *Jesus, it's like Grand Central*, Lexie thinks. Arriving on this train are two more cops. These ones aren't in uniform, but they are clearly police. They must be detectives. They have that aura: confidence, control, authority. If it weren't for the circumstances, Lexie would enjoy the reactions from the Pappas clan when they walk into the living room. This must be other-worldly on every level for father and sons.

The detectives nod. The movement says two things simultaneously: So, sorry you're going through this, and it's business as usual. *It's amazing how cops communicate,* Lexie thinks. No one has said a word, yet it's obvious messages are passing between Yin and Yang and the two other cops in the room. Lexie's friends. Woo Woo's friends.

Boone excuses herself. Terrell stands up to follow. "We'll be right back." He sees the fear on Angela's face. Feels the terror that tremors through Pappas's being. "We have not found them yet. This is an ongoing update."

Lexie wonders if he is lying. How would he know? *Aah, the unspoken language that links all cops*. She hopes there has not been a miscommunication.

There hasn't. Boone and Terrell are back in minutes. As if briefing a squad room full of officers in uniform, Boone says, "The detectives have spoken with Sofia Makri. Her story matches what we saw on the CCTV footage."

There are a few seconds of silence while everyone in the room digests this information and puts it in the context that makes the most sense to them. That context is diverse. Kostas is the first to speak, and he does not try to mask his tone. "Of course, her story matches. Why wouldn't it?"

It's unclear if the tone is animosity toward cops or defensiveness, a protective shield for his wife. Boone does not rise to the bait. She also doesn't answer the question. It is rhetorical, although, she notes with some self-satisfaction, it is Kostas who has planted the seed that his own wife might not be trustworthy.

"What does it mean that her story matches?" Angela asks. "Is that good?"

Boone explains that they are trying to build a timeline, trying to understand Mirabelle's and Woo Woo's states of mind, trying to determine if anything unusual happened at the reflexology sessions. The CCTV footage indicates Mirabelle and Woo Woo were unconcerned, even happy leaving the store. Sofia said the same thing. "Every time we talk to someone, every time we get new information, it helps us to paint the picture and lead us down the path to finding Mirabelle and Woo Woo."

This reassures Angela and her husband. Kostas is still bristling but even he doesn't know why. Dimitri wonders if it is too early to have a drink.

Someone, Lexie is not sure who, arrives with fresh coffee and sandwiches. "Thank you," Angela says. She turns to everyone. "This is my sister, Nancy. I asked her to come over."

Lexie is surprised. When the hell did she call her sister? She turns to look at Boone and Terrell. They are not surprised. I'm definitely doing a bit on cop communication.

In keeping with the mood in the room, Nancy looks awkwardly at the floor. She wipes away a tear. "I'm right here if you need me."

Almost without awareness, people reach for a sandwich, pour themselves a coffee, sit back. The silence has returned. It's not deafening, but it speaks volumes. Benjamin leans forward a millimeter, and the room sits up. Coffee cups pause midway to mouths. Chewing ceases. No one swallows.

"What is it you're not telling us?"

***

There are two ways to play this. *One.* Repeat the key message, make the brass happy, confirm the media training was worth the money everyone knows they wasted. *Two.* Answer the man's damn question.

A look passes between Boone and Terrell. They do not try to mask the look or explain it. Covert is out. Everyone knows now there is merit in the question. The look lets them know the cops are going to answer it. Honestly.

"Our detectives spoke with Sofia. Asked her about the reflexology sessions, asked if Woo Woo and Mirabelle were okay, asked if anything happened. She told them everything went well."

"We already know that," says Kostas. The tone is back.

Boone looks at Benjamin, Angela, Pappas. The look stops at Kostas. "Sofia told us everything went well. The detectives don't believe her. Either of them."

***

It's Sunday. Mac and cheese with wieners. The warden likes to call it comfort food. He believes it brings the boys a sense of home, of familiarity, of reassurance. At least that's what he tells people. The boys aren't buying it. Neither are the guards. It's not about compassion or rehabilitation; it's a budget measure. Macaroni and hot dogs are cheap.

Luke doesn't really care. He likes mac and cheese, and he's hungry. He's three guys from the start of the food line, when a CO taps him on the shoulder. "Castle, you're wanted in the warden's office."

Now this gets everyone's attention. The warden does not work on Sundays. Something is up. Something bad. A loud "Ooooo, someone's in trouble" circulates around the dining hall. Another guard takes his baton and hits the buffet tray slide. Hard. A painful metal screech ricochets around the room. A few guys cover their ears.

"Shut the fuck up," says the CO with the baton. He scans the room and glares at everyone. Then he glares at Luke. "Castle, get the fuck out of line and follow us to the warden's office. Now."

Before Luke can move, a large, very large, form glides in front of him. It's Beast. He doesn't say a word. Neither do the guards. The CO with the baton rolls his eyes and shrugs. There are things he'd like to do to this hulk of a boy. They are not legal.

"Follow me," he says. "Both of you."

***

It's roughly three minutes from the dining hall to the warden's office. This should be time Luke spends trying to figure out what he has done and how to get out of it, at the very least defend it. Whatever it is.

Instead, Luke finds himself thinking about Beast. *I mean how did the guy move from behind him in line to in front of him without so much as a murmur. How could anyone do this, let alone someone the size of Beast?* Luke decides he's going to ask Beast about this. Not now, of course, but someday. Is this a skill the guy has learned or is this just Beast? Luke knows Beast will tell him the answer. Whatever connection they have forged here is titanium. It cannot be broken, and it is founded on brutal honesty.

***

The warden looks up as Luke and Beast walk through his door. Double jeopardy. He sighs and motions the two boys to chairs in front of his desk. He signals the guards to stand on either side of the door frame. No one really wants to be alone in a room with Beast. The warden hates this fucking job.

"You're on your way to Halifax," he says without preamble. "Something has happened, and you're needed."

Luke is about to protest or interject. It doesn't matter which. The warden shuts him down before he can say anything. "No point in asking me what's going on. I don't know. Above my pay grade. All I know is your lawyer called, an HPD inspector called, and a fucking judge. Boy, whatever you have stepped in, it's deep and it smells."

241

The warden may not like his job, but he is good at it. It takes less than five seconds for him to register the look on Luke's face. The kid has no idea what is going on. The warden softens, for a second. "They're not telling me anything, but they're not taking you to the police station. I get the feeling this isn't about you but about what you might know. But then I have been known to be wrong."

"What do you mean?" Luke is confused. A little less frightened, but the unknown is dangerous. He's learned that the hard way.

"Castle, it's time to go." This is from the baton guard. He jerks his head toward the door. "Get moving."

Beast stands up. It's not a question. "You too," says the guard. He moves behind the two boys. He never takes his hand off his baton. "Fuck me."

***

The drive to Halifax is painstakingly long. And terrifyingly fast. The guards don't say a word. Luke and Beast communicate only with facial expressions and body language, and that is limited. They both know there is no point in asking the guards where they are going. The guards won't tell them, and they certainly don't know why Luke is being hauled out of juvie on a day pass. If it's above the warden's pay grade, it isn't even a remote possibility the guards are in the know.

Luke figures it has to be Brandon. Asswipe did something he shouldn't. Same old, same old. Luke would never rat on his brother. Probably couldn't even if he wanted to. How would he know what hell his brother has been up to while he's been in juvie.

For a split second, Luke panics. What if something has happened to Brandon, or his mom. Beast shakes his head no. Luke feels himself relax. Beast is right. In his unspoken understanding of Luke's palpable fear, Beast has reminded Luke of protocol. If this were an accident or worse, there would be a grief counsellor or psych services in the warden's office. There would be no smashing of the baton in the dining hall. The guards would be forced to play nice for a little while.

Could be another attempt to get info out of him about the drugs, but then he'd be going to the police station. His lawyer would also have asked to speak with him in the warden's office. Privately.

So not life and limb. Must be asswipe.

Beast softly shakes his head no. Beast is never wrong.

Chapter 26.

Woo Woo sits up. Pain shoots through her neck and shoulders. Her lower back protests. She swears a hip groaned. Sleeping on the floor will do that to you.

Woo Woo pulls back the three blankets that cover her. They smell, as she discovered last night when she tried to wrap them around her fetal-shaped body. So much for comfort. Woo Woo reminds herself to be grateful. She is alive. She is unharmed.

She is groggy. She feels like a black bear emerging from hibernation, aware there is a world around her but not able to orient herself within that world. Woo Woo wonders if she has been drugged. Perhaps Giannis slipped a little something in the burger and fries he served up for supper last night. Or it may simply be that Woo Woo's body needed to crash, to take her away from all this if only for a few slumbering hours.

Doesn't matter. Today is another day. Breathe in gratitude. Woo Woo also breathed in a little fortitude. She looked around, once more, at the warehouse starting with Mirabelle. The teenager was fast asleep, breathing rhythmically. It is impossible to tell the time in a room with no windows. Or clocks. But there were no sounds from outside the rolling rock. Giannis was either busy elsewhere or not here. Woo Woo hopes it is the latter.

It's Sunday. People will be worried about her and Mirabelle. How can they translate that worry into action? Terrell will be key. And Boone. Woo Woo breathes in gratitude for friends who are cops.

She gets up quietly and makes her way to the far side of the warehouse, the wall of boxes. She starts in the back. It's slow going. Whatever is inside these boxes is well sealed with duct tape, packing tape, staples. Some even have hot melt thermos plastic adhesives. Woo Woo tears firmly but softly at the first box. It takes several minutes to break through the corrugated cardboard. Her hands and fingers ache with the effort.

She's in.

Woo Woo doesn't get far. A hand on her elbow stops her progress, and her heart. A thousand excuses run through her mind. Giannis will buy none of them. Turns out they won't be needed. It's Mirabelle at her side. So much for capture training.

The two of them dive into the first box. Mirabelle literally dives in. There are more accent tables like the one they ate dinner on last night. Mirabelle feels around among the bubble wrap but comes up empty handed.

"Pass me a table."

With some effort, Mirabelle hoists the small table out and over the box. Woo Woo is waiting to grab it. She misses. Actually, she doesn't miss it as much as she drops it. The vacuum-sealed table breaks into a hundred pieces. The pieces are coated in a white powder.

It's time to get the hell out of here. Woo Woo helps Mirabelle out of the box. This will not be a good day for her. Doesn't matter. There is no time to be gentle. Woo Woo has a plan. Mirabelle is central to that plan.

She and the young woman sit down amid the packing chips, the cardboard boxes, the broken table. They go over the plan. They go over the plan again. They play it out. They play it out again.

Then they sit waiting for the rolling rock door to open.

Chapter 27.

The Pappas household is in an uproar. Kostas declares at the top of his voice that his wife doesn't lie. Angela demands to know what it means that Sofia is lying. Pappas claims, loudly, that he never trusted her. Dimitri pours another drink.

In the center of the storm sits Benjamin Aeron. Boone watches him closely, uncertain if he is figuring out what it means that Sofia lied or simply waiting for the furor to die down. Like she and Terrell are doing. And where the hell is Charlene?

Boone doesn't try to stop the ranting and the raving. Sometimes ranters and ravers let important information slip, and she noticed some time ago that Terrell is recording the conversation. Nothing said can be used in court, but that doesn't mean it can't be used.

The silence in the room soon stops the Pappas family from hurling accusations and innuendos. It's an old trick teachers use. They let the room go completely quiet except for those who are speaking out of turn. When the offenders come back to the room, they are both aware of their blunder and embarrassed by it. Admittedly, Nik Pappas does not embarrass easily, but he's smart enough to know there are cops in the room, and they can't unhear something they have already heard.

Fortunately, there was nothing but personal dirty laundry being aired. Pappas is not sure if this is a good thing or if it will have longer-term implications for his family, especially his relationship with his oldest son. Right now, he doesn't give a shit.

Benjamin stands up. Everyone else who is standing sits down. "Perhaps we can pick up where we left off."

Gotta give him credit, Boone thinks. Man knows how to control a room. She glances around that room. "I've told you what I know. I have two experienced detectives who think Sofia Makri is not telling them the truth. They are not usually wrong."

Kostas stands up. His stance is threatening. "My wife is not a liar."

"She is also not your wife any longer," Boone says. She also knows how to control a room.

Kostas sits down. Whatever threat there was is gone. The uproar is back. It's more vociferous than before—How could you not tell us? (Angela) Hope you have a prenup. (Dimitri) This is not information you can keep from me. (Pappas)—but it is shorter lived.

"According to Ms. Makri, she and her husband are separated."

"You think this is a money grab?" Benjamin is figuring out the angles.

"I think this is information we didn't have before."

"This is absurd," says Angela. "Sofia loves Mirabelle. And Sofia has money."

"I doubt very much that Sofia loves Mirabelle." Dimitri says this in the same tone of voice as he would say "pass the salt." Now he has the attention of the room. He takes a slow sip from his glass. Boone doesn't object to a semi-sloshed drug dealer. She'll take information wherever she can get it.

"Come on. Big Daddy announces the other night that Sofia's baby—Suite and Savory—is being ripped out of her arms after, what, five or six years of working her ass off. And it's a decision you don't even have the decency to tell her before you drop it on a bunch of strangers. Christ, you didn't even bother to tell Kostas." Dimitri stares at his father. It's unclear if this is commonplace conversation or bravado bolstered by bourbon.

Either way, there is information here Boone didn't have before. She shoots Terrell a quick glance. He returns the glance. Everything is still being recorded. "Kostas, when did you and Sofia separate?"

Reluctance oozes from the oldest son's pores. He doesn't have to say a word. Sofia left him the night she lost Suite and Savory. "It's not what you think."

"What do we think?" Terrell asks.

Kostas is back on his feet. "You think she married me for money. She didn't—and she didn't leave me because of money. She left because I wouldn't stand up to my father." Whatever Kostas has been holding back, it's coming out now. And it's toxic.

***

Charlene doesn't know what the hell she's walked into, but she knows when she has stepped in it. She breathes deeply. It's like walking back in time. Auditors know this smell. They also know how to freshen the room. Frankly, Charlene can't be bothered. She has something more pressing on her mind.

Terrell can feel her tension. "What's up?" he yells over the din. Not loudly enough. Boone and Benjamin have both picked up on the energy emanating from Charlene. Benjamin raises one hand. Silence descends.

"I found something in the books. Sofia's books."

Now Charlene has the undivided attention of everyone in the room. "I didn't think you had started reviewing the books." Pappas knows this sounds silly, but he opened his mouth, and this is what came out.

"I hadn't, but numbers calm me down. While you were all in here hooting and hollering, I thought I'd do some work. It's like meditation."

"That's nice," says Terrell. His tone is not nice.

"Right," says Charlene. "Suite and Savory rents a property."

"What the fuck," says Pappas. He stares at his oldest son.

His oldest son glares back. "Sofia does not rent another property. She has no need for more real estate. I'd know if she were renting some place."

Boone and Terrell would like this caustic conversation between father and son to continue, but Charlene may have stumbled onto something important. A second property could be a great place to hide people. They need more information. Benjamin Aeron understands this need, and he moves more quickly than the two police officers. "Why is having a rental property unusual? Could be a warehouse for storage."

"Yeah," says Kostas, hands hovering on hips, jaw clenched. "So, what if Suite and Savory has a storage facility."

"Sofia has gone out of her way to mask this expense." Charlene says this simply. The implication is clear.

"Are you sure?" Pappas asks. Boone and Terrell know better.

"This is what I do," Charlene says. There is no defensiveness. There is assurance. "The expenditure is under 'miscellaneous office expenses' and it pops up every month. But you have to go looking for it. It's rolled in with all the other expenses."

"So what?" says Kostas, jaw jutting. He will hang on to the last shred of his marriage until he has no choice but to let go.

'It's $15,000 a month, every month. It comes out of the account on the last day of the month."

"Like rent," says Boone.

"Like rent," Charlene agrees.

The back and forth, like a pro tennis ball bouncing around the court only to be volleyed back, is too much for Angela. She has breathed in and out as much as her body will stand. "Well, what the hell are you waiting for." Arms flail. Spittle forms. Feet stomp. "Go to the damn place. Find my daughter. Don't just stand there."

"They don't know where to go." Benjamin Aeron says this softly. Sadly.

Charlene looks at the floor. "We don't know where to go."

Boone doesn't see this as defeat. This is progress. She's on her shoulder mic. Within minutes a BOLO is out for Sofia's car, a warrant request is in the works to track her GPS, cops are at Kostas's place taking it apart inch by inch.

"Someone has to know something about this warehouse." Pappas can't believe his daughter-in-law could hide this from him. He can't believe he could miss it.

"Officers are enroute to speak with store employees," Boone says. "They'll also see if anyone recognizes the man outside with the gun. If Sofia is behind this, that man is there because she wanted him there."

"Can you trace the property?" Benjamin looks at Charlene. She's already heading for the office and her laptop. "I can, but it will take time."

"We don't have time," Benjamin says. "This isn't about money. This is about getting even."

***

The room collapses. Angela is sobbing somewhere on the sofa. Pappas is looking as if he has been hit by an AK-47. Kostas is holding his head in his hands. Dimitri is holding his drink, mouth wide open.

Terrell has taken to a corner. The silence is more distracting than the yelling. He's missing something. "Figure it out?" Boone comes up behind him. Lexie comes up behind her. This feels better.

"Why does she want another property?" Terrell searches for an answer to his own question. "It's not like she can sell it. It's not an asset."

"But she can use it," Lexie points out, "and no one is the wiser."

"Use it for what?" Boone wonders mostly to herself.

"Not for anything legal, I assume, or why bother hiding it."

"She's a retail store manager, what the hell can she be hiding?"

"Maybe she isn't," Lexie says.

"What do you mean?" Terrell shoots Lexie a look. He's interested in where this is going.

"Comedians do this all the time. You take a job to pay the bills until you get established. You're a waiter, a valet, an accountant. Hell, I knew one guy who was a dentist. Point is, when you're on stage, all people see is that you're a comedian. They don't see what else you are. And that something else brings in a whole lot more money than your jokes."

Terrell and Boone look at each other. "Motherfucker." That was Boone.

"We need Luke Castle." That was Terrell.

Boone reaches for her phone. Everyone else looks at Terrell. "Who's Luke Castle?" Angela asks.

"Your husband or your sons-in-law might want to answer that for you."

Angela turns to her husband, then Kostas, Dimitri. The latter two don't meet her gaze. Pappas is unapologetic. Turns out that is because he really doesn't know who Luke Castle is. Terrell is so glad he is recording this conversation.

Once the latest round of furor, admittedly much more muted, dies down, it is Benjamin who presses for answers. "Who is he?"

Terrell is looking closely for unspoken responses to his answers. "He's a young man currently sitting in juvenile detention for transporting drugs in a pizza van." Aah, so now Pappas knows who Luke is. He's glaring at his offspring. His wife is staring at everyone in confusion. Benjamin has figured it out.

Terrell isn't finished. "He's also Mirabelle's boyfriend."

There it is. More furor. More fear.

Chapter 28.

Giannis walks into the room and looks at the floor where he expects two sleeping bodies to lie. There are no bodies. Before he can fully panic, drop the McDonald's bag he is holding, or reach for his Beretta, Woo Woo is striding toward him. Indignant.

"Do you mind." It isn't a question.

For a few seconds, Giannis has no idea what the hell is going on. Then he sees Mirabelle. On the toilet. Well, the bucket.

"Do you mind." Indignant Woo Woo repeats her question. Without thinking Giannis turns his back to the bucket, and the women. In one well-trained move, Woo Woo reaches between Giannis's legs and grabs his balls. Hard. The big man goes down on two knees. Woo Woo continues to squeeze.

By now Mirabelle is in front of Giannis. She tosses the remnants of last night's soda in his face. She takes her sneaker and whacks it across his face. Giannis is in pain. Mostly he's pissed. As he starts to rise, Woo Woo takes the vacuum-sealed accent table and smashes it over his head. Giannis goes down.

"We don't have much time," Woo Woo says as she reaches in Giannis's pants pocket. Mirabelle is already frisking his shirt and coat for a cell phone. If they're lucky they will be able to make two calls. At the very least, they should be able to make one.

One it is. Woo Woo finds the phone. She has Pappas's number memorized. She dials. Surveillance stations will be set up at both houses, but Woo Woo figured some time ago that Terrell and Boone and her friends would know this was about Mirabelle. The phone rings. No answer. It rings again. Mirabelle is starting to panic. Giannis is starting to move.

"They have to put the recording equipment on and get your Dad ready. One more ring."

Nik Pappas answers the phone. "Is my daughter okay?"

"We're fine. We're at ..." Woo Woo stops. The butt end of a Taurus G2C will do that to you.

***

Boone and Terrell wait for the noise to subside. There is a lot of noise. This takes a few minutes. It's minutes Terrell doesn't believe they have, but police work has taught him patience. Rush and you run the risk of making things worse. Nothing could be worse than this.

257

Pappas is also at the end of his rope, although his voice remains strong. He raises a hand (he's learned that from Benjamin). Nothing happens. Benjamin raises his hand. Silence.

Pappas doesn't have time to be annoyed or embarrassed. His daughter is missing, and it would appear fuck all is being done to find her. "So, there is a boy. Do you think he had something to do with this?"

Terrell would like to hit this man. "No sir. I think this boy loves your daughter. I think he loves her so much he's willing to go to jail for her."

There is a lot to unpack in that sentence. The animosity Pappas can ignore. The content he can't. It's not unpacking time, however. "So, let's get this boy here."

Right on cue, the front doorbell rings.

***

Luke feels like the main attraction in a freak show. He wonders if this is how Beast sometimes feels: apart. There are a bunch of people he doesn't know staring at him: an older man with dark hair, a woman who has obviously been crying, another older man with wire-framed glasses who reminds him of someone, a woman sitting in the corner hunched over a laptop. There are also a bunch of people he does know: the two cops,

Lexie, Kostas and Dimitri. Whatever this is Luke doesn't like it.

Doesn't seem to bother Beast. He walks toward the man with the wire-framed glasses and holds out his hand. Benjamin takes it in both of his. Beast moves forward and hugs Benjamin. It is the gentlest of hugs. He turns toward the two cops. They're in charge. The gangstas might think they own this room. They don't.

"What the fuck?"

Angela and the Pappas clan stiffen. Boone and Terrell take this for what it is: a sign of respect. No bullshit. Still, this will not be easy. Terrell defers to Boone. He's not sure he could get through this, and Boone knows it. She looks Beast directly in the eye. "Woo Woo is missing. She has been kidnapped."

She gives him a second to take this in. Then she turns to Luke. "They also have Mirabelle."

The arm under Luke's elbow is Beast. No one knows how in hell he got from one side of the room to the other. Lexie has given up questioning it.

The next few minutes are spent briefing the boys. And doing introductions. Pappas cannot resist. "So, you are the boy who has Mirabelle's heart." Luke stands tall, and nods. "And you are the boy who used my pizza van to transport drugs."

Luke does not know what to do with this. Neither do Boone and Terrell. WTF.

"That's for later." This is Lexie. "My friend is fighting for her life. Your daughter is, too. Do the business shit later."

Terrell steps in front of Luke. "There is a warehouse. We think they're being held there."

Luke hangs his head. "I didn't work for Sofia. I don't know where the warehouse is." He wants to cry.

"You don't know what you don't know." This is Boone. "We need to take you down memory lane."

Before Luke can nod yes, the phone rings.

***

All Terrell hears is "We're fine. We're at …." Then his heart stops. He lunges over the table, over recording tablets and audio monitors, and iPads. He lunges over Constable Fraser and reaches for the headset. The headset is between Constable Fraser's two ears. Constable Fraser tumbles backward. Terrell grabs the headset before his colleague hits the floor. He scans the closest monitor. He has no idea what the lines mean or the data indicate.

All anyone can hear is silence.

Constable Fraser, with all the experience of his three months on the job, knows what is going on. It was never covered at the academy. Still, he knows. The 6'2" constable rights himself, reaches a hand for the headset and takes over command of the four square feet in front of him. He feels the eyes of everyone in the room on him. He feels their disappointment before they do.

Constable Fraser looks at Boone and shakes his head. "They used VPN. No location data."

"Dammit," says Boone. She looks at the floor. You can't see heartbreak on the floor.

Angela is in tears. She's not sure what just happened, but she knows it isn't good.

It's Charlene who brings everyone back to the here and now—and to hope. "Woo Woo is alive."

Benjamin sags. He doesn't get far. Constable Fraser's left arm, moving of its own accord, takes hold of the older man's elbow. Benjamin straightens. "You are right." He looks at Charlene. "This is good news. My daughter is alive. And if my daughter is alive ..." He turns and looks at Angela and Pappas, "then your daughter is alive as well."

"Woo Woo said 'we'." Everyone looks at Lexie. "On the message." In a split second, Constable Fraser has the file open and hits play. "We're fine. We're at ...." He plays the message over and over again until Boone gives him the signal to stop.

***

261

Sofia Makri is standing in front of Woo Woo. Smiling. "I underestimated you. That won't happen again."

"Glad to hear it. I don't like to be underestimated."

"Aah, glibness. One of three common responses when you know you're about to die." Sofia continues to smile. "I thought you'd opt for pleading. Bet you will before this is over." She turns to sneer at her niece. She turns back to Woo Woo and holds out her hand. Woo Woo hands the cellphone over. It isn't disconnected. Sofia takes the phone. Now it's disconnected. It's only been a few seconds. Sofia continues to smile. "So sorry your call wasn't long enough to be traced."

Woo Woo smiles back. Tracing a cellphone call is almost instantaneous. Terrell has her address. He'll be on his way.

***

Sofia is taking her time. She has waited a long time for this, and she is going to savor every moment. First though, she's got to get Giannis off the floor and find out what the hell happened here.

"Stay tuned ladies. I'll be back in a few minutes." She tosses them the McDonald's bag and reaches to grab Giannis's hand. He's now sitting up. His balls ache, his head throbs, and he may be dying of embarrassment. "Want me to kill them?" he asks from his disadvantage point on the floor.

"Let's get a coffee first."

***

The duct tape chafes her wrists. Woo Woo is not surprised. Not her first rodeo. Mind you, the other rodeos were rehearsals for the real thing. Woo Woo has played by the rules of capture. She has an edge. When Sofia was binding her hands behind her back, Woo Woo leaned forward as far as she could. She did not make fists; she loosely clasped her wrists and forearms together. Now she has wiggle room. Unfortunately, there is no place to wiggle to. She can't even reassure Mirabelle as silly as that sounds. Her mouth is taped shut.

It won't be for long. Sofia is back.

"Ladies, how lovely to see you again. I like this look."

Woo Woo believes, after more than six decades on this earth, she finally knows what it means to wish another human being harm. She doesn't like the urge, but she now understands why many would feel it, nurture it. Sofia would be one of those. She's going to revel in this moment.

Revel away, you bitch. My people are coming for you.

263

***

Sofia, smile glued to her lips, raises her coffee cup. "Sorry ladies. I didn't get any for you. Never a good idea to give hostages hot beverages."

Her grin bounces from Woo Woo to Mirabelle. Self-satisfaction mingles with slight confusion. Sofia expected repartee, anger, defiance, pleading. Of course, the duct tape. She rips it off.

"That's better. Now we can talk."

Woo Woo and Mirabelle are silent. This may help to delay the inevitable. "I hope Giannis has been treating you well." Sofia laughs at her own joke.

She's enjoying this, Woo Woo thinks. It's about more than betrayal and anger. This is hate.

Hate is harder to mediate. It is easier to throw off kilter though. Woo Woo works at her hands. She can feel the tape giving.

"Ladies, don't be shy. Tell me. What do you think of our little arrangement."

"You're a psychopath." Mirabelle spews the word like it is tainted beef.

Sofia sighs. Turns to Woo Woo. "Today's youth. How disappointing. They don't even know what a psychopath is."

Woo Woo bites her tongue. Sofia turns her attention back to Mirabelle. "A psychopath lacks empathy. Is shallow. Easily bored. Ooh, wait a minute. Maybe I am a psychopath." Sofia laughs at her own joke. She laughs so hard she has to put her coffee cup on the floor. Tears stream down her face.

Once she's wiped her eyes and collected herself, Sofia turns back to Mirabelle. "You should know I'm not a psychopath."

Mirabelle's confusion is palpable. Woo Woo shares it. Maybe Sofia has lost it after all. "We're here bitchlet because you stole my store. You've made my life inconvenient. I'll have to regroup. It's not business as usual. I don't like that. Ergo, I don't like you."

Sofia tilts her head. "That's not true. I've never liked you. Stealing my store was just the icing on the birthday cake."

"I didn't steal your store."

"Ahh, Glykeria. Of course, you stole my store. You giggled and preened. Pranced your way into Nikolaos's heart. Kudos to you. I didn't even know the bastard had a heart."

Mirabelle's anger propels her upward. Woo Woo shoots her a look. Mirabelle, chair bound, plops back down. "There she is," Sofia says. "The nasty alter ego that lurks inside. Always has. You've buried her deep, little one, but have no doubt she is there."

Woo Woo wants to kill this woman.

Chapter 29.

Constable Fraser looks blankly at the screen in front of him. Terrell looks at some spot on the wall he cannot see. Luke looks at the corner of the desk. Slowly people start to move to the living room, to next steps, to nurturing hope and suppressing fear. Luke continues to look at the corner of the desk.

"What's up?" There is an edge to Terrell's voice. It's fear. And hope.

Luke puts his hand in front of him. "That's Jonny."

It takes Boone and Terrell less than a second to reach Luke, to pick up the photo he has been staring at. It's a picture of the man standing in front of the van. The van that Woo Woo and Mirabelle were shoved into. The man with the gun.

Boone is all business. "Who's Jonny? How do you know him?"

"He's a customer."

Pappas, Kostas, and Dimitri tense. It's palpable. Terrell couldn't give a shit. But this is important. "What kind of customer?"

Luke knows exactly what the question means. So does everyone else in the room.

"I've delivered pizza to him and the guys." Luke reads Terrell's look. And the one his girlfriend's father is shooting him. "He likes pepperoni and olives. Green."

"How do you know that?" Everyone looks at Charlene like she has descended from an alien craft. Not a cop. But asking questions. Charlene can also read a tense room. "Common question for auditors."

The question doesn't faze Luke. "Big tipper. You remember those." He takes his eyes off the photo and stares directly at Pappas. He's done with this shit. "And he's family."

The furor erupts. Now it's cops against drug dealers. Accusations fly. Denials fly back. It's Lexie who brings the room back to some semblance of order. She gives a weak grin. "Common skill for comedians. Shutting hecklers down."

Before the two senior officers in the room can begin interrogating anyone, Pappas says, with conviction, "That man is not family."

Kostas and Dimitri agree. Boone believes them. She looks at Luke. The unknown in the room. Luke is unfazed, except, of course, for the fact that his world has fallen apart. He shrugs. This is drug dealing crap. He's had enough of that. "The pizza is always comped."

Now it's Pappas and his sons who are shooting glances at one another. It's

Benjamin who interprets the message. "Aah, not your family. Sofia's family."

"Where did you deliver the pizza? Same place every time?" Luke nods. "A warehouse. The park." For people who live in Halifax, the park is Bayers Lake Industrial Park, a huge commercial complex with big box stores, health clinics, hotels. And warehouses.

Boone is already on coms calling for SWAT. "Do you remember the address?"

Luke shakes his head no. "But I can draw you a map."

***

Tears are rolling down Sofia's cheeks. Whatever her joke, she found it incredibly funny. Or perhaps it's the situation she finds herself in. One of her own making. One Nik Pappas can't control. One he'd love to control. *Your daughter's about to die, asswipe.*

One thing capture training can't teach you, at least with any confidence, is when the pendulum swings. When the kidnappers move from the possibility of release to the certainty of death. Woo Woo feels the pendulum move. She begins reciting the loving kindness meditation to herself. She will leave this world a better place than she found it.

May you be happy.

May you be healthy.
May you be safe.
May you live with ease.

Sofia feels the change in the atmosphere. She does not have her hostages' attention. Woo Woo is sitting still with her eyes closed doing whatever it is Woo Woo does. Mirabelle is a mirror image: she does whatever Woo Woo does. This will not do. She pokes Woo Woo. Woo Woo continues to sit quietly, eyes closed. Sofia thinks she might be praying. She wants pleading, and howling, and genuflecting. Well, the symbolic equivalent of genuflecting. The duct tape prevents the real thing.

It's time. Sofia is tired of playing this game, especially with someone like Woo Woo. Someone you can't predict. She just needs to decide who dies first. What is the last thing she wants each of these women to see, besides herself. Perhaps she should take photos. That can be tricky. Evidence and all. One thing Sofia learned from her father-in-law is to be careful.

She lifts the Taurus G2C, a gift to herself after her first major purchase. She had found her path, and she needed a comfort blanket for the future that was unfolding. The G2C is very comforting. Especially when you are dealing powder.

Before Sofia can pull the trigger, a first for her, truth be told, the rolling rock doors whirr. Giannis needs something. Sofia lowers her gun. She is in no hurry to end these women. And Giannis would not interrupt unless it was important.

It is.

***

Sofia turns to tell Giannis it's okay to come in. She can't see Giannis, but she can see the seven SWAT officers who come through the door and the seven Heckler & Koch MP5s they have raised at chest level. Raised at her.

Sofia Makri is no fool. You don't fight cops with guns; you fight them with lawyers. She lowers her weapon and raises her hands above her head. It takes less than a second for two officers to have her on the ground, arms pinned behind her back.

Woo Woo is watching this with amazement, and relief. Her message got through. She can't take her eyes off Sofia. Off this woman who uprooted her life, who taught her to hate. She looks so helpless now. So harmless.

May you rot in hell. Woo Woo is embarrassed by the thought. It came uninvited and instantaneous. At some fiber of her being though, she knows this is not who she is. She will find her way back from this. She will find her way to Woo Woo.

The room is swarming with cops, there is organized shouting, sirens invade the space. Woo Woo breathes in gratitude. She turns to Mirabelle. A woman is quickly making her way to Mirabelle. She has a knife. Before Woo Woo has time to panic, she realizes she knows this woman.

Boone is here.

Oh, thank god. Boone is here.

***

Boone is not alone. Woo Woo feels the arms wrap around her before she sees who owns them. Terrell is holding her. He's crying. Tears cascade down his eyelids, his cheeks, his chin. They pool on his upper lip, his nose, his lashes. Woo Woo takes her hand and wipes away a tear. It takes a second for her to realize her hands are free. That doesn't seem important now. She looks at the tears on her hand, at her hand on Terrell's face. *I've never seen you cry before. I've never touched your face before.*

That is what is important.

Terrell is trying to de-tape Woo Woo. It isn't easy. He can't stop crying and he refuses to let go of her. Her hands are finally free of duct tape. Then her ankles. Terrell reaches down to help Woo Woo stand. She wobbles. Terrell holds her tighter. Woo Woo straightens.

"Are you okay?"

271

Terrell is clasping Woo Woo close to his chest. He whispers three words in her ear. Woo Woo wonders if she has ever felt so wonderful.

"I'm so sorry."

Woo Woo looks at this man holding her for all he is worth and never letting go. What does he have to be sorry for?

"I should have asked you out. I should have told you how I felt. It shouldn't take a crisis for me to tell you I love you."

Woo Woo continues to look at this man holding her for all he is worth and never letting go. She wonders if she is going to faint. She lifts a hand to Terrell's face. She wipes away another tear. Holds it on her finger. Opens her mouth to speak. Nothing happens. Terrell holds her closer. Woo Woo melts into his chest and lets herself acknowledge the terror of the last two days.

Woo Woo looks again at this man. This man she loves. Woo Woo begins to cry. And cry. And cry.

***

It takes upward of an hour for the controlled chaos at the warehouse to subside, for police officers and medical personnel to dot their procedural I's and cross the required Ts. Woo Woo and Mirabelle are both examined by paramedics and given a clean bill of physical health. No broken bones, no bleeding, damage to muscles, organs, or tissues. (This takes a little longer to discern in Woo Woo's case. Terrell won't let go of her.)

Sofia and Giannis are handcuffed and placed in separate cars. They're told the charges, at least the initial charges, against them. They are advised of their right to legal counsel. They are cautioned about speaking their mind. Giannis doesn't say a word. He looks only to Sofia when she is in his view plane. Otherwise, he keeps his head down. Literally.

Sofia is more defiant, smartly so. She tosses her hair, lifts her chin, and, at one point, spits on an officer. (He takes out his hand sanitizer and gets on with the job.) Terrell would like to break her, but he's not moving. Boone would like to break her, but the only thing Sofia has said prevents that. *Lawyer.*

Both Mirabelle and Woo Woo are much more talkative. Mirabelle is recounting in detail everything that has happened. *Good for her,* Boone thinks. What Woo Woo has to say is a little more interesting: the white substance in the accent tables. Constables and detectives and narcotics dogs from the drug unit are combing (and sniffing) through the warehouse. It is not clear from outside the warehouse what they've found, but it is clear from the hollering and hooting they have found something, and it is big.

It's time to leave. Woo Woo knows her dad is at the Pappas home, and Mirabelle knows her parents are waiting for her. All parents have been called. Their babies are safe, but it's not possible for them to come to the crime scene despite what might happen on *Blue Bloods*.

To avoid additional drama, and nosy neighbors, Boone's car has been delivered to the scene. She and Terrell will drive the women home. Further statements can be taken tomorrow. There will be no need to station constables outside Woo Woo and Mirabelle's residences. Terrell is not leaving Woo Woo's side, and Boone is spending the night at the Pappas house. (This is not procedure, but this is not a typical scenario. Who knows, maybe Pappas will confide in the inspector and then they can tear Mirabelle's world apart when they arrest her father. Boone puts that thought in a vault somewhere and tosses the key.)

Mirabelle climbs in front. She reaches for Boone's hand. And clenches. This is excitement. It's also aftershock.

Terrell has somehow managed to get Woo Woo in the back seat without letting go of her. He knows the days that follow will be hard on both women. He also knows they need to move on with their lives.

"Will you go out with me?"

After a few long seconds, Woo Woo manages to speak. "I'm free tomorrow."

***

It's like a scene out of a Hallmark holiday movie and a Quentin Tarantino crime flick. Ten people of various shapes and sizes stand in the shadows. They have coats and scarves and hats and nothing on to keep them warm. They could wait inside. But they couldn't. It is a thirty-minute drive from the warehouse to the Pappas home. It feels like a lifetime. For everyone in the shadows, and those on the outside.

Mirabelle sees her parents in the headlights. She opens the door before Boone has stopped the car. Her feet are already out the door. Boone slams on brakes and Mirabelle runs like she has never run before in her life. Her mother and father grab her as she falls into their arms. She cries and she laughs. They cry and they laugh. For the first time today, Mirabelle thinks she might get through this.

Something in the shadows moves. Or she thinks it does. Mirabelle looks up. This is a big shadow. A very big shadow. She does not know this shadow. Or the shadow beside it. A man, an older man. But the third shadow she knows. This shadow is etched in her heart.

Mirabelle drops her grasp on her parents. She shrugs off their embrace. She shakes her head. *This must be shock.* Mirabelle doesn't listen to the voice. She flies through the air. Luke catches her and holds her close. He doesn't let go. Mirabelle's feet don't touch the ground. She doesn't care. Truth is, she doesn't even realize she is suspended in mid-air.

Pappas and Angela shoot each other a knowing look. This is a conversation for another time. Now is the time to hug their daughter once more and meet the man, properly, that their daughter loves.

***

Woo Woo waits for the car to come to a full stop before she exits. It's hard to get out of the back seat with only one hand. Terrell has the other, and he isn't letting go. Somehow, they manage to extricate themselves. Woo Woo can sense her father. She can't see him yet; it is dark outside, but she can feel him. She follows her heart.

Benjamin Aeron wants to run. He wants to beat Hicham El Guerrouj's speed for running a mile. He wants to stop thinking about inane trivia like who holds the record for running the fastest mile. (Hicham El Guerrouj). He wants his daughter. But he is not sure he can move. Woo Woo will know this, just as he knows everything is okay now, or it will be. If anything happens to him, Terrell has her.

Woo Woo is reaching for her father. He lifts his hand and realizes his sleeve is wet.

He realizes he is crying. Woo Woo's heart breaks a little, but it will heal. The healing starts with a hug. She steps forward. The big shadow steps between her and Terrell.

He looks pointedly at Terrell's hand. The one gripping Woo Woo. "She's not going anywhere. Give them a moment."

Terrell lets go of Woo Woo's hand. His heart breaks a little.

***

The shadows emerge into the light. Everyone gathers in the living room and the dining room and the kitchen. There are hugs. Charlene and Lexie cling to their friend. They cry. They cling some more. They cry some more. At some point, Beast just lifts them up and sets them aside. Gently. Then he hugs Woo Woo. He clings and he cries.

Somewhere in the background, someone laughs. The first-person sounds of joy, of moving to normalcy. The sound comes from Benjamin, and it comes between licks. Madoff has no idea why everyone is so happy, but happy people give treats. Terrell leans forward and extends a hand, Benjamin takes the piece of cheese and holds it out to Madoff. It's gone. It's replaced with more licks. It's only polite to say thank you.

***

The doorbell rings. For the fourth time. The first time it was cops seeking out Boone and Terrell. Updates and next steps. A lot of glancing into the room and at each other. Then the cops left. The second ring ushered in another round of caterers. They brought soup and sandwiches and salads and lasagna and moussaka, and they just kept coming. Everyone in the room realized they were hungry. They grabbed paper plates, plastic cutlery, paper napkins and found a seat. They thanked Benjamin. The man thinks of everything. Including a dog walker. Madoff gave him another lick.

Midway through eating, talking, and clinging, the doorbell rang for a third time. Crown attorney Lauren Edwards. An unhappy lawyer. It's late, she's tired, and it is way too early in the process for her involvement in the case. Yet here she is. Boone and Terrell excuse themselves. There is a hushed conversation, and a note is exchanged. The cops smile. Lauren does not.

So now everyone can rest. Take a breath. Ask a question or two, as appropriate. Grab another macadamia nut cookie.

Constable Fraser is quietly packing up his equipment. He is trying not to smile. He is trying not to cry. When he got the call from Boone saying everyone was okay, he knew he would be the one to tell the families. That is part of the job, and better than the alternative. What the young constable did not know was how the telling would affect him. He heard the words come out of his mouth. *Everyone is okay. No one is hurt. They are on their way home.*

He saw Angela fall to her knees. He saw Pappas raise his face to the heavens. He saw Kostas quietly lower his head and sob. He saw Benjamin stand straighter. He saw Beast come up behind the man and catch him tenderly as his legs gave out.

He did not see Charlene and Lexie come up on either side of him. He did not see as they lowered their hands and took each of his in their own. He felt them squeeze. He did not see, but somehow he knew they were crying. He knew he was crying when they leaned forward and wiped the tears from his face.

God, I love this job.

***

It is the fourth ring of the doorbell that serves to remind everyone that camaraderie and collegiality and the warm feeling of togetherness has its limits. Charlene ushers two newcomers into the living room.

"Everyone. I'd like you to meet Stephanie Kellor and Clayton Manning. Luke's mom and Luke's lawyer. I thought they should be here." Boone sends a quiet signal to Terrell. Her eyes never waiver from the people in front of her.

Clayton has no idea why he is here, but frankly, as a lawyer, he is used to this. And at least there's food. Stephanie has no idea why she is here, or where here is. Her son steps out from behind a police constable, and she no longer cares.

There are more hugs, a few more tears, some brief, albeit cryptic explanations. Clayton knows he has his work cut out for him. He can read between the lines. Stephanie's son is here in her arms, breathing the same air as her. She could care less about work or reading between the lines, although she will come to care. Very much.

***

It is nine o'clock. Terrell is not sure he slept at all last night. He stayed at Benjamin Aeron's house with Woo Woo. The pretext being that Sofia could still have minions out there looking to get even. The reality: he wants Woo Woo within sight at all times. That meant staying awake. Now he has to walk away. A constable from the station has taken over.

Boone picked him up about an hour ago. She got as much sleep as he did. First, she was staying at a drug trafficker's place on the same pretext. Opportunity knocking and all. Second, she had a pile of paperwork and a ton of adrenaline to contend with. She camped out in Pappas's living room. Stephanie was with her, snoring like a stevedore on the couch. Mirabelle was upstairs in her bedroom. Boone had no idea where Luke was, and she didn't ask. She knew he was in the house: he has a tracker strapped to his ankle.

They would normally have stopped for coffee on their way, but Benjamin, who must have been up with the sun, had take-away mugs ready with coffee (something from Ethiopia that Boone thinks might actually be from heaven) and foil-wrapped breakfast sandwiches. He seemed to know where they were going and why. Boone no longer cares. Her body aches and her bones are weary. Terrell long ago gave up trying to figure out how Woo Woo knows what she does. He assumes the apple doesn't fall far from the tree.

***

Perhaps anticipating the tired and cranky crew that has assembled in her office, Associate Chief Justice Louise Redmond also has coffee at hand for the two police officers and the two lawyers seated before her. There is also biscotti and the hint of an apology.

"I understand there have been developments."

The four people on the other side of Her Honor's desk look at each other. This is new territory for them all. Perhaps they'll join a bowling league. The two cops are most reticent. The defense lawyer is most helpful. Lauren Edwards is the cheekiest. She requires at least seven hours of sleep a night. She looks at the judge with a hint of defiance. "My guess is you know more than we do."

Justice Redmond has been on the bench for most of her life. This is not the first contentious or cocky Crown prosecutor she has encountered. She will do what she has always done: squash her like a bug.

"Don't worry about me, Ms. Edwards. Worry about justice. I assume you know what that is."

Terrell tries to hide his smile. It turns into a yawn. "Sorry."

"There is no need to apologize. You have done your job and done it well." Message received. Whatever defiance was in Edwards has dissipated. She just wants to get the hell out of this room.

Boone is trying not to enjoy this meeting, and failing. "Your Honor, we have two people in custody for the kidnapping of Shondra Aeron and Mirabelle Fortin. We are confident those charges will stick, and we will begin interviews once we leave here." Message received.

"I appreciate the update, but that is a case not yet before the courts, and one I cannot discuss. I am inquiring about Luke Castle."

"He is in the custody of the Halifax Police Department," says Terrell.

Edwards snorts. Apparently, there is a little defiance left. "He's at a drug dealer's house drinking imported coffee, cuddling his girlfriend, and watching Netflix."

"He is wearing a tracker. He is being watched over by a constable," Boone says.

"And he is innocent," Clayton Manning points out.

"That is the issue," says the judge. "Have we ascertained that innocence."

"We have," says Clayton.

"We have not," says Edwards.

"Let the games begin," says Boone. To herself.

Louise Redmond is running out of patience. "Conduct the interviews. Fast-track the forensics. We'll meet back here tomorrow at two o'clock after which time Luke Castle is either a free man or he is spending the rest of his life in jail."

***

Sofia doesn't like jail. And this is only a holding cell. She realizes this will be a problem if she is sentenced to federal prison. She can work around any drug charges they lay. *Not my drugs. I had no idea there were drugs in the warehouse. I rarely go to the*

283

warehouse. The kidnapping charges are harder to explain away. So, she needs leverage. She has leverage. Is she willing to use it?

***

By the time Boone and Terrell arrive at the station, caffeinated enough for the week ahead, detectives from the drug unit have already interrogated Sofia and Giannis. Well, interrogation is a strong word. They've both lawyered up, and legal counsel has restricted most of what they might be willing to say. It would appear there is nowhere to go but down, and by down, the cops mean into the abyss that is the criminal justice system.

Appearances can be deceiving.

***

Terrell is mulling an idea. Well, really, he is mulling Woo Woo's idea. It's likely a good one although it is one Terrell does not like. Nor does Boone. Neither can say why, but both are trying to be open-minded.

Woo Woo isn't pressing. She is simply proposing. Trying to help. Trying to get back to being Woo Woo. She's looking at her friends across a soy latte with maple syrup and vanilla bean (to hell with healthy eating, she's soothing her soul with sugar). Her friends, the four of them who are trying to look nonchalant and failing miserably, aren't sure whether to be honest, to discuss the idea frankly, or to agree with their friend as a show of love and support.

"It's not working," Woo Woo says. Everyone knows what she means just as Woo Woo knew they would understand.

"There's something about this that doesn't feel right," says Boone. She's being honest. She also knows Woo Woo lives much of her life by what feels right, and this will resonate.

"I think it makes sense," says Lexie. She takes a long slurp of her Americano and looks Terrell directly in the eye.

"Me too," says Charlene. She has yet to see the dividing line that is making its way down the café tabletop.

"Well, that settles that then," says Terrell. He is operating on little sleep, and there is a knot in his stomach that has attached itself to his organs.

Boone snorts. It's exactly what the quintet needs. Now they are all laughing. "We don't even know that we'll get past go," says Woo Woo grinning. Everyone knows what she means. Boone reaches for her phone and dials. They just moved closer to go.

***

285

It takes Pappas about fifteen minutes to reach the café. The group has a deep roast waiting for him. They didn't realize he'd have company. Mirabelle and Angela are in tow. Mirabelle wanted to see everyone, mostly Woo Woo, and her mother is never letting her out of her sight again.

Mirabelle likes the idea. Angela thinks it has merit. Pappas sees the chasm that is opening in front of him. Why the hell would he jump into the abyss? Because he loves his wife and his daughter. Nope, not because of that. Because he wants to end this? Nope, not that either.

"I'm in," says Pappas. Terrell's jaw drops; Boone sits back in surprise. Woo Woo sips her soy latte. Spite can open doors that would otherwise remain closed.

***

The young guard stands to the left of Sofia and nudges her and her shackles forward. It's too early for lunch, and she has no scheduled court appearance. Something is up. That conclusion is confirmed when Sofia is led into an interrogation room. Her lawyer is sitting in one of the two metal chairs. He doesn't look comfortable.

The guard exits. Sofia leans forward. Her lawyer tries to work out a kink in his neck. It's not coming out. It's never coming out.

"They want you to meet with Pappas."

"Fuck them."

"Sounds good to me." Her lawyer stands up.

Sofia raises a hand to stop him. "I'll need a little more."

"I don't have a little more. Apparently, someone thought it would be a good idea for you to have a face to face with your father-in-law."

Woo Woo. Sofia doesn't trust Woo Woo, especially now. What does Woo Woo think will happen? Sofia will break down and beg for forgiveness? Sofia will admit everything in his presence like a penitent in a confessional? Not going to happen.

Sofia grins. Screw you Woo Woo. She looks at her lawyer. "I'll meet with him."

***

Turns out, "him" is outside. The same guard that nudged Sofia into the interrogation room takes Pappas to the same unit. It's agreed her lawyer will not be present, there will be no cameras or audio equipment, it will be two former family members squaring off on their own. Sofia feels safe. Pappas feels the chasm opening wider.

"Nikki, nice to see you."

Pappas hates the nickname. He hates this woman. He smiles. "Just had hot

287

chocolate with Woo Woo and Mirabelle. They send their regards."

"Tell them I enjoyed our time together."

Pappas will kill this woman. He's not sure when or how, but he will. For now, he will play along as he promised. He knows how to play this woman. "Is that all you've got? A few jabs. I thought you wanted to box."

Sofia feels the heat in her belly, between her legs. She refuses to be baited. "I've already won the match."

Pappas looks around the room and smiles. That superior smile Sofia loathes. "You call this winning."

"I do indeed. I'll be out of here in no time."

"That's unlikely to be healthy for you."

"I should be fine. I imagine witness protection will keep me alive and well for decades to come."

There it is, the gauntlet. The threat is overt. Pappas is rethinking his reluctance to be here. This just might work in his favor. "I doubt you have anything to bargain with."

Now Sofia is laughing. Loud and long. "Nikki boy, I have so much to bargain with they may put me up in a palace."

"I wouldn't get too comfortable. My guess, and I'm merely guessing, of course, is that your information is out of date." It's Pappas's turn to grin. "You know how easy it is to reroute, reorganize, rethink your

288

business model. I've been doing a little of that myself.

"And I have plans for Suite and Savory, bigger and better. Bolder. It needs fresh new ideas."

Sofia will kill this man. She's not sure when or how, but she will.

***

Boone's small, functional office is intended to hold three people somewhat comfortably, and two people most comfortably. There are five people crammed around her desk, over chairs, against the wall. The inspector would like to remove everyone but her detective and Nik Pappas. Apparently, that is not going to happen. The Triad has wormed its way further into the investigation and into her office. Pappas seems comfortable with them here, and right now only Pappas knows what went on inside the interview room.

The young constable arrives with Tim Hortons coffee and Timbits. This is followed by several minutes of rustling and awkward maneuvering as six people suddenly realize they are hungry and nervous. That may be excitement they're feeling. Whatever it is, they want something to do with their hands and something to look at should the need arise.

It well may. Pappas has learned two things from the woman his eldest son married. Stupidly. First, she is cunning. He did not give her credit for that. His mistake. Second, she is ambitious. That he knew. What he did not know, or failed to realize, was the extent she would go to achieve her ambitions. Pappas dismissed her as arm candy. Someone to pacify while those with real brains and balls forged ahead. He was wrong.

Pappas will kick his own ass later. Now, he needs to decide how much to share of what he has learned from Sofia. The chasm and all.

Five sets of hands have finished fiddling with their doughnuts and their coffee cups. Five sets of eyes turn to him.

"What do you want to know?" he asks. It was the wrong question.

Lexie rolls her eyes. Terrell shakes his head. Woo Woo stares at the floor. "What we want," says Boone, "is to find out what went on in that room. If you're not comfortable telling us, fine. But let's not drag this out. We can't survive in this room much longer."

Pappas is not sure how to finesse this. He's heard honesty is the best policy. It has never been his policy.

"No time like the present," says Woo Woo.

"She's running powder."

There it is. The foot in the door. Pappas knows he'll walk all the way through. If pushed. Boone pushes. "We kinda knew that. There are two hundred accent tables with crystal meth shoved into every crevice. It was a dead give-away."

Pappas doesn't rise to the bait, but he opens the door and walks through. "That's the tip of the iceberg. She's running powder across Canada and into the northeastern U.S."

Boone sits back. Terrell whistles. The Triad look at each other, then they look at the two police officers. Terrell is the first to speak. He may be speaking to himself. "If she's running that much, she's a major player. And she's nowhere on our radar. That doesn't seem likely."

"You were looking elsewhere," says Pappas. There is a hint of satisfaction in his voice.

Boone reaches for the phone. "You'd better send someone up here right away."

The someone is Ryan Ford, head of the drug unit. Now there are seven people in the room built for two. Stash, as everyone calls the narcotics officer, tries to shoot Pappas's intel down. "There is just no way. We'd know. That much meth. We'd know."

"You'd only know if she was selling locally," Pappas points out. "She wasn't."

"Doesn't make sense to use the gateway here and not sell to the local market," Stash says.

"It does if you know who her father-in-law is," says Pappas.

Stash reaches absently for a Timbit. "Sonofabitch."

"There is," Boone interjects almost reluctantly, "the small matter of proof."

***

The group of seven move to the conference room so they can breathe (everyone), use the whiteboard (Charlene), do a child's pose (Woo Woo). "She's got to be cleaning the cash," says Stash.

"If there's a paper trail, I can find it," says Charlene.

"She isn't likely using Suite and Savory," says Pappas. "Too risky."

"But selling meth isn't." Lexie points out.

Boone gets someone to bring in the GPS printout from Sofia's car. Terrell calls property valuation to find out who owns the warehouse. Then they have it: a company name and likely locations. Stash leaves to meet his team. Within the hour, four teams, including SWAT, descend on the four property locations on Sofia's GPS that couldn't logically be accounted for. Within that same hour, Charlene uncovers a network of numbered companies that trace back to Sofia. Actually, they trace back to Suite and Savory.

Nik Pappas is not happy. *I'm going to kill the bitch.*

Daily Thoughts–
Shondra (Woo Woo) Aeron

Monday, December 19ᵗʰ

We did good today. We helped put Sofia away for a long time (at least we think we did). Her secrets are no longer secrets. Stash found three warehouses with trucks, manifests, and enough meth to make El Chapo blush. (I'm not sure who El Chapo is, but I heard one of the drug unit cops say this.) He also found the condo where she has been living, and they are tearing it apart now.

Charlene is in seventh heaven. She has her laptop, spreadsheets, and a calculator that is faster than a speeding bullet. She's the calm at the center of the storm, handing over information and insight that have the drug guys spinning. Boone is beaming.

I'm glad it's over. I know it's not over, over, but all this is moving past me now. It's not about what Sofia did to Mirabelle and me so much anymore. It's about Sofia the drug lord. Bet Pappas is pissed.

This isn't wishful thinking. I know we are moving forward because we are moving back to normal, to familiar ground. We had supper at Char's tonight (we are not allowed to call her "Char"). Michael walked Madoff, Lexie ran through her show at Enigma, like a special production for friends. Even Dad came. I think he likes Michael. Michael is terrified of him.

I talk to Mirabelle every day. Only for a few minutes, but long enough to know she is resilient. She is fighting her way back. Luke is helping just by being Luke. I worry though what will happen if he goes back to juvie. I can't quite figure out how Sofia and Luke are connected but everyone seems to think they are. At least everyone with a badge. Michael can't say much, confidentiality and all that. Sofia isn't saying anything except through her lawyer and the one air-gapped conversation with Pappas, who seems to have said all he is going to say. And Luke is like a nest of monasteries. Not a word. At least not a word to anyone who is talking to me.

But it shouldn't be all about me. Lately it has been. There is a lot of hovering. A lot of touching: my hand, arm, back. Reassurance I'm here.

Well, I'm not going anywhere anytime soon. Screw you, Sofia.

Sincerely,

Shondra Aeron

PS I went back for the pewter figurines today. They were gone. I'll go back next week to see if any more come in.

Chapter 30.

It's decided. Well, Woo Woo has decided. Terrell is going to work. Her father is not dropping in for a visit that lasts until Terrell gets off work or the girls drop by casually for a cuppa that surprisingly lasts until Terrell gets off work. When he takes over the night shift.

Woo Woo is going to yoga. Then she is going for coffee. Then she is going to the office. Then she will do whatever the hell she wants. Woo Woo is at peace with her decision. No one else is.

***

Terrell is at work. He's fussing. Moving some papers around as if he is actually doing paperwork. "Nice shuffling." That's Boone. And that's sarcasm.

They head to the local Timmie's for a coffee and a donut. They both need sugar and caffeine.

"So, the kid is going back to juvie?"

"Looks that way," says Terrell. "We've hit a wall. Nothing from Sofia. Nothing from Pappas. Less than nothing from Luke."

"Well, you have four hours."

And nothing to lose.

***

Luke has something to lose. He knows that intellectually. (Not the word he uses.) He knows it in his heart, but that knowledge sits on the surface of his heart like a small, clogged artery. There is no pain. There is no danger.

Right now, there is only a light snowfall visible through the breakfast nook windows, a French press is brewing something that smells like heaven (and is about the same distance removed from the coffee in juvie), and Luke is finishing off his third croissant (there were no croissants in juvie).

His mom went home last night. Today she will go to work at Suite and Savory. Mirabelle's dad asked her to stay on. Luke isn't sure if Mirabelle pushed for this or if the request came directly from her dad. It doesn't matter. His mom has a good job. That will be good for her, for his brother. Luke can live with that. In jail.

***

Mirabelle can't. She picks at her first croissant like a cat walking on snow. Luke seems oblivious (her word). She wonders if he is. She picks another flake from her croissant and considers eating it. She's not hungry.

***

It's 11:18 when Terrell's phone rings. It's Lexie.

"Luke wants to talk to you."

***

The interview room has coffee, donuts, and even napkins. It reminds Luke of vet clinics that try to make clinic rooms homey when a dog is about to be put down. (He does not know how he knows this, but he knows the feeling all too well.)

Terrell breaks the silence. "This is your meeting."

"This is hard." Luke picks at his donut like a miniature excavator. He does not want to be here. He knows he has to be.

Terrell waits. He eats his donut. He reaches for another. Boone says something in his earpiece. Terrell ignores her.

"Tell her I'm getting there," says Luke and goes back to excavating the donut hole.

298

Luke got there. Then Boone got filled in. Then Luke's lawyer got called in. (He was pissed about not being called in for the first meeting. Luke wore that one.) Then the Crown prosecutor got called in. She's pissed at missing lunch.

"Do you people not have a calendar?" Terrell passes her a Timbit.

***

There are chocolate chip cookies and tea (and, strangely, four bottles of Coke) on the table to the left of the three chairs that frame Associate Chief Justice Louise Redmond's desk. She waves toward the refreshments. "I heard you didn't have lunch."

She looks at the three people in front of her. Her gaze lingers for a split second on Edwards. "I appreciate that."

Edwards returns the gaze. She's hungry. She's frustrated. She's spent eight weeks of her life on this case. This shit case. Now it's going down the drain. Like her career. Okay, that is a little over-dramatic. But the Crown attorney is pissed. And hungry.

"We have an agreement." Clayton Manning looks directly at the judge. He doesn't dare look in Edwards's vicinity. She's annoyed, and you never know what a Crown attorney will do when they're cranky. Job security and all that.

Edwards continues to stare straight ahead. She's smart enough not to openly defy the judge. Job security and all that.

Honey couldn't give a rat's ass about the Crown prosecutor's mood. The Associate Chief Justice looks at Terrell. "You tell me."

Now Terrell has all eyes on him. *Let the prima donna deal with that.* Honey smiles.

"We have new evidence, credible evidence, that Luke Castle did not know what was in the truck he was driving. In fact, he was not supposed to have been driving the delivery truck that night."

Terrell has the judge's attention. "Are you telling me wrong place, wrong time?"

"We are," says Edwards. She wants control of the room. "The Crown has determined given this new evidence that we do not have enough to proceed against Mr. Castle. We have withdrawn the charges."

"I have reached out to the detention center to inform them the charges against my client have been dropped. He has been formally released as an inmate."

"So that's that." Honey looks at the three people in front of her. There is much she wants to say. Truth is, she wants to rail. She wants to yell, "How the hell did we get to this place? Why the hell did some kid spend the last three months in juvie? How could he be so close to a life in jail, and we eat biscotti?"

Instead, she presses the intercom in front of her. "Bring them in."

***

There is a flurry of activity at the door. Seven more people enter the room. Justice Redmond's office is large. It is not that large.

Woo Woo, Lexie, and Charlene hug the back wall. Luke moves into the chair his lawyer has just vacated. Stephanie Kellor isn't sure whether to join the three women at the wall or move closer to her son. Maternal instinct wins out. Beast heads for the biscotti and opens a bottle of Coke. You don't get biscotti in juvie. Or Coke, for that matter.

Honey waits for the rustling of chairs, beverages, and humans to settle. "The Crown has some announcements to make, and we wanted you all here so that we could deal with things efficiently." Honey realizes she could have been more charitable to the Crown. She also realizes Lauren Edwards pisses her off.

Edwards shoots Terrell a look. He is in her sightline, and she can't shoot that particular look to the Associate Chief Justice. "Effective immediately, we are dropping the charges against Luke Castle."

The rustling is back in full swing. The Triad gives each other a high five. Stephanie covers her mouth but not before her squeal fills the room. Luke and Clayton clap each other on the back. Edwards rolls her eyes. (She really does piss Honey off.)

"Mr. Castle, on behalf of the court and the people of Nova Scotia, I want to apologize for your unnecessary incarceration. You are free to go."

Stephanie and Woo Woo are in tears now. Charlene is hugging Stephanie. Beast is doing something with his feet. Luke thinks it might be a dance of joy.

There is a movement of chairs and shoes and files. The judge stops the movement before anyone makes it to the door. "We're not done." She turns to Edwards. "I understand Mr. Gloade's fine has been paid in full."

Edwards nods. She wants to spit. "We are releasing Conall Gloade effective immediately."

Charlene and Lexie look at each other and shrug. Stephanie turns to Luke. He shrugs. Clayton turns to the man-boy behind him and extends his hand. Beast belches. Honey really likes this kid.

The man standing in the center of the room steps forward. He hands an envelope to Justice Redmond. She takes the envelope. "Thank you, Mr. Aeron. The court thanks you Mr. Aeron."

She turns to the crowd that has now inched further away from the wall and the biscotti, and closer to her desk. "With the permission of legal counsel, I am able to tell you that twelve inmates at the Waterville

Youth Center have been released from custody. Their fines have been paid in full."

The pronouncement makes sense to those in the room who arrest, defend, and prosecute. Beast knows what is happening. It has happened to him. Benjamin also knows what is going on. He has put these wheels in motion. Everyone else is in the dark.

Honey shines much-needed light. "When individuals are charged with a summary conviction, such as a noise violation in Mr. Gloade's case, a fine is often levied. If that fine cannot be paid, the individual is incarcerated."

Charlene gasps. She can't believe this is true. That we would put people in jail because they are poor. Beast hangs his head. He knows it is true. Benjamin and Woo Woo step up beside him. Beast raises his head.

Honey waits for the silence she knows is coming. "Thanks to a generous and ongoing donation from Mr. Aeron, this situation will not happen again to young men and women in this province. We are setting up a fund to pay fines for youth and adults unable to pay." Honey looks at the people before her—friends, colleagues, strangers. "Justice has been served here today."

***

Mirabelle is not letting go of Luke. Literally. She has his right hand clasped in both of hers. That is not as easy as it sounds. They are sitting at a table at Enigma. It's Lexie's big night. It's Dimitri's big night. It's Mirabelle's big night. Luke is here with her. Luke is not going to jail. Her father has not forbidden her from seeing Luke. Her mother opted to sit on the other side of him. Mirabelle forgets for a minute that she nearly died. That her aunt hated her so much she wanted to wipe her from the face of the earth.

Tonight is about gratitude. Mirabelle scans the faces at her table, and the table next to her. These are family members and friends. New friends. Firm friends. Lifelong friends.

Mirabelle is happy. Her mother can sense this happiness. She knows its source. Her father knows his daughter is happy, and he knows why. He's not happy about it, but he is smart enough not to intervene. Not now.

The night is a success by any measure. Lexie is on fire. She has the crowd eating out of her hand. She's not sure if this is nerves, excitement, the thrill of being back on stage, or a mixture of all of this. When she listens to her inner voice, as she is learning to do, she knows this is joy.

Dimitri is finding joy in the bottom of a bourbon glass and in the sidelong glances he throws his father's way. Comedy Night at Enigma has drawn a huge crowd—a crowd with money, a crowd that likes to drink.

Dimitri believes he has proven his point: he's ready to lead. It's time his father stepped back—or down—and let him assume the helm.

That is not what his father is thinking. The night is a hit. Pappas is pleased. He has emerged as a leader in the community, as a philanthropist. This is, in part, Dimitri's doing. Mostly it is the Triad as somehow the three women have come to be called. Dimitri was played. Pappas was played. The difference: Pappas knows he was played.

The drug lord with a thirst for respectability looks at the table next to him, the table with the cops. This makes him uneasy, but he is savvy enough to know having blue bloods here gives him a veneer of trustworthiness. His status is elevated by the mere presence of Boone and Terrell. His guests.

It doesn't hurt that they just raised $65,000 for ElderDog Canada, one of Mirabelle and Madoff's favorite pet charities.

Pappas has invited everyone back to his luxurious office upstairs following the performance. There will be smoked trout croquettes, goat cheese and salami stuffed dates, and spicy crab salad tapas. There will be sugar cookie fruit pizzas and caramel apples with sprinkles. There will be Ruinart Blanc de Blancs. (Mirabelle will be allowed one small drink; she likes the bubbles.)

Terrell is out of his element. First, it's fancy here. There is champagne and something that looks like a fig vomited. He prefers beer, albeit craft beer, and burgers. Second, he is a cop. This party is being hosted by a man who traffics drugs across Canada and into the United States. Tonight, however, is a night for exceptions.

The detective first class is not here as a police officer. He is here as a friend of Lexie's—and Lexie deserves a round of applause for tonight. He is here as Woo Woo's boyfriend (and doesn't that sound silly), as Charlene's friend, as the would-be-son-in-law of Benjamin Aeron. Terrell reaches for a glass of Ruinart although he does not know that is what the drink is called. He takes a small gulp. Who knew he liked bubbles.

The detective is learning to mingle. It may be the champagne. He reaches for his second glass as Lexie walks through the door to loud clapping, hooting, and back slapping. She grins. Terrell, who let's face it is always a police officer, takes a quick look at Mr. Bourbon. Someone isn't happy.

Dimitri is the odd man out. Almost. His older brother is equally unhappy. Kostas is waiting for the axe to fall. His father hasn't said a word to him about Sofia and her side business. He will. He's biding his time. Testing Kostas and testing his nerves.

Everyone else is laughing and chatting and smiling. Stephanie is floating. Charlene is stuffing a trout croquette in her pocket for Madoff. Boone is asking Lexie about being on stage. Luke and Mirabelle are looking at each other. It's getting a little old.

Benjamin spends time with his daughter and the man who will replace him. He can breathe easier now. He can rest more soundly. He makes his way to Nik Pappas, to thank him for tonight and for this week. He knows that will be important to Pappas, and it requires nothing of him. Angela joins the two men, but she only has eyes for her daughter and the boy who may one day replace her.

***

It's time to call it a night. Dimitri is getting loud, Mirabelle is yawning, Charlene is worrying about Madoff, Terrell is wondering if his underwear is clean. Pappas scans the room. He has made a decision.

"I want to thank you all for coming. Tonight was an important night for all of us and for our community. Lexie and Dimitri organized this event, and Lexie wowed us on stage. I'm still laughing."

There is more applause for Lexie, and she is the center of attention for a few

307

seconds before everyone turns back to Pappas. "In five days, we will celebrate Christmas, and we have much to celebrate this year. Many of us in this room did not know each other last year, but we have been brought together.

"I have been raised to believe there is a reason for this. Angela and I are hoping you can join us for dinner on Boxing Day. It will be a buffet. It will be relaxed. It will, we hope, be fun. It is our small way of saying thank you." There is something wrong with Pappas's throat. There is never anything wrong with his throat.

To everyone's surprise, Mirabelle lets go of Luke's hand. She moves to the front of the room, to her father. She takes his hand in both of hers (it's a thing). She smiles at her dad. She looks out at the group of people. "Please come."

***

It's not that Woo Woo has forgotten about Christmas. It's that she has been, well, tied up. But Pappas's remarks reminded her the clock is ticking, and gift-giving has changed this year. She knows her dad's likes and dislikes. He will not be a problem. She has Lexie crossed off her list (a fine art print by Paul Klee, the *Comedians' Handbill*, and coasters that resemble the walk of fame with Lexie's name on them). She's considering a

308

charm bracelet with a yoga mat, a calculator, and a Westie for Charlene. She's not sure if she should get Boone something. She's decided she will get Beast something. (She's also decided she is not going to call him Beast anymore.)

Then there's Michael. That has to be perfect. She has something in mind, but she is worried it may be too much, too personal, too intrusive. She also has a water bottle that cleans itself for him. She has no idea why. She bought it at Suite and Savory. It spoke to her at the time. Now it just seems silly.

Woo Woo starts Wednesday morning committed to finishing her shopping. After yoga, she'll head downtown, maybe even to Suite and Savory. She can say hello to Stephanie.

Yoga is just what Woo Woo needs. The poses push her to her edge, but not beyond. She opens her hips and groin with dragon and gives her quads a much-needed workout. Frog stretches the inner thighs and nudges her range of motion to expand. Melting heart tickles her spleen, calms her nerves, and tightens her core. Not to mention what it does for her spirit.

Coffee with the crew, as always, reminds her that what you learn on the mat you bring with you into your day and into your life. There is laughter, there is camaraderie, there is an ease of being with friends, lifelong and otherwise. Then there is Michael.

Literally. Standing by the table holding an herbal tea and an organic brownie. This does not bode well.

When the yogis retreat to their lives, Terrell gets down to business. He doesn't need a reason to join these three women for a break. Today he has one. They are well aware. He could lead into the reason for his sudden appearance, pave the way for the second-hand request he is about to make, the request that makes him nervous. But not for himself.

"Sofia wants to meet with you." Terrell looks at Woo Woo. A piece of his heart breaks.

The statement has taken everyone by surprise. Lexie instantly says, "No way." Charlene agrees. "That's a terrible idea." It's Woo Woo who asks the question Terrell can't answer. *Why?*

"She says she wants closure. For her and for you. She says she's had time to reflect on her life and her behavior. She says she owes you an apology."

"She's lying." Lexie says this as if there is no doubt in the world. Charlene nods her agreement.

"You're probably right. All we know for sure is that Sofia wants something and whatever that 'something' is, she thinks she can get it from Woo Woo."

As the conversation swirls around her, Woo Woo picks absently at her brownie. She nibbles on a corner, sips a mouthful of her lemongrass tea. She's trying to figure out what she is feeling. She fails.

Terrell places a hand on hers. Lexie follows suit. (Different hand.) Woo Woo comes back to the present, where she believes we all should live. "I don't know what to do?"

"You do whatever you want," says Lexie.

"Whatever your heart tells you to do," says Charlene.

"They're right," says Terrell.

***

In the end, it's Mirabelle who decides. Her father picks her up and drives her to the café. He tells her what's going on as they drive. Terrell gets more brownies and real coffee for everyone.

"We should buy shares in this place," says Lexie. Charlene makes a mental note to see who owns Muggs.

Mirabelle swooshes in, a flurry of hair and arms. She hugs Woo Woo. She hugs Lexie a little longer. Everyone sits down and takes a few minutes to repeat what they have already said to each other and to themselves. As the recap is coming to a close, Luke walks in.

He nods at Mirabelle. "She texted me." *Of course, she did.* Woo Woo can't help but grin. Pappas tries his best to mirror her smile.

Terrell is about to start again at the start. Luke waves away the explanation. "I'm caught up. Sofia wants to mindfuck Woo Woo."

And there it is. The thing no one has said, even to themselves. (Mirabelle thinks "mindfuck" is such a brilliant word. Her father does not. Doesn't matter. It's the right word and everyone knows it.)

"This is about protecting Woo Woo." Terrell looks at Luke, at this seventeen-year-old kid, and thanks god he is here at the table with them.

Woo Woo starts to protest. She's silenced by the same look from the six people sitting at the table with her.

"This is one hundred percent about you. About what you need," Lexie says.

"But I don't want to hurt Mirabelle by doing something she doesn't want me to do."

Mirabelle gets up and hugs Woo Woo. "Whatever you decide is the right decision. I don't doubt you for a minute."

Woo Woo can feel the welling in her heart, in her eyes. "But Michael what if she might say something that would help you?"

Terrell squeezes her hand. God, he loves this woman. "Sofia is going to jail for a long time. I'm good."

"What are you afraid of?" Charlene recognizes Luke's question is not a challenge, it's an invitation to itemize. She reaches in her purse for pen and paper. After a round of tea (everyone is off caffeine), they have identified five concerns:

- Sofia may get inside Woo Woo's head and stay there. (Indeed, this may be the whole reason she wants to meet.)
- Woo Woo may be a pawn in Sofia's plans to continue messing with Pappas and Mirabelle.
- The meeting may remind Woo Woo of everything she went through, and this could impede moving forward.
- Sofia may actually want to apologize, and Woo Woo may not be ready to forgive.
- Woo Woo simply doesn't want to give Sofia what she wants. And that's just mean.

"It's all of them, isn't it?" says Woo Woo. It isn't a question, and although it may have been said aloud, it wasn't really intended for anyone else to answer but her. Everyone knows this, and they give Woo Woo the time she needs to think.

It takes her three minutes and twenty-two seconds to decide.

***

The interrogation room is still grey: grey walls, grey cement floor, grey-topped table, grey chairs. Sofia is tempted to give the HPD a gift card to Suite and Savory. *Would it hurt to have a little color in this room?*

The color is outside the room working up her nerve to go through with this. It's not so much nerve as reaffirming her conviction this is the right thing to do. Woo Woo doesn't trust Sofia. I mean, who would? Once trust is gone, so is Woo Woo's footing. She knows how to engage, to interact when the foundation is firm. This foundation is not just cracked, it is shattered.

Still, one can always dress for the occasion. Woo Woo is wearing a retro boho dress in bright yellow with what looks like polka dots on it. If you look closely, you'll see the polka dots are actually submarines. Woo Woo appreciates the humor. She hopes it will remind Sofia she has little laughter in her life. Then she tells herself that is mean. Herself says, "Who gives a shit?"

And there is all the resolve Woo Woo needs. She opens the door to the interrogation room and walks in. She pulls out the grey chair from the grey table and sits down. Sofia's wrists are handcuffed to a metal hook in the middle of the table. Woo Woo wasn't expecting this. In hindsight, she should have been. The shackles somehow make Sofia look smaller. And here is an emotion Woo Woo never expected to experience in this room: pity.

There's a knock on the door. Terrell props it open with his right foot and thrusts a cardboard tray into the room. Two herbal teas and two morning glory muffins. Woo Woo takes the tray and says, "Thank you." It's the nod that lets Terrell know everything is okay.

The handcuffs give Sofia just enough leeway to raise the cup to her lips but not enough to throw a hot beverage at anyone. Woo Woo isn't sure she has the inclination let alone the energy.

"Love suits you."

"Jail suits you."

"I wasn't being snarky."

"Neither was I."

Things are clearly moving along well. "What do you want?"

"To talk."

"I don't have all day." Woo Woo hears the words coming out of her mouth. She feels the syllables forming on her lips. They are her words. They are not her words.

Woo Woo stands up. She walks around the room. That takes six seconds. She completes another lap. Then she sits down. "Let's try this again. From the top. Are you okay?"

It is clearly not what Sofia expected, but perhaps somewhere in her cellular network it is exactly what she knew would happen and exactly what she needed. "I am okay. I will never be okay again."

Woo Woo lets this sink in. For Sofia and for herself. It is part of the reason why she believes Sofia wants her here, but there is also something else.

"What do you need?"

"I need to rewind the last five years of my life." Sofia doesn't wait for Woo Woo to answer. There is no answer.

"I want to apologize to you and to Mirabelle. Things got out of hand. Pappas can do that to you. I let Pappas do that to me."

"Pappas didn't kidnap us. Pappas didn't hold us hostage in a warehouse full of drugs. You did that."

"I'm sorry."

Two simple words, and they say so much. Woo Woo knows what Sofia is telling her and she knows it is bullshit. Time to play along. Time to let Sofia think she has the upper hand. Even if it is handcuffed to a grey table.

"I'm going to cut a deal." Sofia tries to make this sound nonchalant, but every tense bone in her body says otherwise.

Woo Woo sits up. Michael didn't tell her this. Perhaps he couldn't. Sofia reads Woo Woo's surprise. "The boyfriend doesn't know. No one knows. I didn't know until just this minute. Here with you."

"What does that mean?"

"It means I am not alone in this." Sofia looks at Woo Woo. There is no animosity.

Woo Woo thinks there is sadness here. After all, they were once friends of a sort.

"I have information the cops in this country and the U.S. would like. I have information about drug pipelines, drug players, traffic routes, cargo holds. I'm willing to give it up in exchange for .... In exchange for what I don't honestly know. The lawyers will work that out."

"Sounds like a good plan."

"It's the only one that doesn't have me staring at grey walls for the rest of my life. I'm tired of grey walls. Lord knows I saw enough of those at the warehouse on Topsail."

"Have you seen Kostas?"

Sofia smiles, but there is no joy in this smile. "Not a word."

"That must be hard."

"It's not unexpected. He is under his father's thumb."

"Maybe he'll visit you in jail."

"I won't be in jail in Nova Scotia. That will be one of my conditions. The only condition other than witness protection that I am sure about at the moment."

"Why leave here? He might come. I might come."

"Pappas is not a man you thwart. I'm safer somewhere he doesn't know about. Somewhere he can't reach me, although those places are few and far between."

"You could forgive him."

"I would rather die."

There's nothing more to say. Woo Woo stands up and walks slowly out the door. She doesn't look back. Sofia doesn't look at her leave. She's staring straight ahead at the grey wall, a small smile playing at the corners of her mouth.

In the hallway, Woo Woo reaches for her phone. She texts her friends and Michael. Supper at my place. 6pm. Bring Boone. Stash is invited too if you want.

***

Supper is a Costco special. Woo Woo stopped on her way home and picked up three barbecue chickens (at only $7.99 the deal of the century). She loaded her cart with deli meats, cheeses (two Baldersons), coleslaw, olives, brioche buns, cherry cheesecake, and anything else she thought would work well for a smorgasbord. Or a picnic.

***

Stash doesn't have time to pick his jaw up off the floor. Before he can really appreciate the house he has just stepped inside, Lexie has thrust a leash in his hand. A small cream-colored dog is on the other end.

"There's poop bags in his collar."

318

Madoff is not overly thrilled with this new addition to the group. There is no cooing or belly rubbing. Most seriously, there are no treats. Still, Madoff has to do his business, then he makes it clear, it's straight back to Woo Woo's.

By the time man and dog return, there is a feast spread out on the ten-foot island that is the heart of Woo Woo's kitchen. Everyone digs in, and everyone (except for the man who smells remarkably like skunk) remembers to feed Madoff a treat.

***

No one wants to push Woo Woo. They know she will tell them why they are gathered here when she is ready. (To be accurate, this is not the case for Stash. He has no idea why he is here or who owns the dog. But there is food, and he can always eat.)

Charlene is cutting the cheesecake into remarkably even triangles, Terrell is serving up freshly brewed decaf, and Lexie is squirting whipped cream in Madoff's dish when Charlene is out of earshot. It's time.

"You've all been so patient. Unnecessarily so." Everyone smiles at Woo Woo. This is support, support she doesn't really need. "I wanted you to hear what Sofia had to say. It may mean more to you than it did to me."

"Tell us," says Stash. He just figured out what is going on.

Woo Woo reaches into the pocket of her retro boho and brings out her phone. She places it on the island and presses "play." For the next twenty-three minutes no one says a word.

Woo Woo reaches for her phone and stops the playback. Boone turns to Terrell. "Did you catch it?"

"I did."

"Catch what," Lexie wants to know. So does Stash.

"The warehouse isn't on Topsail," Terrell says. He and Boone have locked eyes. They are communicating as only two cops who have worked together for decades can do.

Stash is in his element now. "Do you think this is a mistake? Did she just slip up?"

"Sofia doesn't make mistakes like that," says Woo Woo. "This is the reason she wanted to meet."

"So what does it mean?" It's Stash who asked. It's the question on everyone's mind.

***

There is more coffee, more cheesecake, and more whipped cream from a can in Madoff's bowl. (Best night ever.) There is also a lot of discussion, a back-and-forth of plausible ideas, possible explanations, and outrageous conclusions.

Madoff yawned, noticeably, for the third time in ten minutes. The group decides it's time to sum up where they are and what they need to do next. Charlene runs out to her car for a portable flip chart and markers.

She writes "Conclusions" across the top of the first page. After another forty minutes, everyone agrees there are three conclusions to be reached from Woo Woo's meeting with Sofia and three next steps. It looks like this:

Conclusions
1.   Topsail is important. (Why is unclear.)

2.   There may be an opportunity to cut a deal with Sofia. (This is news to all the cops in the room.)

3.   Sofia hates Pappas. (Hate will color her decisions. This can open doors. This can also shade the truth.)

Next Steps
1.   Boone will reach out to Sofia's lawyer for a sit down.

2.   Boone will alert the Crown prosecutor about a possible deal.

3. Terrell will get the tech unit to go
    through Sofia's laptop again looking
    for anything with Topsail.

It's what's not on the lists that has everyone worried.

Daily Thoughts–
Charlene Kurtz

Wednesday, December 21st

It's late. Madoff is tired. He's even tired of yawning, although point taken. We made progress tonight. Slowly. Two steps forward, one step back. I'm glad I'm not a cop (even though I would be good at it).

I'm sipping some herbal thing Woo Woo swears is good for me. Has echinacea in it. Smells like feet. Doesn't matter. I'm not really tasting anything. I'm too busy thinking about tonight and what tonight might mean. Lexie says the best way to get a great punchline is to walk away from the joke. Stop thinking about it. Take a bath. Squeeze a dog. Drink something that smells like feet. So far it isn't working.

I have made progress on my shopping though—and I'm so glad we'll be doing Christmas dinner together. We decided to do it at Lexie's. Well, we really didn't decide; we drew a name out of a hat. Lexie won. Madoff will be thrilled. She'll have treats hidden all over the place.

I hope she likes the customized headphones I got her. Let's be honest. I hope she loves them. I'll say it's from Madoff. After all, it has his picture on both sides of the headset. Woo Woo is getting a yoga mat. A Bennd chakra ayurvedic yoga mat made from ethically sourced raw cotton with rainbow shades from medicinal dyes meant to align the chakras. I know she'll love that. But Woo Woo will love whatever we give her because she loves us. That's the best gift.

Great. Now I'm getting sappy. It's not something auditors do. Bad for business. I got Boone and Terrell gift certificates for Dry Dock. I also laminated two of the pub's placemats with their names on them. The manager said if they don't use them, he'll tack them to the photo board.

Still not sure if I should send him a gift. I mean it's not like we've ever spent Christmas together before or any holiday for that matter. Perhaps I could get him a lifetime subscription to Ancestry DNA or send him a framed family portrait. I know that's mean. I just don't know why this topic makes me unpleasant. I mean I know why— diddling dad and all that—but why am I taking it out on this poor sod I don't even know. And when did I start using the word "sod?" That settles it, the man is getting a gift. Woo Woo says it's important to send positive energy out into the world. Gift card from Amazon?

I can do better. On all counts. I'll order something tomorrow. I have time. Apparently the HPD tech people are going to go through Sofia's laptop. Again. They didn't find anything the first time. Bet I would have.

That's not fair. I know that's not fair. These people are good at their jobs. Very good. I mean, they aren't auditors, but they are educated professionals. If there is anything to find, they'll find it.

They didn't the first time though. I have to let go of that. Think positive energy. Flip the question: why didn't they find anything the first time?

Shit. Shit. Shit.

They're looking in the wrong place.

Sincerely,

Charlene Kurtz

Chapter 31.

It's 5 a.m. when Charlene texts her friends and her friends adjacent. She simply can't wait any longer. By 5:30, she's heard from everyone. Muggs after yoga. Check.

Kristi is leading the class through a series of poses to release tight hip flexors. Charlene doesn't know what a hip flexor is, but hers are clearly tight. Dragon nearly killed her; high saddle is likely to finish the job. Truth is her mind is elsewhere, a yoga no-no. Yoga is about being present. Charlene is too nervous to relax and find her way to the here and now. Truth is she's not nervous; she's excited.

By the time Lexie, Woo Woo, Terrell, and Boone make it to the café, Charlene has a plate of goodies (including the organic stuff Woo Woo likes and Terrell pretends is edible), coffee, and tea in the corner area with the comfy chairs and couch. She's not aware she's sitting on the edge of her seat. Everyone else is.

Charlene can't wait for the four bottoms to settle on seats. *What takes these people so long?* "Topsail isn't in Sofia's laptop. It's in Kostas's."

Boone shoots Terrell a look. It's a look he knows, and it mirrors his thinking. "We'll need just a little more."

"Sorry." Charlene can breathe now. She's been holding that in. "It's something Sofia said. I don't know if it was deliberate or unintended."

"And she said ..." Lexie prompts her friend as she goes over the conversation in her mind. "Shit. She said, 'I'm not alone in this.'"

"Yes," says Charlene. "That's exactly what she said." Charlene inhales a deep breath. She looks at her friends. She smiles. She likes being in the present. Her hip flexors feel great.

***

The table erupts. It's a hushed eruption, but there is a lava field of questions, suggestions, counter-suggestions, and one request for more treats. The first issue, raised by Terrell, is how to access the information. The police can get a warrant, but that alerts Kostas and Pappas that legal action is under way. That, in turn, might make them get rid of evidence, change plans, thwart investigations already in progress.

"Why don't you just ask Kostas for access to the computer? Make sure Pappas is in the room and make it sound like they would be helping build evidence against Sofia. Helping the community." Woo Woo can't believe those words are coming out of her mouth. Nor can anyone else, but the words have merit.

"We'd have to guarantee we can't use anything unrelated to Sofia or Topsail," Boone says. She's looking at Terrell.

"The warrant would limit us anyway," Terrell points out. "But if they say 'no,' we've given them an opportunity to wipe the computer before we get access."

"Have the warrant in your back pocket. Literally." Everyone looks at Woo Woo. Lexie may actually be gaping. Woo Woo takes a sip of her pomegranate raspberry tea.

***

"I shouldn't be telling you this," Boone begins.

Woo Woo puts her tea down. "We are so past that."

Terrell leans forward and feels her forehead. Perhaps she has a fever.

"I checked the visitors' log for Sofia. She's telling the truth. Kostas has never been to see her. She's lying about why. Sofia has put his name on the restricted list. She doesn't want to see him."

"Are you suggesting she's taking her husband down with her?" Lexie asks.

"I'm saying only that she doesn't want to see him."

Woo Woo thinks back to her conversation with Sofia. "She seemed more hurt than pissed at him when we spoke, but she does hate Pappas and, if she can hurt Pappas by hurting his son, she might well do it."

Boone and Terrell stand up. "We'll loop Stash in and get started on the warrant. Thanks ladies. This could be the foot in the door we need."

Terrell bends down and gives Woo Woo a quick kiss on the forehead. She does feel warm.

***

Pappas and his sons have a weekly meeting to discuss business operations, legal and otherwise. The cops know this. Pappas and his offspring know they know.

Still, the three men were surprised when Terrell and Boone unexpectedly appear in their office. "We're hoping to speak with Kostas. It shouldn't take long," Boone says. "If this is an inconvenient time, we can wait."

There it is, Pappas thinks. *Something's up, and we're cornered.* "May we ask what this is about?"

"Woo Woo met with Sofia yesterday (was it only yesterday?), and we'd like to update you. We also have a few follow-up questions." Terrell is lying and not lying.

Pappas knows the drill. "Certainly. We'd be delighted to help. Would you mind giving us fifteen minutes to finish up here? Zoe will make you some of that coffee we all like so much."

There is nothing for it. Boone and Terrell nod their acceptance and thank the three men for being so accommodating. As they're leaving, Pappas stops them. "Sorry. I do have one request. I hope you won't mind." More nodding. "I'd like Charlene to be here. She's reviewed the books thoroughly and may have insight we don't."

The request surprises both cops although they don't show it. "No problem. We'll text her while you finish up. Hopefully she's available."

"Well, if she's coming, I'd like Lexie to be here." This is Dimitri, and this is an absurd request.

"Bring them all and get it over with." This is Kostas, and this is the sound of defeat.

***

It's closer to thirty minutes by the time the three women arrive, the coffee is brewed, and the Pappas clan have concluded their conversation.

330

"Thank you for coming," Pappas says as if they're meeting for high tea and possible incarceration is not on the menu.

Boone takes the next few minutes to brief Pappas and his sons. "Sofia makes a reference to Topsail, and we wanted to learn more about this."

Everyone is watching the reaction of the three men. It's the same look: blank. The word doesn't mean anything to them. "Are you sure she said 'Topsail'?" Kostas asks. It's a smart question, indicates a willingness to help and a reason why they can't. Too bad there wasn't a recording to confirm what Sofia said. *Oh, wait a minute. There is.*

Boone and Terrell are prepared for this. They've asked Woo Woo if she would mind Pappas et al listening to the conversation although this is pro forma. The recording is now evidence. Sofia requested that the HPD not record her talk with Woo Woo or listen in when it was happening. They did neither. And they did not know the conversation was being recorded by the one other person in the room. HPD is in the clear.

"The conversation was recorded." Boone says this matter of factly. It's a fact that has the three family men sitting up straighter. Much straighter. By the time the recording ends, two of the men are more relaxed. One of them is dejected.

"Topsail it is," says Pappas. He looks at his son. Kostas shrugs his shoulders and shakes his head "no."

"Man, she hates you." This is Dimitri. This is not the time or place. Everyone knows this but Dimitri. Lexie pinches his upper arm. "Sorry," he says to his brother. "That just came out."

Dimitri's comment was inadvertent. It was also spot on.

***

Here's the deal. Kostas (read Pappas) will let HPD indirectly access the laptop. They will let Charlene access it directly. Along with the Pappas family, HPD can have a presence in the room when this happens.

It happens quickly. Kostas's laptop is already in the office. He always brings it to the weekly meetings as Boone and Terrell well knew. Sofia's husband hands over the computer. It's like he has just handed over the dirty dishes from a condemned man's last meal.

There's an awkwardness in the room. What is everyone to do while Charlene works. Polite chitchat seems wrong on so many levels. Humor is out. For everyone but Dimitri, it seems rude to take out their phone. Boone thanks Kostas (really Pappas) again for helping. It hangs in the air.

It doesn't hang for long. It takes Charlene seventeen minutes to find the bank account. It takes her twelve seconds to access it. She is not a hacker. This info was intended to be found.

It's Kostas's computer. He gets to look at the screen first. He's gobsmacked. At least, that's what Woo Woo says later in her daily thoughts. Kostas likely doesn't know what gobsmacked means, but he knows this: whatever the hell is on his screen has nothing to do with him.

Somewhere between gob and smacked, Pappas nudges his son to the side and takes over looking at the screen. He's not sure what he's looking at or how much trouble his son may be in.

"It's a bank account," Charlene explains. "It has a lot of money in it—more than $375,000—and it appears to be money obtained illegally."

"What makes you say that?" Pappas asks. Kostas sits down with a thump.

"At first glance—and that's all I have had time to do—there are a number of warning signs." Everyone wants to know what they are, but not everyone wants this information shared. Charlene doesn't know this, and there is no way for anyone to stop her.

"The account belongs to a shell company in Panama. That's an offshore jurisdiction, and there is no reason to have an account there unless you don't want the CRA to know about it. There are also large sums of money coming into the account from numbered companies."

Pappas is beginning to squirm. You have to look closely, but the discomfort is there. Boone is also ill at ease. This may be bigger than she thought, and she's wondering if they should have confiscated the laptop as a first step. Terrell pats his back pocket. *Warrant.*

"What happens now?" Unexpectedly, it's Lexie who lays the real question out on the table.

"Someone needs to do more digging," Charlene says. "We have no idea really what we're dealing with."

"I would like that someone to be you." Pappas makes this request sound like a cross between a lullaby and a military command. He places his hand softly on the computer like a dog marking territory. The move is not lost on the two police officers in the room. Fact is, it's not lost on anyone.

"We'll need to get sign-off on this," Boone says. She tries to sound nonchalant. She fails.

While the inspector is speaking in hushed tones to someone on the other end of her phone, Zoe makes more coffee (decaf) and a selection of macarons appear seemingly out of nowhere. (Woo Woo knows they are from Costco. She buys them all the time.)

Fifteen minutes later, the group is sipping coffee, nibbling French cookies, and chatting quietly. Détente has been achieved. Charlene has agreed to scour the laptop.

She'll summarize her findings (this will likely be a PPT) and submit those findings simultaneously to Terrell and Kostas.

Until then, there's no point in letting macarons go to waste.

***

Benjamin Aeron has been busy. Frankly, busier than expected. Not busier than desired. He's been meeting with lawyers and potential executive directors for the new justice initiative. He was horrified to learn people—including and especially kids—were being locked up because they couldn't pay court fines. He's hoping the new initiative (Re:Fined has a nice ring to it) will put an end to that.

But Benjamin is old enough and rich enough to know that he might be able to put a plug in the flow of Nova Scotians being incarcerated for a few thousand and sometimes a few hundred dollars, but this is a big country and there are many more thousands facing the same fate. If he thinks too long about this, he'll feel the weight of the world and the weight of a few billion dollars on his shoulders.

So, he thinks about his daughter. She's at Charlene's helping to make supper for friends old and new. And the dog. Something is up, and he has been briefed. He understands she is telling him what she can, and he does what any good father does. He calls the boyfriend.

He and Terrell speak every day now on some pretext or another. Terrell realizes this is a process: he is earning his future father-in-law's trust. Benjamin simply feels better when he knows Woo Woo has someone else in her life who puts her first. If she needs help, she'll ask. If Terrell thinks she needs help, he'll ask.

In the meantime, there are others who need help. For Benjamin, this is a fine line to walk. He can help. Should he? He doesn't want to be the rich man who rushes in to make things right for people who are perfectly capable of fending for themselves. He also doesn't want to be the savior for people who don't need saving.

He has found a balance. At least this week. He has located new apartments for Stephanie Kellor and Beast's grandmother. The rent is subsidized. It's nice to have rich friends. It was easy to explain to Stephanie that the subsidized apartment was an employment perk, and Pappas was happy to go along with the semi-truth. In fact, he offered to move the family at his expense. The offer did not surprise Benjamin. He appreciates consistency.

Luke was not fooled by the offer of an apartment, but he is no fool. This is a man-in-the-making who takes time to think things through. He understands the advantages of a new school district for his brother and a better residence for his mother. More opportunity, less guilt.

Beast was a little trickier to convince. The kid is not one to take charity, and Benjamin is reluctant to proffer unwanted solutions simply because he can. In the end, the family is moving into their new digs on the condition that Beast devotes serious time and energy to school. His grandmother will join him. She's going to become a paralegal. In the interim, Beast will help the apartment superintendent with odd jobs around the building as needed.

The new living arrangements work for everyone. They don't address the housing crisis or the power of the one percent, but these are issues for next year. Benjamin is going to give his conscience a break for the holidays. He now has to buy something for Terrell, appropriate and not off-putting.

That will have to wait until later today. Woo Woo has called. She needs a lawyer. Not something a father likes to hear. The few details he got reassured him this was not about his daughter but about further resolving the situation with the woman Benjamin has come to call simply, "Her." He hopes she rots in hell.

***

Madoff is confused. Mama C. came home, scratched his head (perfunctorily, he noticed) and immediately went to her office. There were no cuddles, no assertions about his number-one place in the canine universe, and, most importantly, no treats. Madoff is not sure what to do. This is unprecedented.

The doorbell saves him from abject anxiety. It's Lexie. She seems to sense there is nothing funny about this situation. There are cuddles, confirmation he is the best dog in the world, and, most importantly, treats. The beef tendersticks from Costco. Madoff's favorite. Lexie knows this. Madoff loves Lexie.

Before Lexie can get the leash on him, Woo Woo has arrived. A catering van pulls up behind her. Without turning around, Woo Woo says one word to Lexie: Dad.

Lexie has a few more words to say. "What is he, the food whisperer?"

Madoff wonders if perhaps they should postpone his walk for a few minutes.

***

Post-macarons the group gathered in Pappas's office dispersed. Boone and Terrell went back to the station. Woo Woo and her father went shopping. Lexie and Dimitri went down two floors to Enigma's main stage. There is talk the comedy night might become a regular thing. Kostas went back to Kimolos and, truthfully, a new level of depression. Pappas remained in his office. Charlene assured him he wouldn't bother her.

Now they have come back together again at Charlene's. (Madoff prefers to think of this as Charlene and Madoff's.) Benjamin has joined them, and he has brought food. Well, he has arranged for food to be brought. There are three hot pasta dishes, two types of garlic bread, and two salads. There are no macarons. There is, however, home-made baklava compliments of Pappas, who is wondering if he may be losing his mind. The gathering looks and sounds like friends coming together for a pre-holiday festivity. All that's missing is Santa Claus and a few elves. Pappas knows there is nothing jolly about the reason these people have come together. This night could land his son in jail. Or himself.

Turns out, Santa has other plans.

***

Everyone is eating in the living room. Charlene's idea. She has a PPT, and this is the best room for everyone to see the slides. Despite the awkward balancing act that juggling paper plates, wine glasses, and napkins involves, no one is complaining.

They're too focused on the white wall with the words "Kostas's laptop" in large print.

Charlene dives in. The account in Kostas's name turns out to be a joint account. The other account holder: Nik Pappas. (At this pronouncement, Pappas drops a forkful of moussaka on the floor. Madoff graciously helps out.)

Without missing a beat, Charlene continues. The account is five years old. It is based in Panama, a known haven for ferreting money offshore, and also for getting laundered money out of the country. There is no trail, paper or otherwise, leading back to the CRA, so no taxes have been paid on this money or recorded (although they well might be now).

The account doesn't yield much more information. Charlene notes that the only access to the account seems to have come from Kostas's laptop. All debits and credits are accounted for from this one source. In a footnote, she recommends that this finding be confirmed by HPD's forensic accounting team.

Aside from the crunch of lettuce, small sips of wine, and the occasional gulp (usually Madoff), the room is quiet. It's about to get quieter.

"There is a file on the laptop called 'Topsail,'" Charlene says. "It's not out in plain view. It certainly isn't well hidden."

"What is it?" Kostas asks. He wants all this to be over with.

"From what I can gather, it's a property," says Charlene. "In Sheet Harbor."

"Do you mean it's a house?" Lexie asks.

"I don't know what it is," says Charlene. She presses her remote and the address of the property comes on the screen. Under the address are the property records. They list the two owners: Kostas and Pappas.

Boone is quick off the mark. "Do we have your permission to investigate? Check out the property?"

Pappas, and let's face it the decision is his, is caught between a rock and a hard place. Say "no," and he looks guilty. The assumption would be he has something to hide. Say "yes," and a bunch of cops will descend on a property he knows nothing about and has no idea what secrets it may unveil.

Before he can decide what option to pick, his son solves the problem for him. "Yes, investigate. Please." So much for the decision being Pappas's to make. Now he has no choice but to agree. Saying "no" would make him look even guiltier and more difficult.

Boone doesn't wait for any discussion. She's on the phone to Stash explaining what is going on. By the time she puts her phone back on the table, the narcotics detective has started to assemble a team and has called the Sheet Harbor RCMP to alert them city police are on the way.

"What's the big deal if Kostas owns a property?" Lexie asks.

"I don't own a property," Kostas protests. He looks at his father. "We don't own a property."

"It's not owning that's the problem. It's hiding the ownership," Charlene says. There is no judgment in the pronouncement. It is a simple statement of fact.

It's a fact that scares the shit out of Pappas. Charlene recognizes fear. It's the emotion auditors most commonly see. She reaches a reassuring hand out to Pappas and leans in. "Panama was a mistake."

***

It doesn't take long for things to fall in place and go to hell in a handbasket. Less than two hours later, Stash calls Boone. At the same time, Charlene's doorbell rings. While Stash is explaining to Boone what is going on in a remote area of Sheet Harbor, two uniformed officers are arresting Nik Pappas and his son. By the time the furor has died down, Benjamin's lawyer has joined the group. Apparently, he has two new clients.

While Pappas and Kostas are charged with drug manufacturing, trafficking, and money laundering, HPD's big brass are staking out a boardroom in central and are working through the implications of what their team has uncovered. They're also listening intently to the two senior detectives. Both Boone and Terrell are making it clear that whatever this is it has nothing to do with Pappas and his son.

HPD brass finally agree. As the sun is inching its way over the horizon, Pappas and Kostas are released on bail. They understand why they have been arrested; they also understand their freedom is thanks to two police officers who may not like them but who are convinced of their innocence.

Everyone not wearing a uniform heads home for some shut eye. It won't be long before the nightmare hits replay.

***

The Triad has been busy. While Boone and Terrell were convincing their superiors that known drug dealers were innocent, the three women were trying to unearth the proof, or at least the path to proof, of that conviction. Madoff was trying to sleep.

Here's what the cops found in Sheet Harbor: a fully functioning meth lab. Here's what the cops did not find in Sheet Harbor: any attempt to hide that lab. Cables for security cameras were disabled; alarms were spiked; and windows, once blackened, were clear.

For cops, this is a goldmine of evidence. For cops, it is also a landmine. Anyone smart enough to operate a powder keg from rural

Nova Scotia is smart enough to make access to that lab at least a wee bit difficult. As Boone and Terrell were heading out the door, Pappas and Kostas in handcuffs, they said to their friends. "Figure this out." They said it within hearing distance of the two handcuffed men and their lawyer.

***

Charlene was able to access the property records; Lexie snapped a photo of the signature, and they compared it to documents Charlene had on file from her work with Pappas. Woo Woo made a note on the flipchart: get handwriting expert (Dad or lawyer). Already on the flipchart:

- Get account documents from bank – confirm date, signatures (Dad)
- Check fingerprints on any paper documents (HPD)
- Check fingerprints on lab (HPD)
- Surveillance footage from the bank in Panama
- Lie detector test (?)

By six o'clock, when everyone else was heading off to bed, the three women were heading to the yoga studio. They needed to connect with mind, body, and spirit. Kristi led them through a breathing exercise, centering poses, and several breaths of joy. By the time class ended, the three women were ready for coffee.

***

The three women and Terrell are huddled around mugs of coffee and bran muffins. Several items on the flipchart—photo'd and sent to everyone—have already been checked off. The lab has been dusted, or at least enough had been dusted, to confirm Pappas and Kostas have never been there (unless they hung from the ceiling). Police officers retrieved a copy of the deed from the Land Registration Office, and a handwriting expert is examining the signature (thanks to Benjamin Aeron).

Calls are in to the president of the bank in Panama, but it is early there yet. At this point though, the answer seems obvious. If there is footage, neither Pappas nor Kostas will be on it. And documents will be released to the police.

"It's a misconception that bank secrecy is still alive and well in Panama. In fact, the country signed a broad agreement that stripped its secrecy regulations and opened the door to access from other countries." This is a fact and is stated as such. What has everyone at the table gaping is that it came from Woo Woo.

"Father. Billionaire," she says by way of explanation.

***

The next stop is HPD. A large boardroom, the same boardroom where the brass gathered last night, is set up with water, cake, and more coffee. There are eight people around the table. More wanted to be there.

It's agreed that Pappas and Kostas did not operate a meth lab out of Sheet Harbor, that they did not distribute meth in Nova Scotia or beyond its boundaries. It's also acknowledged that there is evidence they did both these things, but there are holes in that evidence big enough to drive a tank through. There is also no evidence that Pappas or Kostas have ever been to Panama or opened an account there. (That said, they may be entitled to the money sitting in the account.)

It's also agreed the last 24 hours happened because Sofia Makri wanted them to happen. It's not clear if she wanted Pappas and Kostas to go to jail and her plan failed, or whether she just wanted to scare the bejesus out of them, and her plan succeeded. It may not matter, and that is why everyone is here (by necessity or invitation).

"Let it go." This is Kostas. He is tired. He is embarrassed. His heart is broken. How could he have been so blind for so long.

"There is merit in that argument," Terrell says. "It will take a lot of time and resources to prove this was Sofia, and it may not add much to her sentence. Opening the accounts will not get her a lot of additional time; the meth lab might, but we already have her on drug trafficking."

"Is she getting a deal?" Kostas wants to know.

"It's likely she will, another factor in why additional charges are unlikely to amount to much." Terrell pauses. "What is less likely to be glossed over is the kidnapping charge. That will be taken seriously."

"What does it mean in years, months, weeks?" Woo Woo asks.

"Sofia will do prison time. It will likely not be in a maximum prison. She'll negotiate that."

"Years, months, weeks?" Woo Woo asks again.

"Five," says Terrell. "Years."

Silence fills the room. It makes its way into the sofa cushions, the half-eaten torte, the dog treats. Madoff feels the hush. Those with only two feet sense the stillness at a cellular level. It is part anger, part defeat, part sadness. It is love for Woo Woo and an echo of the unanswerable question: how much more can she endure?

Woo Woo is not angry. She will not be defeated. She will not succumb to sadness. But she will get even. She'll call it karma, but it is payback.

She looks at this man she loves, for that is what this is. She knows part of his heart broke with those two words: Five. Years. Woo Woo's heart is just fine.

"Five years is a lifetime." Everyone stops looking at whatever inanimate object they had their eyes glued to and turn to Woo Woo not certain how to interpret this pronouncement from their friend. Wisdom? Acceptance? Idealism?

None of the above. "Sofia is pregnant."

***

It takes several minutes for the furor to die down. Stillness, it appears, is fleeting. Pappas is on his feet. Charlene is making a note on the flipchart. Lexie is fanning Kostas who is semi-upright. Terrell is on the phone.

"Sofia can't have children." Kostas says. "She told you she was pregnant?"

"No."

"Then how do you know?" Pappas demands. There is a rustle of activity as everyone in the room jumps in to explain how she knows. Everyone but Woo Woo. She just shrugs.

Pappas is tired of playing pop the bubble with these women, with these cops. This is beyond ridiculous. He says so. In no uncertain terms.

Terrell shoots him a warning look, woman he loves and all. Lexie laughs at the drug lord and at the woman she has become—the woman who knows her friend is one hundred percent correct. Charlene shakes her head. Ignorance is not bliss. Woo Woo shrugs.

Kostas turns to his father. "What if she's right?"

At this point, Pappas realizes he has raised an idiot, which explains why they are in the situation they are in, why they are in the room they are in. He is about to blast his son. Clearly changes need to be made. He catches Boone's eye en route to a well-controlled tirade. This is a woman who operates on logic, on evidence, on the tangible. This is a woman who is not bedazzled by the absurd or deceived by good intentions. Boone meets his glance directly. She holds her look, and for reasons she will never know, she says, "Woo Woo is right."

Now the conversation has come down to these two people. Criminal and cop. Rule breaker and rule keeper. "How do you know?"

"Because Woo Woo said so."

Madoff looks up quickly. He swears a bubble just burst.

The group agrees Woo Woo's announcement needs to be dissected. Charlene is so glad they are in the boardroom. There is a whiteboard. She writes the intro: If Sofia is pregnant. Then she crosses out "If."

"Is it my kid?" Kostas wants to know.

Woo Woo shrugs. Then she remembers kindness. "Sofia always spoke of you with love, and while we were not close, she never mentioned anyone else to me."

"That gives you parental rights," Boone says. Charlene writes "parental rights."

"You'll need a paternity test," Terrell points out. Charlene writes "paternity test."

"And you'll need it quickly," the eighth person in the room says. "Sofia is being moved later today once we sign the agreement. Tomorrow is Christmas Eve and the whole correctional system will grind to one giant festive halt." Charlene puts an exclamation mark on the board.

"What does this mean for Sofia?" Lexie asks.

"She's between a rock and a hard place. She'll be in jail and won't be able to keep the kid. When she's out she goes to witpro and has to cut all ties with family. If she doesn't opt for witness protection, she's on her own, and she has shared a lot of information about a lot of dangerous people."

"Five years is a lifetime." Pappas looks at Woo. She smiles.

***

Associate Chief Justice Louise Redmond is looking forward to the holidays. Her daughter and family are coming to town. She will get to hug two delightful grandchildren, watch them open presents, and talk about important issues like Santa Claus. She will get to fart to her heart's content.

One more meeting to go. Associate Chief Justice Redmond is looking forward to this too. It has been a while in coming and the end is in sight, a justifiable end. Honey sighs. It's a sigh of contentment. It's not often justice is served.

The first to arrive is Detective Terrell. He's fifteen minutes early, at the judge's request. The others arrive en masse, a murder of legal crows descending. And one self-satisfied criminal. They're in the conference room scattered by lawful genre around the square mahogany table. There is an assembly line of paper to be signed and notarized. The agreement regarding charges. Check. The agreement regarding punishment. Check. The agreement regarding protection post-jail. Check.

Lawyer number one is starting to pack up. He's halted mid-paper shuffle by the judge's expression. "We have one more matter to conclude." Now all the lawyers in the room and one slightly less self-satisfied criminal are looking at one another in confusion.

Justice Redmond is enjoying this. "We have a request for a pregnancy test."

Lawyer number one is rising from his chair. The look on the judge's face has him sitting back down. Promptly.

"We did not know about this." Lawyer number one sounds slightly offended.

"I only just found out about it myself," says Justice Redmond. "Nonetheless, the request is reasonable."

"The request is absurd." Sofia is composed. She's smiling. "It's a blatant attempt to manipulate me. I cannot have children."

"Then you cannot be manipulated," Honey says reasonably.

"This is a last-ditch attempt by my husband."

"This request did not come from your husband. It came from the HPD."

Now everyone is looking at Terrell. He knew this was coming. He's prepared. "We have a confidential and reliable source who says you are pregnant. That potentially complicates the agreement you have with the Crown."

"This is Pappas."

"This is not Pappas," Terrell responds calmly. "And I tell you that with his permission. We thought you'd point a finger of blame in his direction."

Justice Redmond is really enjoying this meeting. The lawyers are silent. (She marks the date and time in her notebook. This may be a first.) Sofia is obviously trying to assess what the hell is happening. The detective is sitting quietly. Inside, Honey knows he is grinning from ear to ear.

Lawyer number one starts to rise. This time it is his client who brings him down to earth. "Fine. I'll take the damn test. I'm not pregnant."

There may be an invasion of privacy here. There may be prisoner rights being violated. Both have been blithely waived by lawyer number one's client.

Justice Redmond savors the moment. Then she explains what is about to happen next. "We have two pregnancy test kits from a local pharmacy. A nurse, who will accompany you to the washroom, will also take a blood sample for testing in a lab."

"I'll take your damn tests. But I want assurances now that my agreement is not in jeopardy. Pregnant or not pregnant."

"The papers are legally signed. Your wishes are crystal clear. The agreements stand." Justice Redmond is smiling inside.

***

Sofia is leaning against the countertop in the Halifax Law Courts washroom. She has three minutes before she can officially gloat. Sofia likes gloating, and she will enjoy the moment when it comes. She's trying to figure out Pappas's angle. She can't. There doesn't seem to be any advantage in doing this. And the cop did say this wasn't Pappas. Would the cop lie? Of course, he would. Sofia chuckles.

The nurse looks up from her kit bag. She is ready. Blood drawn. Kits in a sealed bag. The nurse heads out the door. Sofia follows. Terrell is waiting. Sofia shoots him a big grin. He grins back.

Shit. Shit. Shit. Not Pappas. Woo Woo.

***

Terrell has decided his favorite location in the world, at least at this moment, is that point between a rock and a hard place. That point where Sofia found herself after two pregnancy tests sported plus signs. No one doubts the blood test will yield the same result.

There is little Sofia can do. She tried. She wailed. She yelled. She berated her lawyer. She pleaded with the judge. But everyone in the room knew exactly what position she was in: rock/hard place. She is pregnant, and she is locked into an agreement with the Nova Scotia judiciary that will keep her from ever seeing her child grow up. She can rip up that agreement, she has that right, but in doing so she will spend her life in jail, and she will likely sign her own death warrant. The police will find a way to use the information she has given them. In doing so, Sofia may well sign her child's death warrant although no one said that out loud in the hour-long discussion that followed the second + sign.

Perhaps it was weariness, perhaps the first nudge of maternal hormones, perhaps resignation but Sofia agreed that Kostas could be told. Arrangements could be made. The court didn't need Sofia's agreement. Things are easier when it is given, however. Terrell is on his way to the Pappas house now. There is paperwork that will need to be drawn up; there are lawyers that will need to be involved, there are congratulations to be given. Such as they are.

Angela answers the door. She knows what is going on. She knows better than to ask. The entire family is here. They're gathered in the living room. There is a table with coffee, water, and a plate of cookies. Terrell realizes he is hungry. Now is not the time.

As a cop, Terrell has delivered bad news to many, many families. He has also delivered good news. He prefers the latter although when a cop gives you good news it's often nestled in anguish of some sort. Like today.

Terrell takes out the two pregnancy tests and hands them to Kostas. He doesn't know what he is looking at. Angela and Pappas do. They are both in tears. Pappas hugs his son. His son continues to stare at the two tests.

It is Dimitri who brings him back to earth—and to joy. "You're going to make a great dad."

Pappas has brought out champagne. As Terrell sips a small glass of bubbly and eats his third cookie, he explains the process, the paperwork, the judicial stamp of approval that will hover over Kostas's child until birth. Sofia has agreed to relinquish her parental rights to Kostas, but she may well change her mind and then there will be a fight. It is a fight Sofia cannot win. Rock/hard place.

There will be many more questions. Now is not the right time, and Terrell is not the right person. As he stands to leave, he asks Pappas if he has a minute. There is a split second of concern. Terrell brushes this away. "Just wanted to follow up on a small matter."

***

Pappas takes the chair behind his desk. This is a power move, like a dog urinating on a tree trunk to mark its territory. It's also precautionary. Gives Pappas distance from a threat. Terrell is not a threat.

As he thanks Pappas for taking a few minutes away from celebrating with family, he reaches in his pocket. He hands a piece of paper across the desk. "I thought you might be interested in this."

Pappas stands up, takes the paper, reads it quickly, looks up at the detective and back down at the paper. "What is this?"

"It's a weekly driving roaster for Kimolos. A very particular week."

Pappas peers at the paper. He sits down. Terrell swears he heard a thump. "What is it you want me to do with this?"

"What you do with the information is up to you. What I wanted you to know was that Luke Castle could have brought an early end to his incarceration if he had shared this with us before now. We would have protected him. His family. They would all have been safe."

"I have never threatened Luke Castle." Pappas looks up at Terrell. It's a statement of fact.

The paper hovers in Pappas's hand. "This is a copy. How do you know it's real?"

"I've seen the original."

There's always an angle. Pappas is used to angles. "So, I am being blackmailed. If not you, then by the boy."

"No one is blackmailing you. I'm just letting you know Luke Castle was never supposed to be behind the wheel the night that pizza truck was pulled over. Someone else was on the roster. That someone took themselves off the roster."

"Are you saying my son made this mess?"

"I am."

At this point, Pappas would usually stand up and physically threaten the man (or woman) who dared accuse his son this way. He doesn't have it in him, and he knows why. So does Terrell.

"Why are you giving me this?"

"I thought you should know." That sounded good even if it isn't the truth. Pappas recognizes it as fiction. He smiles. "Let me ask you again."

Now Terrell smiles. "Sir, I don't want to get in the middle of a family fight, nor do I want to cause one, but someone put $6 million worth of street cocaine in one of your trucks. Someone will have to pay for that. It will not be Luke Castle."

"Why didn't the kid show you this before?"

"My best guess, he was protecting his family. And he was avoiding a trial, a very messy trial that would have aired all your dirty laundry. For all the world to see." Terrell pauses. He meets Pappas's eyes. "He was protecting your family."

"I don't even know the boy."

"He was not protecting you."

There is a sadness in Pappas's face, and joy. "He was protecting Mirabelle."

"With his life."

Chapter 32.

The beer mug is almost empty. Terrell nods at the waitress for another Galaxy IPA. He shakes his head in Boone's direction. And another white wine. The two cops are settling in for a nice night: fish and chips, lots of libations, and a little gossip. First, it's business.

"Pappas will give us someone. It might not be Dimitri, but it will be someone."

"Can you live with that?"

"It's better than no one." Terrell has had years coming to terms with the detective's dilemma. Justice will be served albeit in smaller doses than it should be. "Luke is also safe. Win-win."

"Except Dimitri walks free."

"Free is a relative term. If he goes to jail, great. If he doesn't, Pappas will keep him under an iron fist. I don't envy him."

"You don't think there is any way we can arrest him on what we have?"

"I doubt it. Doesn't matter. Crown says no way they prosecute."

"Makri could tell us. We both know she's behind this."

"She's shut up tighter than a clam in a windstorm. Now that she's pregnant she needs to play nice with the family that will be raising her child."

"So, we wait for Pappas to give us a Christmas gift."

"We wait."

"For what?"

The third voice scares the crap out of the seasoned detectives. Lexie laughs and plops herself down in one of two empty chairs at the table. "I thought cops were supposed to be observant."

"Must be the beer," says Boone. She bends backward and hauls another chair over. "I assume the triumvirate will be convening."

"We've been shopping." Lexie gives both of them a big grin. "Who's buying?"

***

Madoff is sniffing the packages. There are lots of packages. Not one of them smells like a dog treat. Perhaps he's been over exuberant. Madoff starts back at the first package.

Lexie reaches into her pocket and hands Madoff a liver treat. He feels that is the least she could do after all the sniffing he has just done. Madoff also gets a belly rub. He is prepared to forgive Lexie. He likes this babysitting thing. That's what Lexie calls it. She told him Mama C is meeting with Pappas but will be home soon.

First, they'll go through the bags. Madoff loves bags, and Lexie is such a good commentator. She tells him what's in each bag and who it's for. The first bag is booze. That's what Lexie says. It is a Bonterra chardonnay. "It's organic. Will drive Boone nuts." According to Lexie, Woo Woo is giving Boone some fancy bottle opener to complement the wine. Madoff eats another treat.

Terrell is getting a yoga mat, a good one. Lexie was going to get him a hot pink one, but all she'd do is laugh through class every time he came so she thought better of it. For Charlene, there is a magnetic dry-erase whiteboard, double sided with its own easel. "It's perfect." Madoff agrees. He gives the box a lick and gets another treat.

Woo Woo was tough. First, she has everything. Second, she's been through hell. Third, she has everything. Now she will have a grounding mala necklace. Lexie does not know what that is. Woo Woo will, and they will both agree the necklace is lovely.

Madoff is on his sixth treat and the packages are all put away when Charlene comes home. It's eleven o'clock. "Everything okay?" Charlene looks tired, and she has been with Pappas. Lexie feels the first pangs of worry.

Charlene puts those to rest. "It's been a long day, but a good one."

"What did Pappas want?"

I'm not sure. I think he wanted me to tell him whether he should turn his son over to the police."

"What did you tell him?"

"To do what he thought was right."

"Good answer."

"Probably not helpful though."

"Is that what you're fretting about?"

"No, something Pappas said. Gave me an idea. Like a really, really stupid idea."

***

It's December 24th. There is no yoga class, no coffee afterward. Asana is closed. The three friends have scattered to the winds: shopping for last-minute gifts, wrapping parcels, dropping presents off, spending time with family. Tomorrow afternoon they will come together just the three of them to open gifts and have a traditional Christmas dinner: turkey with stuffing, mashed potatoes with gravy, sweet-potato something. They've divvied up the cooking and will put the whole meal together after the presents are unwrapped and at least one cup of hot chocolate with Baileys and one helping of fruit cake with rum has been consumed. It will be their time.

At least that is the plan. Plans change.

***

Woo Woo is fretting about her gift for Michael. It's too much. It's not enough. Lexie is trying to wrap the whiteboard. It's bigger than it seems at first glance. Finally, she covers it in bows. Charlene is thinking about her really, really stupid idea. Then she thinks she should call her brother. Half-brother. Really, really stupid idea.

***

By three o'clock on the 24th everyone descends at Charlene's. Lexie drops by to walk Madoff. Woo Woo has holiday pajamas for her friends—a Christmas Eve tradition. Terrell comes by with gifts. Boone is right behind him. Benjamin shows up about 20 minutes later. (Terrell texted him.)

Just as the group is trying to decide what to eat for supper, the doorbell rings. It's Beast and his grandmother. (Benjamin texted them.) They've brought Stephanie, Luke, Brandon, and Mirabelle with them. Charlene wonders if she should move to a bigger house.

"We wanted to say thank you." This is from the mother and the grandmother in the room. It's echoed by Luke and Mirabelle. (Brandon is too cool for unbridled emotion.)

Almost everyone in the room waves away the thank you. "We didn't do anything." "This was you." "You made your own way." Boone says, "You're welcome."

Amid the laughter the doorbell rings. It's pizza. Twelve pies from Kimolos with garlic fingers, Greek salad, and fruit pizza for dessert. "From dad," says Mirabelle. (She texted her father.)

The group is starting to wind down. Benjamin is walking the dog. Boone is washing dishes. Lexie is drying them. Woo Woo is putting leftover bags together for everyone.

Terrell is clearing the last remnants from the table. Luke comes over to help. It's not really why he comes over. "Everything okay?" Luke is not asking about the table.

"Everything is okay—for you and your family. Pappas has some decisions to make. As do you, I would guess."

"I've made it. I don't have the original anymore."

"Who does?" This is not Terrell. This is Mirabelle. She has come up behind them. They jump.

"Scared the crap out of me." Luke is watching his language. He leans in for a kiss. Mirabelle leans away.

"You have to stop treating me like a kid." She turns to Terrell. "You both have to stop treating me like a kid."

"Fair enough," says Terrell. He hopes this ends the conversation. It doesn't.

"I know what my father does for a living. I know what my brothers do. You can stop protecting me."

"I will never stop protecting you," Luke says. And everything is right with the world.

From the doorway to the kitchen, Woo Woo watches the hug that turns into a group hug. She texts Pappas. "It's time."

Daily Thoughts–Lexie Hill

Saturday, December 24ᵗʰ

We had a great night. Unexpectedly so. Dropped by to walk Madoff and suddenly there was a house full of people. Friends and friends adjacent. Really good pizza from Kimolos—and didn't cost us a cent. Best kind. There was some fruit thing for dessert that was amazingly good. Who knew.

I'm all set for tomorrow. Everything is wrapped and ready to go. I'm doing potatoes, but I'll do them at Charlene's after the hot chocolate and Baileys. I hope everyone likes their gifts. Time to be honest. I want everyone to love their gifts.

The one I'm worried about the most is Nathan's. I asked Woo Woo to give it to him. Just a little something. That's not true. It's a big something, but not too big a something. Well, maybe a little big.

I don't know why I'm dangling the gift like it's some unknown. I am writing to me about me. It's a surfboard. Firewire. Signed by Kelly Slater. It was part of a charity stand-up night years ago. He was there. We met. We talked. I will never surf. He will never do stand-up. Somehow, we remembered each other.

Obviously, Woo Woo didn't give Nathan the board. I mean, I can't even wrap an easel. The board is at the gym. In the storage closet. He can get it on Tuesday. Until then, he'll have to settle for some photos. I hope he likes it. God, please let him like it. Please, don't let him think it is too much. Oh god, I should have gotten him a gift card.

Too late now. Nothing I can do. What I can do is enjoy this time with my friends. Tomorrow will be our day. I could use the break. Good food. Good drinks. Cuddles with Madoff. Hugs from everyone else.

It's easier to do that knowing Luke and Beast are okay. Are going to be okay. If I ever have a problem, I'm calling Benjamin Aeron. Man is amazing. Then again, so is his daughter. She's fretting though. Said something about her gift for Terrell. I thought she also said something about her Dad's gift for Terrell, but that can't be right.

Doesn't matter now. Too late to change anything. Including the surfboard. Really, really stupid idea. Like's Charlene's secret idea. I'd like to know what that is. Last one made me a co-owner of a gym and a yoga studio. Can't wait to hear what this one does to disrupt my life.

Now, I'm going to bed, and I'm going to sleep. Reading a new mystery, borrowed it from Charlene. Going to curl up in bed, fluffy covers, warm socks, and no damn surfboard.

LH

PS I really hope Nathan likes the board. Mostly I hope he likes me. I love him.

Chapter 33.

Santa has outdone himself. The three friends are surrounded by bows and paper and gifts and bags and mugs of now-cold hot chocolate. Woo Woo and Lexie are asleep on the couch and the chair, respectively. Charlene is speaking with Madoff, quietly, about all the wonderful gifts he got for Christmas.

Uncle Terrell got him an East Coast bandana for their walks and an East Coast water bowl for when they get home. From Aunt Woo Woo, there is an over-the-top dog coat made of leather with faux-fur trim and faux diamonds. Madoff will be a rock star. Woo Woo found the coat at Value Village for $3. It's perfect. Aunt Lexie also went over the top. Charlene holds out a piece of paper. Madoff is not usually fond of paper, and this piece made Mama C cry. It doesn't smell like dog treats, but he's assured it is special: a gift card to a gourmet doggie bistro that serves meals like lama lasagna and venison and veggie vindaloo. "It's for four," Charlene whispers. She starts to cry. This is the best Christmas ever.

And it's not over. It's time for Charlene to move forward into a new year and a new way of thinking. She picks up her phone and dials her half-brother. She makes a mental note to call him her brother from now on. By the time the call is over, Woo Woo and Lexie are awake, and Charlene is in tears. She doesn't know how much they heard. She does know it doesn't matter. These are her people.

"Sam's coming for a visit." Now there are more tears, and hugs. Madoff isn't sure what's wrong, or right, but he knows everything is okay if Woo Woo and Lexie are here. He wonders if it might have something to do with that piece of paper. It smelled a little funny.

The holiday meal is a success on every level: nothing is burned, the pecan dressing is moist, the gravy lump free, the potatoes whipped to white-peak perfection. Madoff is stuffed. So are the humans. But the meal is not over.

It's time for dessert. Right on cue the doorbell rings. It's Terrell and Benjamin. Five minutes later Boone arrives. There is a new flurry in the kitchen as more wine is opened, coffee is brewed, tea is steeped, and pie is put into the oven.

Terrell is clearing the table. Benjamin is coming with new plates and cutlery. He seems a little hesitant. That is a look Terrell has not seen before.

"Everything okay?"

"Everything is perfect." Benjamin feels tears somewhere at the back of his eyelids. "I have something for you. It's a little much. It's the least I can do."

Terrell is on alert. Not sure how to interpret this but knowing instantly the bottle of wine he got for Woo Woo's father is not going to measure up. Benjamin hands him a card. Cards are good. Perhaps there is a gift certificate inside.

There isn't. There is a letter from Dalhousie University thanking the Terrell family for their generous donation to establish the Clara Lewis scholarship to help Black women complete their nursing degree. Terrell reads the letter. He reads it again. He looks up at Benjamin. He is about to tell him he cannot accept this gift.

Right on cue the doorbell rings.

***

Terrell can't see who's at the door. He can't really see much of anything; something seems to be swimming in his eyes. He does, however, recognize the laughter that quickly makes its way from the front door to the dining room.

His sisters are here.

Before he can even register what is going on, four wonderfully strong, soft, familiar arms embrace him. "Baby brother." "Little one."

370

Good god.

He manages to extricate himself, but not too quickly. "What are you doing here?"

His oldest sister, Pearl, points to the letter. "We knew you'd say 'no'."

Savannah, his other (also older) sister takes his arm and starts to lead him into the kitchen. "We're not going to let you do that."

***

It's midnight by the time all the pie is consumed, wine tasted, and tea sipped. Everyone is scattering to their respective winds and contented sleep. Terrell is driving Woo Woo home. They settle comfortably into the front seat of his SUV. Still Woo Woo feels the pea in the mattress. "How are you doing?"

"It's a little much."

"It's my father. It's always going to be a little much. It was either the scholarship or a Patek Philippe watch." Terrell laughs. Woo Woo doesn't. "I'm not kidding."

"I love my water bottle." Terrell shifts gears. "Who knew you could get one that cleans itself?"

"It's the silliest thing ever. Somehow though it spoke to me."

"It also spoke to me when I first saw it at Suite and Savory."

Now that makes sense. Woo Woo smiles. "The essential oils are lovely. And you'll know they will be used."

"They're the safe gift."

Woo Woo sits up. "What do you mean?"

"I have something else for you, but somehow it seems silly. Somehow it doesn't."

"I have something for you too. Something inappropriate or just right. You'll have to tell me which."

***

They're in Woo Woo's family room. The fireplace is on. She's made hot chocolate with marshmallow bombs. They play rock paper scissors. Terrell wins. Or loses. (Paper covers rock.) He reaches into his pocket and brings out a small box. Woo Woo knows what it isn't. It's way too early for that. She also knows it can't be "safe" jewelry or Michael wouldn't be fretting.

Woo Woo takes her time unwrapping the gift. In part, to extend anticipation and potentially gird against disappointment. In part, to delay having to give him her real gift. The paper is off. Inside the box are three miniature pewter figurines: lotus, shoulder stand, plow. They're perfect.

Terrell wipes away her tears. Then he wipes away his own. Woo Woo puts the three figurines on a shelf. She returns to the sofa

372

and leans in. Terrell thinks it's for a kiss. He's wrong. From behind the sofa, Woo Woo removes a painting. It's a portrait of a Black woman in a nurse's uniform. She's smiling at the artist. She's smiling at the world.

Terrell is not sure he can breathe. Neither is Woo Woo. "It's my mother."

And with that Woo Woo knows her gift is, like, his. Perfect.

"Where did you get this?"

"I've had the photo for some time. Almost since we first met, and I said your name was Lewis. I got it from the Dal archives. I don't know why. It seemed like it was something I was supposed to do."

"How did you get the portrait?"

"I showed the picture to Dad and said I wanted someone to paint this. He called around."

"He called my sisters. This is my favorite artist."

"That explains a lot. Like how the scholarship idea came about."

Terrell looks at Woo Woo. He looks at the portrait. "I love you," he says to both of the women in his arms.

***

The house is lovely. Soft holiday lights fill every room, a majestic balsam fir reaches to the ceiling, ornaments are scattered tastefully (and deliberately no doubt) throughout the main floor. Christmas music plays quietly from speakers in every room.

Lexie wonders where Pappas and his family found the time to do all this, kidnapping blip and all. Charlene wonders where they found the energy, holiday demands and all. Terrell wonders how much the whole thing cost. He knows most of it was paid for by drug money, but tonight (for most of the night anyway) he is off duty. Boone has given him special permission to attend an event at the home of someone who is of active interest to the Drug Unit.

Terrell has to give it to Pappas, he knows how to make guests feel welcome, even cops who are undoubtedly not welcome. The 62-year-old greets them at the door and ushers them in. Coats, scarves, mitts, and muffs are removed and a drink—eggnog with rum—finds its way into everyone's hands.

"Something festive to start with. Then, please, the choice is yours." Pappas waves to the bar set up in the living room. Rudolph with his red nose blinks from one end. A ceramic Mrs. Claus offers napkins from a tray in her hand at the other end.

The men get handshakes, warm for the most part. The women get hugs. The embrace for Charlene seems genuine. Terrell makes a mental note. This could be useful when he is a cop once more.

Mirabelle rushes over in a blur of cashmere, leggings, scrunchie and gives everyone a hug. All genuine. Luke is beside her. There is more hugging and shaking. Clearly, she is doing well. That says a lot about the young man at her side. It says more about her.

Appetizers keep coming—hot/cold, comfort/gourmet, familiar/unpronounceable. Terrell is on his third sweet potato and feta bourekas when it hits him. He's having a good time. *Dammit.*

Woo Woo finds his hand. "You'll be fine. You won't go over to the dark side. It's a Boxing Day party, and it will be over in a few hours."

Benjamin finds his other hand. "That said, you might go over to the dark side."

Terrell shakes them both free and reaches for his fourth boureka.

***

Dinner is duck. Lexie thinks it was raised in heaven. Woo Woo apologizes to Donald and Minnie and digs in. Charlene wonders if it is polite to ask for a doggy bag for Madoff.

Amid the clatter of cutlery and the clinking of glasses, there is animated talk and laughter. The laughter surprises Terrell, but he is not sure why. Part of him thought Dimitri would be chagrined, Kostas would be bereft. Apparently not. Everyone appears to be having a good time, including the seasoned detective who swore he wouldn't.

Dessert is a selection of traditional Greek cookies—melomakarona, kourabiedes, diples, and mamounia—all homemade by the entire family Pappas tells everyone. The delicious coffee made in a briki signals an end to the meal. Everyone leans back and savors the aroma; at least two people undo their top button.

There have been no speeches. Until now. Pappas stands. He thanks his guests. He looks at the people around the table and smiles at each of them. "Tonight, I have something special to share with all of you." He turns to Mirabelle. She gets out of her chair and goes to her father. Angela joins them. The two women are in tears. Pappas is struggling to hold his back.

"We are a family, and as a family we want that bond to be unbreakable." Pappas looks at his sons. They meet his gaze. Kostas might even be happy. "Tonight, I share with you—our friends—the wonderful news that I will be formally adopting Mirabelle."

The room erupts in applause, back slapping, table thumping. Kostas stands up. "To Mirabelle. My sister. Always my sister."

Everyone raises a glass, a coffee cup. The room tinkles with happiness.

***

It's impossible to top that moment. The group senses that and the beginning of the end is under way. There are still a few more drinks to be had. Benjamin and Luke are sharing a cigar outside. Mirabelle joins them. Dimitri is trying to talk business with Lexie, but it is half-hearted. She's too full. He's too drunk. Charlene asks one of the catering staff if it's possible to get a little duck to go, but before anyone can bring her some leftovers, Angela arrives with a bag full of plastic containers. Each one is marked with the name of the food inside and the word "Madoff." Charlene likes these people.

Terrell is starting to look for an exit. It's time. He's lived in the other world for long enough. He searches the room for Woo Woo. His glance lands on Pappas who nods in the direction of his office. Terrell follows. *WTF*.

Pappas is sitting behind his desk by the time Terrell walks over the threshold. And just like that, Terrell is a cop again and Pappas a criminal. "Thank you for coming."

"It was a lovely evening. But you know I'm here for Woo Woo, and Mirabelle, and Luke."

"I appreciate that. I also appreciate the consideration you showed me."

Terrell doesn't bite. Waiting for people to fill the space is basic interrogation 101. "I have something for you." Pappas reaches into his pants pocket and removes a piece of paper. Terrell wonders how many times he touched that pocket and that paper tonight.

There is a name and an address typed on the paper. "January 6th. I'm told a shipment of fentanyl will arrive. I trust the source of that information.”

“This is helpful. Thank you.”

“I assume we are even.”

“I’ll let you know on January 7th.

“Fair enough.” Pappas rises. He extends his hand. “I could not send my son to jail. I’m sorry. But what I can do, and what I will do, is make sure he works only at Enigma running the bar and the comedy series.”

“Do you really think that will be enough?” Terrell looks at Pappas. “If we’re being honest here, it was your son who sloppily shoved cocaine into sacks of flour. It was your son who couldn’t even bothered to drive the drugs to the airport for shipment. This mess is squarely in his lap.”

Pappas meets Terrell’s eyes. “I will make sure my son does not have the opportunity to make mistakes like that again.”

“What about Luke?”

“What about him? He is a youthful fling of my daughter’s. He will be replaced soon enough.”

“You may want to rethink that.”

“Surely you don’t believe two seventeen-year-olds will fall into a happily ever after fairytale life?”

“I don’t. No. Woo Woo does.”

Pappas sits back down. “So that is that then.”

“It would seem so, and I ask again, ‘What about Luke?’”

“You want a favor?”

"I want an assurance."

Pappas nods. "You have it."

"Just like that."

Now Pappas is laughing. He stands up and comes out from behind his desk. He leaves the power position behind him and slaps Terrell on the back. "Just like that. Mirabelle is my world. I will not jeopardize her world. Luke will have a great job, and I might add a very legal job, with one of my companies now and when he finishes university, which I will pay for. You have nothing to worry about. My daughter has nothing to worry about."

Chapter 34.

The eight yogis sitting, bending, and stretching on their mats are keen to get started. There has been too much good cheer, good food, and good drink over the holidays. There have been too few downward dogs, warrior ones, and triangle poses. It's time to get back to reality, to breathing, flowing, and strengthening.

Kristi leads the group through a series of poses—lizard, pigeon, plow—to wake up muscles, flex fascia, and improve circulation. The group ends where they began: with melting heart pose. Woo Woo brings her chest toward the mat and feels her rib cage open. Lexie bends and feels her back protest inches from her destination. Honey farts.

"Melting heart stretches, strengthens and lengthens," Kristi says. "It is good for your back, your spine, and your organs. And it is an emotional release."

Two minutes into the pose, Terrell's chest moves slightly closer to his mat; he lifts his forehead and tries to put his chin on the floor like Woo Woo and Kristi. His shoulders protest. His midback strains. His heart melts.

***

Coffee is taking forever. No one is leaving. They're all sitting there smiling, laughing, munching away like they have all the time in the world. *Please don't let them have all the time in the world*, Charlene thinks. She's on edge. It's that really, really stupid idea of hers. Time to put it out there into the world.

When she last had an idea like this, she and her friends became partners in Vitality+. However, she knew that idea had merit, what she didn't know was if everyone had the money and the inclination to own a business. Turns out they had both.

This idea is different. It's about a new business. A *new* business. The three of them forging new paths. New challenges with a hint of danger, thrills around the corner. Charlene pushes her coffee cup away. Clearly, she's had too much caffeine.

Honey is crumpling her napkin. Charlene sits up. That's a sign the dismount is near. Sure enough, two people are standing. Two more follow. (Big crowd today.)

And suddenly it's just Charlene, Woo Woo, and Lexie.

And suddenly it's not. Honey has remounted. She stops at the table, tilts her

381

head. "I just wanted to say thank you." Honey's gratitude is met with confusion. That confusion reaffirms her faith in humanity. "For helping Luke. He was looking at a lifetime in jail. Now he's looking at a life."

"We didn't do much," says Lexie.

"You did everything," says Honey. "Thank you."

Honey's gone before Charlene can get her bottom jaw to meet her upper lip. It's like Honey knew this would be the perfect segue. *It's a sign.*

"Spit it out," says Lexie.

"Spit what out?"

"Whatever has you chomping at the bit."

"Your idea," says Woo Woo. "It's time."

"It's just an idea," says Charlene. "Way out there. No commitment. But maybe something we'd like to consider. No pressure."

"It's time," says Lexie. Woo Woo nods encouragement.

Charlene breathes in. Not a meditative breath practiced in yoga class, a deep, pluck-up-your-courage breath. *Here goes.*

"I think we should open our own detective agency."

There it is. Real. Out there in the world. Charlene waits for the laughter. The dismissal. The kind but firm, "No."

Lexie looks at Woo Woo. She nods. Lexie turns back to Charlene. "We'd like to see the PowerPoint."

The End

donalee Moulton books also published by BWL Publishing

Hung Out to Die
(A Riel Brava Mystery #1)

Conflagration!
(The Trial of Marie-Joseph Angélique)

Bind (Lotus Detective Series #1)

donalee Moulton's first mystery book *Hung out to Die* was published in 2023. A historical mystery, *Conflagration!*, won the 2024 Daphne du Maurier Award for Excellence in Mystery/Suspense (Historical Fiction). *Melt* is a follow-up to *Bind*, the first in a new series, the Lotus Detective Agency. donalee's short stories have been published in numerous anthologies and magazines. "Troubled Water" was shortlisted for a 2024 Derringer Award and a 2024 Award of Excellence from the Crime Writers of Canada. donalee is also an award-winning freelance journalist. She has written articles for print and online publications across North America including *The Globe and Mail, Chatelaine, Lawyer's Daily, National Post,* and *Canadian Business.*